A Majestic Affair

Sharon G. Clark

Yellow Rose Books
by Regal Crest

Texas

ISBN 978-1-61929-178-2

First Printing 2014

9 8 7 6 5 4 3 2 1

Cover design by AcornGraphics

Published by:

Regal Crest Enterprises, LLC
229 Sheridan Loop
Belton, Texas 76513

Find us on the World Wide Web at
http://www.regalcrest.biz

Published in the United States of America

Acknowledgments

To my wonderful beta readers: Linda A., Hope V., and Nancy Hoist, my heartfelt appreciation and gratitude for your assistance and input.

To my coworkers: Linda Matthies and Diane Busch, for listening when I vent about my writing (and other things)—nothing to do with our jobs.

Thank you, too, Patty and Judy Kerr. You're fabulous editors who managed to keep me on task—without cracking the whip too hard.

Dedication

Special love for *Mi' Corazon*, Hopi, you'll always be my Boo.
Also, for my son Jeremy, my other heart.

Chapter One

THE SEVENTY OR so miles seemed longer than Tiara remembered. Stuck behind the numerous eighteen-wheelers and tractors chugging along at turtle speed on the country roads hadn't helped her get there any faster. Neither had stopping for dinner at the small restaurant boasting of pure country charm on a sign attached to its entrance door. Nervous energy had made her hungry. The meal was the first in eight months that wasn't from a drive thru or heated up in a microwave.

Tiara turned onto the county road marked MM, wishing she had a bag of them right now, with almonds, and headed east. Her father's property was six miles farther. She let up on the accelerator when a tractor, this one with a large round bale of hay, came into view.

She groaned loudly. All she wanted was to get to her father's place, preferably before Christmas, and make the trip a quick one. It wasn't that she didn't love her father. She adored him, but being with him made her feel awkward, as if she couldn't do anything right. And he would ask questions about Angie that Tiara didn't want to answer.

Above all, she wanted to lessen any chance of running into Jayce.

Dusk sped toward darkness as her truck's headlights brightened the path. The tractor in front of her slowed and she hoped it was about to turn off the road. It wasn't. Inching left, Tiara tried to see if it was safe to pass and instead, saw another tractor and an RV coming toward her. As she waited for them to pass, her mind flashed on the memory of the last time she'd seen Jayce.

Tiara had been fourteen, with a big case of puppy love. Even at seventeen, Jayce was a fine specimen of what the female physique could achieve and still be sexy. Unfortunately, Jayce's brain hadn't caught up to her body. Jayce's ideas of being pleasant during that last particular summer consisted of such antics as giving her a fish-gut bath, locking Tiara in a storm cellar, and dowsing her with sticky horse feed and straw.

Of course, there was also the incident of the kiss...

The tractor and RV had gone by and she had a chance to pass. She pressed down on the accelerator and skirted around the tractor. Tiara had driven less than fifty feet in front of the tractor when she realized she'd almost missed the road to Falling Down Acres. She jerked the wheel left and made a sharp turn onto the long dirt drive. She barely missed the mailbox tilting to one side on a four-by-four post. In her rearview mirror, she saw the red tinged dust cloud churned up by her speed on the dry gravel road.

A quarter-mile of road later, Tiara came upon the dark house. She wondered if her father had gone to bed early or was possibly out for the evening. She stopped on a concrete slab beside the house, which she'd never seen before, and guessed it to be a driveway. Tiara shut off the engine and sat.

Since her father had mailed her a key, she assumed he had anticipated the probability he might be away when she arrived. She had no idea how long Slim would be gone.

Tiara's options were simple. She could sit in the dark truck and wait for an unknown amount of time, or grab ner gym bag and go inside the house. The smartest course would be the latter.

She walked up the stairs and onto the porch, dropped her bag by the door, and fished the key from her jeans pocket. Her actions were rewarded with a bright beam of light directed squarely on her face before she could pull the key free.

"What are you doing here?" asked a voice too sultry to be her father's.

"Going blind," she said, raising a hand over her eyes to see beyond the light. "Could you lower that a little?"

"You didn't answer my question."

"I don't do interrogations."

The beam, though lowered from her face, slowly ran over the length of her body. With no moon tonight, Tiara could only make out a silhouette of a shapely woman.

"Red?" the voice asked. "Is that you?"

Tiara felt as if she'd been doused with iced water. No one had called her Red since she was fourteen, and then only by one person. "Jayce. What are you doing here?"

"Keeping an eye on the place while Slim's away."

"I thought—" Tiara wasn't sure she wanted to hear the answer, but asked, "For how long?"

Jayce didn't answer, but asked a question of her own as she turned the flashlight beam on Tiara's gym bag. "Do you plan on staying?"

"I don't think that's any of your business."

"Look, Red..." A heavy sigh. "I can let you inside."

"I have my own key."

"Maybe we can talk," Jayce said as if uninterrupted. "You can tell me why you're here."

Tiara pulled the key from her pocket and unlocked the door. Twisting the knob, she pushed the door open, kicked her bag into the hallway, and turned to face Jayce. The last thing Tiara wanted to do at this moment was talk to her. Hit Jayce, maybe. Yell at her for making a fool of Tiara that summer ten years ago, definitely. Invite her in? Not if Jayce had a plate full of chocolate chip cookies.

"Come on in," she heard herself say. Tiara mentally groaned. Why didn't her mouth ever agree with her brain? Maybe because Jayce knows more about your father than you do, right now. Darn, she hated when common sense won over emotions.

Jayce strode past her and entered the house first, switching on lights as she went. Tiara followed more slowly. Everything appeared to be about the same as when she'd lived here. Surprisingly, the inside was clean and in much better repair than the outside, especially for bachelor quarters.

The living room consisted of a sofa and a matching chair in a burgundy striped design, a low oak coffee table, a worn leather recliner, and a large fireplace in the back wall. Above the fireplace sat a thick mantel cluttered with framed pictures coated with a fine layer of dust.

One snapshot in particular caught Tiara's attention. She stood in front of it and stared. The picture was from their last summer as a family unit. Her father wore a broad smile with an ever-present toothpick poking out of his mouth and her mother showed her usual deadpan expression.

Tiara pulled the frame down for a closer look. Her own eyes, they looked so —

"Sad, weren't you," Jayce said from over her shoulder. She made it a statement, not a question.

"I never realized it was this obvious." Stunned that Jayce had seen the expression too, Tiara was unaware of Jayce's hand on her arm until she leaned forward to replace the frame on the mantel. When Tiara turned to face her, Jayce let the hand drop back to her side, but Tiara could still feel the warmth left by the contact.

"It hasn't changed," Jayce said in a low tone.

"What?"

"The sadness. It's still there."

"Thank you, Dr. Mansfield, but I beg to differ. I'm happy and have a good life."

Jayce tilted her head and studied Tiara. "Maybe," she said, after a quick assessment, a review that made Tiara's heart rate increase. "But you're not happy with your life, are you?"

Tiara did her own evaluating. Jayce's eyes, still the same incredible blue, gazed directly into hers. She wore faded jeans, weathered cowboy boots, and a cotton shirt with the sleeves rolled above her wrists. Her dark brown hair was longer than Tiara remembered and neatly combed back and over her ears. She had a thin nose, slightly curved at the tip from being broken when she was sixteen, and sensuous full lips.

Tiara didn't want to think about Jayce's lips. Thinking about them started the memories. Memories she desperately wanted to forget. Didn't she?

Clearing her throat, Tiara moved away from Jayce and plopped down on the sofa. "I thought you wanted to talk, not analyze." She groaned. "You know, I think I like you better with a bucket of fish-guts. Why don't you tell me where my father is, so you can go away?"

"I'm not that easy to get rid of, Red."

Or easy to forget. Tiara shook her head roughly. "Don't call me that, I hate it." She closed her eyes, laid her head back against the sofa and threw an arm across her face. If Tiara ignored her, maybe Jayce would take the hint and go away.

JAYCE HADN'T MEANT to annoy Tiara, but she'd given her the nickname over a decade ago. It suited her then, but as Jayce stared down, she realized Tiara wasn't a girl anymore. She'd grown up. Her height hadn't changed much, she was still petite. Her strawberry-colored hair had more gold than when she was a kid. Though Tiara had flung an arm over her eyes, Jayce could see the mass of freckles had disappeared, only a couple of strays remained on skin tanned a beautiful honey-brown.

Until Jayce witnessed the sadness in Tiara's eyes a few minutes ago, she had forgotten about the gold flakes scattered in the gray depths. That wasn't right, exactly. She hadn't forgotten. Jayce had only let the memory hide away. Tiara's eyes were striking reflecting her every emotion. If the eyes were the mirrors of the soul, Tiara Summers had come home with the same personal inner-demons as those from many years ago. It wasn't Jayce's job to chase them away, so it might be better to find out how long Tiara planned to stay and then go home.

"Okay, I'm sorry I called you Red." Jayce sat on the coffee table facing her, pulled Tiara's arm away from her eyes, and gave what she hoped passed for an apologetic expression.

It must have worked, because Tiara grinned. "Apology accepted."

"Now," Jayce said, "I don't know specifically how long Slim will be gone, so you don't need to stay here." What Jayce didn't say was how much she had missed her, how fantastic she felt seeing Tiara, and how much she wanted to beg Tiara to stay. "He asked me to watch over the place until he got back. I'll do just that."

"I plan to stay as long as it takes to get a few answers," Tiara replied, jutting her chin defensively. "When I get those answers I'll go, but not until then."

Jayce was confused. "Answers to what?"

"The stuff in the note he sent."

"You've heard from him?" That explained Tiara's return after so many years. "When?"

"I don't really see where it's any of your business."

"I do." Jayce shook her head slowly. "You're not going to make this easy, are you?"

Tiara jumped up from the sofa, but the distance between them was minimal. All Tiara achieved was to shove her breasts into Jayce's face, not that Jayce minded. Tiara smelled good, like jasmine.

Jayce slid sideways off the coffee table and stood. Tiara's face was deep red. The courteous thing to do would be to pretend the contact hadn't happened, but Jayce couldn't help herself. "That was great for me. How was it for you?"

IF TIARA COULD'VE crawled into a hole at that precise moment, she would have; but the floor didn't open up and swallow her. "I've had a hard day and a long drive, and don't feel like playing games with you."

"Then tell me about Slim's note."

If it would make her leave, she'd tell Jayce anything — almost, anyway. "He said he's in trouble and mentioned a horse."

"What horse?"

"He doesn't have a horse?" Tiara gauged the answer from the surprised look. What game was her father playing? Could he have lied about his trouble, too?

"He didn't last I checked. That was about fifteen minutes ago." Jayce grinned and Tiara wanted to slap the smile off her face. Tiara had left work for a wild goose — no, make that horse — chase.

"Then I guess I can answer your earlier question. I'll be leaving in the morning."

"It's probably best that you do," Jayce said.

"Yeah, right." She moved to the front door and stopped. "Look, Jayce, I'm ready for sleep." Tiara had never gone to bed this early, at least not since she was a pre-teen.

Jayce took the hint. She opened the door herself and stepped onto the front porch. Tiara was about to close it when Jayce turned around and stared at her. "Will your next visit be this long in coming?"

Tiara clenched her teeth and bit back the response she wanted to shout. Jayce shrugged and stuffed her hands into her jeans pockets. "I know, I know, none of my business. Have a good night, Re — Tiara."

"Whatever." Tiara watched Jayce disappear into the darkness. Then she shut the door and leaned against it wearily. What she needed was a hot bath. No, she needed cable, and wondered if her father even had a television. Was there one in the living room? She didn't remember seeing one. Then again, other things had been on her mind when she'd entered the house. What about munchies? She'd run out of Twizzlers on the drive here. Food of any sort would do. This would be a very long night if her father didn't have either.

She knew of only one way to get answers and that was to search for them.

Tiara went back to the living room. An old television sat in a walnut cabinet located beneath the picture window. "Yes. One quest down." She headed for the kitchen and pulled open the first set of cabinet doors. Numerous cans of tuna were stacked in rows of six and piled four high. Her father obviously liked tuna. She moved to the next cabinet and found canned soups, stews and spaghetti, three boxes of Corn Flakes, and a super-sized jar of green olives.

"Gosh, Dad, now I know where I get it." She was about to give up and check the refrigerator when a pastel blue Post-it note on the pantry door caught her attention. Moving closer, she read: *Tiara, for you. Love Papa Slim.*

She doubted he'd put the mysterious horse in there, but was hesitant to open the door. Finally, curiosity got the better of her. Inside was everything from cases of soft drinks, to cookies and chips. Tiara shook her head. How did he know she'd come? Or did her father eat like this regularly?

She grabbed a bag of ruffled chips and a can of soda and closed the door with a quick swing of her hip. If Tiara didn't know better, she'd believe her father had set this whole visit up. Why?

The answer came quickly and she didn't like herself for it. Under normal circumstances, she wouldn't be here. He was probably as nervous as she was about their reunion, though she didn't understand the elaborate charade. Why didn't he just call?

As if the thought were an omen, the phone by the refrigerator rang and she jumped, dropping the items in her hand. The chips fell with a crunch, the soda can a thud before spraying its contents wildly over the kitchen.

Tiara cursed the disaster anticipating it would take the better part of a half-hour to clean up if she expected to avoid a sticky floor in the morning. She lifted up the receiver. "Hello?"

Silence was her only answer.

Chapter Two

TIARA LISTENED FOR breathing or even some kind of background noise from the caller. She heard nothing.

"Hello?" she repeated loudly into the receiver, in case of a poor connection.

"Princess? You really came?" Her father sounded shocked. He shouldn't have been, not after the letter he sent. "I've missed you," he said.

She missed him, too, but didn't have the courage to tell him. "Dad, please tell me what the heck is going on. You're not here, and neither is the horse you mentioned."

"I know. He arrives tomorrow."

"And when do you arrive?"

He cleared his throat and Tiara could tell he was stalling. His next statement confirmed it. "I saved your collection."

"My what?" she asked.

"You know, your collection," he said in a conspiratorially lowered voice. "It's hidden so no one can find 'em."

For a few seconds Tiara had no idea what he was referring to. Then the memory hit her with the force of a cement truck and she groaned. "You act like they're worth something, Dad."

"To me they're important and for you, too, if you'd just listen to your heart instead of your head all the time."

She didn't like where this topic was going. "It's just junk from childhood."

Through the receiver, she thought she heard sorrow in his sigh. By denying the importance he'd placed on her collection, she'd disappointed him once again. A pounding headache began at the base of her skull.

"When are you coming home, Dad?"

"Soon." He paused. "You know, you used to call me Papa Slim, Princess.

Sheesh! He continually changed the subject so he didn't have to give specific answers. Tiara felt her temper heat up. If he didn't start providing direct responses, her irritability would boil over before they ended the conversation. "I can't help if you don't talk to me."

"But we are talking, honey."

Granted, they were, and more than they had in the last ten years. Still, she knew nothing more about the horse or his alleged trouble. All she'd gleaned so far was that he preferred she call him Papa Slim, and that he'd saved a worthless collection of carvings she'd made as a kid. These tidbits of information told her more about her father than she cared to admit. She didn't want to change their relationship. No, to be honest with herself, Tiara was afraid to change it.

She leaned against the wall, then slowly slid down and landed on the floor in a small puddle of soda. The mess around her brought an earlier question to mind. "Dad, how'd you know to fill the long cabinet with junk food?"

"Um, just a guess." His answer was as evasive as all the other answers he provided.

"Forget it. Tell me about this horse."

"Majestic."

"Majestic?" she repeated.

"The horse, his name's Majestic. I won him," he said in a prideful tone.

She felt an instant twinge of envy toward the horse. "Won a horse? Gambling? You haven't changed a bit," she said icily.

"I've upset you," he said.

"No, not really." I just hoped you'd changed, her heart whispered. "What am I supposed to do with the horse?"

"Just watch out for him 'till I get home. Jayce can help, if you need it."

"No thanks. I'm sure I'll manage until you get here."

"That's my girl."

"When will you tell me what kind of trouble you're in? Is there anything I can do right now?" Tiara asked, trying to pin him down on at least one answer.

"Don't fret over it. It'll work out."

He sounded so certain; Tiara wondered why he wouldn't talk about it now. "By not telling me, I worry it's worse than I can possibly imagine."

"I wouldn't feel right telling you over the phone, Princess. It should wait for when we're together." Finally, Tiara felt they'd gotten somewhere.

She waited. He wasn't giving any more information. "When is that going —"

"Love you, Princess." The distinct click told her he'd hung up.

"Damn," she groaned in frustration. A temper tantrum would feel good, but she couldn't picture herself stomping her feet and yanking out chunks of her hair. Pulling his hair, maybe; stomping on his chest, definitely. "Yeah, right," she said loudly to the empty kitchen instead. "Don't answer the important questions, Dad."

Not nearly as satisfying a result as she'd hoped.

She stood and replaced the receiver. Tiara looked around the kitchen and evaluated the mess she'd made when the phone rang. Despite what she told Jayce earlier, she'd be here for a little while longer, which meant the spilled soda could wait until morning. The day's events had worn Tiara out. She grabbed a dishtowel off the counter and threw it on the largest of the caramel colored puddle, then picked up the chip bag and tossed it on the table.

Tiara rubbed her temples roughly remembering Slim's mention of her collection. Some collection; a bunch of carvings she'd done as a foolish little girl who'd hoped it would make a father love her and a mother forsake the liquor bottle. Neither response had happened. The one person who seemed truly impressed was Jayce. She'd complimented Tiara with more than words. When she'd presented Jayce with a carving, her reward had been a kiss.

The kiss, warm and intense, had made Tiara feel worthy and had set her heart on fire. Then Jayce had doused the fire, though it was probably Tiara's own fault. Tiara's heart must have hammered a warning only Jayce could hear, and one that had frightened her. Seconds after the kiss, Jayce had scowled and quickly walked away. Tonight was the first time Tiara had seen her since the kiss, and it brought a resurgence of the pain she'd carried these past ten years. Pain from knowing she had disappointed Jayce, too. "When haven't I disappointed my loved ones?"

The room didn't answer, but the silence was enough. Suddenly, Tiara wanted nothing more than to find her old room and go to sleep. She could hate herself tomorrow, when the horse arrived. Then she could add ignorance to the long list of her negative traits.

Why did dealing with her father make her feel insecure? She didn't really hate herself. Her competence and hard work had driven her construction firm to the top of the need-to-have list, despite the current financial trends. She was proud of her achievements. So why should she care whether her father was proud of her?

Part of their conversation nagged at her. Hadn't he been proud enough to save the collection? He had to be or he'd never have kept them. So why hadn't he ever told her before?

Maybe if I were a horse to bet on...

JAYCE HAD A routine she'd followed since she was sixteen; however, this morning the routine had been jinxed. She'd managed to fill her mug with black coffee, and take a steamy shower before derailing. Nothing drastic, something as simple as the wooden horse displayed on her dresser. It shouldn't have affected her. The palm-sized carving had been in the same spot for over ten years. Her hair was still wet and uncombed; the drops of water falling on her bare shoulders chilled her. After yanking on a T-shirt and jeans, Jayce reached out, picked up the carving, and took it to the seat under the east window.

The memories flooded back as if they'd happened only yesterday.

Jayce found Red hiding in her dad's old barn, Swiss army knife firmly in hand. Tiara had been concentrating so intently on her work that she was unaware that Jayce watched her. When she did notice, Tiara jumped in alarm and nicked her finger on the sharp blade.

"What are you up to, brat?" Jayce asked, pretending not to notice Tiara hide her hand from view.

"N-nothing."

"Nothing, huh? What are you hiding?" Jayce moved closer, ignoring Tiara's nervous step back. "From what I did see, it looked like something."

Hesitantly, Tiara produced the small hunk of wood.

Jayce gently took it from her and examined it. The carving was an intricate design of a horse. "Oh, gosh, Red. This is incredible." It wasn't even a lie, either. Tiara had managed to capture every nuance, the very essence of the animal portrayed.

Tiara's cute freckled face looked stunned, her eyes watering as her lips quivered. "You really think so?"

Jayce nodded. Blood from Tiara's wound had soaked into the wood. "You cut yourself, though. Maybe we should get Aunt Edna to bandage that up for you."

Tiara shook her head and asked, "You really like it?"

"Yeah, it's awesome." Jayce bit the inside of her cheek when she realized, at that moment Tiara meant more to her than simply a neighbor or a friend. The eyes were Jayce's undoing, as Tiara, apparently surprised by her compliment, stood transfixed, undisguised adoration in her expression. There was only one thing for Jayce to do. She kissed Tiara.

Jayce was startled by how right the contact of their lips felt. She pulled Tiara into a tight embrace and moaned when Tiara closed her eyes. Then, immediately she realized how wrong she was to virtually attack Tiara, a mere child, whether she responded or not. Jayce firmly pushed Tiara an arm's length away, dread weighing uncomfortably in her stomach.

Before Tiara opened her eyes, Jayce bolted from the barn.

Jayce had pushed those memories so far back into her subconscious that it should have taken a search party to find them. All it took was seeing Red last night.

Jayce looked out the window in the direction of Slim's house. From her second story bedroom, she had a clear view across the quarter acre or so separating them. What Jayce saw made her yank on her boots and race out of the house.

It took a couple of minutes to run to Falling Down Acres. Parked behind Red's truck was a green king cab Dodge with a horse trailer attached. Why it was here at six-thirty in the morning Jayce couldn't imagine. Apparently, Red found herself with the same problematic question.

"What am I supposed to do with it this early?" Red was asking of the short, plump man before her, as she eyed the horse.

"I was told to deliver him, he's here." The man spat tobacco juice onto the ground, wiped his chin with the back of his hand, and then crossed his arms over his protruding belly. "The rest ain't my problem, young lady."

"I realize that, but I'm not sure I know either." The horse nudged Tiara, sending her back a step. "Calm down you brute." Raising his head, the horse snorted. Her eyes widened. "Please?"

Jayce observed how lost Tiara looked in her gray sweats, unlaced running shoes and her hair in wild disarray. "Maybe I can help." Jayce moved forward and positioned herself between Red, the horse and the man.

"Good," the man said. "Your sister's not being too helpful."

"I'm not her sister." Red snapped the declaration over Jayce's shoulder.

Jayce shrugged. "We're just friends."

"Not even that," Tiara mumbled.

Not one to miss an opportunity to tease when it so readily presented itself, Jayce shrugged helplessly. "She's cranky without her morning coffee."

The flab on the man's multiple chins quivered in what Jayce assumed to be restrained laughter. He motioned Jayce aside with a stiff jerk of his head. When they reached the rear of the trailer, he whacked Jayce on the back. "Argument, huh? Mrs. Rand and I have 'em all the time. My son's...ah, not-even-friend is temperamental in the morning, too."

Jayce nodded, letting Mr. Rand draw any conclusion he felt comfortable with, more than a bit surprised by the ready acceptance. "Do I need to sign anything for this delivery?"

"Yeah, but the horse ain't all." He went into the trailer, and soon a commotion echoed from the darkness, followed by an ungodly honk. An indignant goose exited the trailer. Mr. Rand came out and pulled wrinkled pieces of folded paper from his back pocket as he glanced over Jayce's shoulder. "Jittery, ain't she?"

"Jittery?" Jayce turned to see Tiara, a death grip on the lead rope, eyeing the horse with a cautious stare, her body tensing for flight. Tiara would spook the horse if Jayce didn't get over there, fast. Hastily, she opened the wad of papers. "Pen?"

After she signed the shipping invoice, the last page removed for Slim's files, Mr. Rand left. Jayce rushed toward Tiara. "I'll keep him at my place, if you'd like." Tiara frowned. "It is my business, after all, to train and board horses. Remember?"

Tiara bit her lip and glared at the horse, then turned her attention to Jayce. "If Dad expected him, I'm sure there's a place to...ah...um..."

"Corral him?" Jayce offered. "Yeah, but it's in sad shape. Most of the fence needs repairing. Can't guarantee he'll be content to stay put.

The barn is in worse shape than before you left."

"Then I'll repair them."

"It's a lot of work," Jayce said.

"I own a construction company, or did you forget what *I* do for a living?" Tiara said, placing a hand on her hip and tapping one foot. The goose took the action as a personal affront and nipped at her ankle. Tiara sidestepped a bit to get out of his way. "I'll do the house, too, for that matter."

Jayce had remembered her occupation, and Slim brought it up every chance he got, whether part of the conversation or not. "Red, I'm offering help. Don't be stubborn."

"Tiara! And I'm not stubborn. Quit analyzing me."

Jayce knew she'd messed up. It was too early in the morning to argue. Hell, she hadn't even finished her own coffee. "I only meant—"

"I don't need your help. Just point to wherever he's supposed to go, then you can leave, too."

"Why are you doing this?" Jayce asked, barely able to contain her flaring temper. "Acting like I'm the enemy," she stated, genuinely confused.

"Aren't you?" Tiara asked.

"No, I'm not." Jayce sighed. "Can't we talk without losing tempers?"

"You're angry? Well, I'm not sorry."

Jayce's temper became harder to rein in. She backed up a step and pointed with her thumb over her shoulder. "Corral's in the back."

"Fine."

"Fine." Jayce strode away just short of running. She'd never run from a fight, against a man or woman; she didn't intend to make this her first occasion.

What had happened to the kid who tried so hard to make everyone happy, even at the expense of her own happiness? Tiara had changed, going from a caring kid to a nasty, pigheaded woman. Jayce now knew why she'd seen the sadness in Tiara's eyes last night. She probably turned people off as fast as a light switch. Probably didn't have a friend in the world. Well, Tiara could very well manage single-handedly.

Jayce would go home, get a fresh cup of coffee, and go about her own business. She certainly had enough work to do without trying to help an ungrateful neighbor.

"I wouldn't help her if she begged me on her knees." Jayce felt proud of herself for reaching her steadfast decision.

Until she heard Tiara's scream.

Chapter Three

TIARA HADN'T MEANT to scream.

Of course she hadn't expected to be dragged across the yard by a beast hell-bent on reaching a particular patch of grass behind the house, either. However, both had happened. Early morning dew dampened the knees of her, now, grass stained sweats as she tried to stand. She'd almost achieved her goal before the horse took off again. In an instant, she was back on the ground. The goose noisily voiced his opinion of Majestic's pitiable treatment and then snapped at Tiara as if to confirm his estimation of her inadequacy.

"The grass isn't going anywhere, you brute," she said, eyeing the horse's destination. "You're definitely male. Obstinate. Thick headed. Brutish. And—" She stopped her tirade as the horse paused and she had the misfortune of being in the wrong position at the wrong time while glancing upward. "Oh boy."

"Well, he's not a gelding," she heard a voice from behind her.

Tiara hadn't noticed Jayce's reappearance. "I guess not," she said. The horse decided to stay put, for the moment at least. The goose also took that as a signal to desist his tirade. Tiara stood and retrieved the running shoe she'd lost during her short haul. Jayce pried the lead rope from her fingers and moved to the horse's muzzle.

"Are you all right?" Jayce asked, rubbing the beast's nose.

Tiara couldn't believe her ears. She'd been the one taken for a ride, an undignified one at that; yet, Jayce seemed more concerned with the horse's welfare. "He should be fine. I didn't drag him around."

Jayce's brows drew together before she laughed. "I meant you, silly."

"Oh," Tiara mumbled. "Yeah, I'm fine."

Silent, Jayce stared at her for so long she began to feel self-conscious. Not to mention it was early, Tiara hadn't had a shower, and still had her pajamas on—thank goodness she didn't wear baby dolls to bed. When Jayce finally spoke, her voice was low and soothing. "Look, Red. You won't accept my help, even though I handle horses for a living, but will you accept a trade?"

As if Tiara hadn't heard that line a few times. "A trade?" she squeaked. "I know it's the new millennium, but I'm not as modern as you must think." Jayce laughed, this time a deep sultry sound that would have been comforting, under different circumstances, and if it weren't directed at her.

"I'll remember that, but it's not what I had in mind. I thought more along the lines of my corralling the horse and you fixing us coffee. Nothing devious intended, unless you want to throw in breakfast."

Tiara hoped her father had coffee in the kitchen. A trade meant she wouldn't owe Jayce a favor. And the horse wouldn't get to drag her, or the miserable fowl to snip at her. Breakfast was out of the question, as Tiara couldn't cook. "I'll get coffee started," she told Jayce then slipped her shoe on and made a mad dash for the house.

Inside, Tiara ran to the kitchen and began her frenzied search for a coffee maker. She found it in a cabinet below the sink, filters and a new can of coffee beside it. Thankful the coffee wasn't decaffeinated, she started a carafe brewing. Tiara wondered if there was enough time for a quick shower before Jayce came inside, then realized it didn't matter. Jayce knew the layout of the house. Hopefully, Jayce would come get her cup of coffee and leave before Tiara finished showering.

Heading for her room, Tiara was stopped by the squelching sound made by her running shoes, and reminded she hadn't cleaned the spilled soda from last night.

"Damn." Tiara picked up the dishtowel she'd placed on the puddle. The towel made a ripping sound as she jerked it from the floor and she realized why she'd never left a mess to clean later. She glanced out the kitchen window, no sign of Jayce yet.

Tossing the soiled cloth in the sink, she turned on the hot water full blast. When the towel was soaked she grabbed it to wring the excess water out, but the water had heated faster than she'd expected. Tiara alternated hands, jerking them free quickly to cool them. If anyone where watching, they'd believe her a possessed marionette. After adjusting the water's temperature to a manageable level, she stole another quick glance out the window, still no sign of Jayce.

Tiara vigorously cleaned. And after four trips to get all of the spilled soda removed from the floor, cabinets and wall, she tossed the towel in the sink and rushed to get into the shower. She had no idea what was taking Jayce so long, but thanked whatever it was, even if the nasty beast were the reason.

When Tiara reentered the kitchen twenty minutes later, Jayce stood in front of the stove, a spatula in one hand and the frying pan handle clutched in the other.

"Hope you like your eggs scrambled," Jayce said with a grin.

"I thought I was supposed to do that." She gave her best imitation of shock while cheering inwardly. Jayce had unwittingly let her off the hook, even if she hadn't agreed to make breakfast. Tiara's breakfast usually came from the frozen food aisle to be toasted or nuked, or picked up in drive thru lanes.

"I didn't think you'd mind. You did do the coffee," Jayce said putting down the spatula and lifting a mug. "You can finish if you want."

"No, no," Tiara said hastily, "I wouldn't want to spoil your fun."

Jayce raised an eyebrow. "You want to set the table?"

"Sure." She took a hesitant step forward. Tiara didn't remember which cabinet had the plates, or from which Jayce had retrieved the coffee mug.

"Plates on the left, silverware in the drawer below the plates," Jayce stated as if aware of Tiara's predicament. "If you want coffee, the mugs are over here." Jayce indicated the cabinet by her shoulder with a quick tilt of her head.

It was a challenge, and Tiara never turned down a challenge. Tiara had the impression Jayce waited to see if Tiara would ask her to pull one down, or come and get it herself. The atmosphere in the kitchen had subtly changed. It was too friendly — too cozy.

"Afraid I'll bite?" Jayce asked quietly.

"Yes, *you* would." Part of Tiara wanted to forget the coffee. Another part wanted to take up the dare, if only to get close to Jayce. Would Jayce brush her with a touch? Tiara simultaneously hoped she would and wouldn't make physical contact.

"I guess you're not thirsty," Jayce teased.

Tiara swallowed the nervous lump in her throat. Tiara was thirsty, but not for coffee, instead she longed for one small touch, one kiss, anything would do if it involved Jayce's body and hers. The thought terrified her.

Her terror must have registered on her face or in her manner because Jayce's next words startled her. "I didn't mean to frighten you. I was kidding."

"You didn't frighten me."

"Oh? You always look like a scared rabbit ready to flee? I'll get a mug for you, Bugs."

"Don't be ridiculous. I can get one myself." Jayce had given her a chance to avoid any possible touching and satisfy her logical side. Instead, Tiara had taken the dare — most illogical.

With legs feeling heavy, Tiara walked forward. Jayce shifted slightly to allow room, little though there was, and, edging close to the counter, Tiara squeezed into the space. She managed to open the cabinet door without touching Jayce. Then she inwardly cursed. The mugs were on the middle shelf and with her size — or lack of it at five-foot-two — she had to stand on tiptoe to reach.

"Would you like some help?" Jayce asked.

Her breath was warm on Tiara's ear. "I've got it." She really didn't. Lifting herself onto her toes, Tiara lost her balance as her fingers grasped the mug's handle. She fell against Jayce.

Goose bumps rose on her flesh and multiplied like the rabbit Jayce had mistaken her for only a moment ago. Tiara put her empty hand on Jayce's abdomen and pushed herself away. She felt surprise at how solidly Jayce was built, yet how unmistakably female she appeared outwardly. Her fingers trembled and Tiara didn't know if it was from her awareness of Jayce's physical strength or that Jayce sapped Tiara's energy, leaving her paralyzed in both mind and body.

Tiara took a deep breath to calm her rapidly beating heart. Her brain didn't register the scents she inhaled because Jayce bent her head forward and Tiara became mesmerized by the blue of her eyes.

"You're more beautiful up close," Jayce said. "I'm glad you've kept a few freckles."

"It...um...wasn't a choice."

"I'm glad anyway."

Jayce moved lower, closing distance. Tiara wanted Jayce to kiss her. Her lips were a breath away when Tiara recognized the mysterious scent. "Your eggs are burning."

Spinning around, Jayce mumbled, "Damn, so much for breakfast." She tossed the pan and its contents into the sink, ran water into it and stared at the resulting steam.

Tiara felt a blend of relief and disappointment. She'd come here to help her father, not be mixed up in an old relationship. Not that it ever had been one, except in her childhood daydreaming. Tiara was better off not starting something she wouldn't stick around to finish. Nevertheless, their physical contact made Tiara's heart leap. Even a simple kiss from Jayce could rekindle those old feelings, and dreaming was better than having nothing at all.

What would it mean to Jayce? Would a kiss from Tiara send Jayce rushing home with another scowl? Would they avoid each other? Tiara didn't want to find out. Of course, if Jayce responded that way again, it would be one less distraction for Tiara. "I wasn't hungry anyway," she said, as she clutched the cup and walked to the coffee pot. She had to concentrate to control the trembling in her hand as she poured.

"I could try again," Jayce turned toward her with a smile and crossed her arms, "if you promise not to distract me."

Tiara choked on the coffee. "You could've saved breakfast if you'd taken two cups down in the first place."

"Spoil sport."

If Jayce hadn't said it with an exaggerated pout, Tiara would have lost her temper at Jayce's implying her actions were a game. Jayce looked so beautiful with her eyes sparkling with mischief and her lower lip pushed forward that Tiara could forgive her anything at the moment. As it was, Tiara found it difficult not to reach up and tug at the extended lip.

Tiara needed a distraction. "What'd you do with Majestic?"

Jayce must have recognized the question for what it was, since she leaned casually back against the counter. "Put him in the corral, then went over to my place for the feed and other items he'll need later. Not sure what to do with that damn goose, it's not in my critter repertoire. It seems content enough just to be with the horse. You'll need to make those repairs to the fence, though. One misplaced bump and the whole thing will come down. I can make a call for supplies."

"Great, I can work on it today." Tiara felt relieved to have the topic on safe ground. "You know what to order. I'll get you my credit card."

"Did you mean what you said earlier?" Jayce asked.

Tiara frowned, knowing she'd said a lot earlier. "About what?"

"Fixing the house, too?"

Actually, Tiara hadn't given it much thought as she'd made her comment in anger. Did she mean it? "The house could use it. Since we don't know when Dad will get back, it would keep me busy."

"Good." Jayce seemed genuinely pleased.

"What?"

Jayce appeared to do some internal evaluation. Her eyebrows almost met in the center of her forehead in her concentration. "It will make Slim happy."

From her frown, Tiara expected her to say something different. What about you? Tiara wanted to demand. Would it make you happy, Jayce? Instead, she said, "I'll get my credit card."

After Tiara handed the card over, she walked Jayce out the front door and toward the driveway. "How long do you think it'll take for them to deliver?"

"I'll have it here in a couple of hours. Brad, who owns the lumber company, is a friend of mine. He owes me a favor or two."

"That always helps," Tiara added with a dollop of sarcasm.

"Yup." Jayce grinned. "I'll bring this back later." She stuffed the card in a shirt pocket.

Much as she wanted it returned, Tiara wasn't sure she liked this messenger coming with it, creating a flurry of emotions in her head and the pit of her stomach. "No hurry."

"Oh, yeah? What if I use it for my own purposes?"

"Just keep it under the limit."

"Which is?" Jayce lifted an eyebrow.

"For you?"

"Who else?"

"Maybe a lady love," Tiara said, suddenly saddened by the prospect, confused by the surge of jealousy she felt. What if Jayce had a lover? Why do I care?

"Nope, none—yet. If your credit's worthy, I could find a temporary one fast enough."

Tiara was tempted to slap her. "I bet you could. Your limit's the cost of a day at the gym."

"Don't need that, or didn't you notice when you were mauling me in your kitchen."

"I wasn't mauling," Tiara felt her face flame with embarrassment.

"Well, maybe you could later." Jayce winked. "I'll leave the stove off next time."

"There won't be a next time," Tiara hissed through clenched teeth.

Jayce laughed, and Tiara realized that the tall beauty was enjoying her discomfort. "I'll go call this in. It'll give you time to see what you're up against. The fence is a lot of job for anyone, much less a little thing like you. I'll be back later."

"Don't hurry," she shouted as Jayce walked away. Tiara stared after her—observing that cute little swagger—until Jayce reached her property. "Sexy, arrogant witch," she finally breathed when certain that Jayce couldn't hear.

Tiara turned and surveyed the house, noting it wasn't as bad as she'd originally thought. Okay, maybe it was bad. A new roof, replace most of the siding, build a garage on the existing concrete slab, reinforce the porch and it would be good as new. Better, even.

Tiara couldn't understand how her father had let the house go for so long. Didn't he care? Or had her leaving with her mother, Angie, ten years ago destroyed any love he'd had for the house?

To Tiara, the deterioration had started with her mother's sullen moods. The house had been alive once, beautiful, comfortable and warm. Perhaps whatever demons had driven Angie to hide in the bottle had seeped into the wallboard and the hand-carved moldings, causing the house to become sad and depressed.

She would follow through and make the more immediate repairs. Tiara couldn't rebuild the last ten years, but she could infuse a new look, some new life. If it wasn't enough for her father, so be it. At least she'd have given it a shot.

If only emotions could be as easily repaired. Plaster, sanding and painting could mend a hole in a wall to sleek perfection. But how did a person fix a hole in the soul?

Maybe Tiara couldn't fix a soul. Instead, she'd focus on the house. When completed, Tiara could start rebuilding her relationship with her father—if Slim ever came home. It wouldn't be easy, but neither was construction work. Both took sweat and exertion.

"I'll do it."

The affirmation was like a deeply drawn breath, refreshing and cleansing. It didn't last long, and the tension returned. "How does Jayce really feel about this idea?" she asked aloud.

A beam of sunshine hit the windows and Tiara almost believed the house smiled at her. She blinked and the image disappeared; yet she felt happy with her decision knowing the house was pleased. Having something to do would make the time go faster, take her mind off Jayce, and keep her busy until her father arrived.

Good as she was, Tiara knew she couldn't do this alone in a short time. She rushed into the house and to the kitchen telephone. Tiara punched the numbers to the company's cellular phone Harry kept with him.

She laughed softly as a plan formed in her head.

Chapter Four

"SUMMER'S CONSTRUCTION, HARRY Carter speaking."

"Hi, Harry, it's me," Tiara said.

"Boss Lady. How's it going?" His tone became serious. "Everything okay?"

"Just fine." Tiara couldn't help smiling; his concern warmed her. "How's the work on the chiropractor's house coming along?"

"Great. We're ahead of schedule. Any adverse summer weather's been holding off here. Unfortunately, probably means drought later."

"Glad to hear the work schedule's good since I need to take a couple of the guys off the project. Kind of cosmic, you know, with the job going so quickly."

Harry snorted. "What's going on in that head of yours, Boss?"

She shrugged, though he couldn't see it. "Can you spare Craig and Mark?"

"If you need 'em, you got 'em."

Tiara didn't want to disrupt their personal lives, but she couldn't do the work alone, either, not with the schedule she had in mind. "Make sure they don't have a problem with this first, but I need them immediately for an extended stay. If Mark agrees, he can certainly bring Darla. I've enough room here for all of them. I'll understand if Mark prefers not to come, considering Darla's current health issue."

"Your father doesn't mind the extra company interrupting your reunion?"

"Dad hasn't arrived yet."

"But..."

"Don't ask." Tiara sighed. "It's a long story."

"Just remember to tell me all about it when you get back," Harry ordered playfully.

"Not like I'll have a choice in the matter. You'll nag like an old woman until you get all the details." After a few more moments of banter, Tiara gave him the directions to the house, her father's house phone number, and a list of supplies and equipment she needed. Anything else she could probably get locally from Jayce's friend. "Honestly, if this is inconvenient even a little bit, to any of you, let me know, Harry. Maybe you could recommend somebody else I could use."

"You'd be the first to know. I gotta ask, Boss, fixing or rebuilding? This is quite the list."

"A little of both, and I don't know what might be available here without a backorder. Besides, you know I like busy work." She chuckled. "Okay, then. That leaves the corral for me until the guys arrive with everything else."

"Do I have to wait for you to explain that, too?"

"Trust me, Harry, I've a feeling the story will be worth the wait. You'll get one heck of a laugh, and at my expense, as usual."

Harry's tone turned serious. "Tiara, the teasing is never meant—"

"I know, Harry," she replied honestly. Tiara didn't want him to feel a need to apologize. Harry was the closest she'd come to having another father around her. Fatherly-types were supposed to laugh at a child's antics, especially when the child was as clumsy as Tiara. The mood shifted, and she didn't want that to happen, didn't want Harry worrying. Cheerfully, she added, "It's all good, honest. Talk to you later, Harry."

She hung up, excited. A new project always pushed her adrenaline into hyper-drive. She ran upstairs to her room and took her work sunglasses from the gym bag; then, as she turned to leave, stopped short noting the picture of her mother and father on the wall by the door.

Tiara hadn't really noticed it this morning and was too tired last night. It was an earlier picture of her parents, from right after their wedding. They looked so happy. Tiara wondered what had changed their relationship so drastically. Whatever had happened to them came before her birth. From her earliest memory, her mother had a drinking problem and her father bet on anything he could. Which started first?

A thought nagged at her, like an itch she couldn't reach. Had their problems resulted from her birth, her disruption to the family? Was she the reason their blissfulness had gone? Tiara shuddered. It was too late to change what had occurred. All she could do was move on. With one last look, she rushed down the stairs and out the kitchen door.

The fence material arrived two hours later. Jayce, on horseback, was not far behind. Tiara had already inspected the corral, which covered a three-acre area, and made mental notes of what needed to be done and prioritized the jobs. The project would be a bit of a change from building homes, and would expand her repertoire. She was excited and it must have showed.

"You won't be so happy once you get started," Jayce said, dismounting.

"How can you be so sure?"

"I've been there. It's a lot of work, and physically exhausting."

Tiara frowned. "What's with you?"

"What?" Jayce squinted.

Was the squint because of the sunshine or confusion? Tiara decided she couldn't care less. "Why is it so hard for you to believe me capable of hard work? I never expected you to be a—a—chauvinist. Guess I was wrong." Tiara said, shaking her head.

"Ouch. I'm no chauvinist," Jayce replied.

"Whatever." Tiara walked over to the lumber truck's driver and indicated where to deposit the material.

Jayce followed her. "Wait. I didn't mean to imply you couldn't do the job."

Tiara spun around to face her. She remembered they had an audience and entertaining the locals was the last thing she wanted to do. "The implication is strong enough, Jayce, meant or not. Now, there's work to accomplish, so please leave."

"We should settle this misunderstanding first."

"Okay," Tiara said, "then go ahead and tell me."

Jayce frowned. "Tell you what?"

Crossing her arms, Tiara said, "That you believe I can do the job, and do it right."

"If you say you can, I can't argue. It's just a fence, after all."

"But you don't think I can handle even that task," Tiara snapped.

"All right, let's be honest." Jayce shoved her hand out with her palm up. "Look at yourself. You're too little for the kind of work that will be needed here, let alone do it by yourself."

"Thanks for your honesty," she said sarcastically.

"See. Truth hurts and you forced me into voicing it."

"You're right, Jayce, the vice grip on your arm as I twisted the confession from you was too much pain to stand. Oh, poor little baby."

"Now you're mad," Jayce said.

"As hell." Tiara closed the distance between them and jabbed a finger into Jayce's firm stomach. "I've nothing to prove and I'll be damned if I'll kill myself trying. I couldn't possibly care what you think I'm capable of doing."

"Then why so bent out of shape?" Jayce asked, slapping Tiara's hand away.

"Because the sexier you got as you grew, the dumber you became." The two deliverymen stopped unloading the truck. Tiara sighed and lowered her voice. "Size has nothing to do with any of this. All those years of training and breaking horses have knocked the last shreds of brain-matter from your thick, albeit gorgeous, skull.

Throwing a quick glance at the men, Jayce lowered her voice, too. "We aren't getting anywhere by arguing, especially about something so trivial."

"You're wrong. We each know where we stand. I didn't ask for your help, and I won't. So get on your horse and ride away, cowgirl."

Jayce was still scowling when she rode off.

Tiara hadn't intended to call her dumb. She hated to believe people could be entirely stupid, really, but Jayce made her so furious.

The mature thing to do would be to apologize, but the idea of an apology was unthinkable while she was still angry. Tiara sniffed. If Jayce were like most people, she'd take any well meant—somewhat well meant—sorry for agreement that Tiara was wrong. "Ugh, phooey with an apology. Better Jayce think what she will and just leave me alone."

JAYCE REINED THE horse into the stable and dismounted. After loosening the cinch and removing the saddle, bridle, and blanket, she gave Arabelle's shoulder a nudge sending her out to the other horses currently with the stable hands. Jayce had enough work.

Actually, Jayce had hardly accomplished any training today. Since Tiara had arrived last night, she couldn't focus on much of anything, unless she counted Tiara, which she had no rational reason to do.

If she thought the reasons through, Jayce knew she'd conclude she just worried about Tiara's well being, stuck in that big old house by herself, waiting for her father to return, and taking on repair jobs bigger than she was. "Hell, seven-year-old boys are bigger than Tiara." Not that she originally meant any insult, at least not until Tiara got all fired up. Then, Jayce had felt duty bound to continue pushing Tiara's angry button.

As Jayce thought the situation through she reached different conclusions. Those were the last reasons Tiara was on her mind. Last night she'd seen the sadness in Tiara's eyes. This morning she'd felt the warmth of Tiara's hand on her abdomen and come so close to kissing Tiara that not doing so had left her feeling empty. If Jayce had kissed her, would Tiara be out of her system? Would Jayce be able to turn away and finally forget the petite woman?

Why was she asking herself these ridiculous questions?

Jayce had meant nothing to Tiara for ten years; she was a grown woman, no longer some lovesick seventeen-year-old wanting to play Galahad. Tiara was the one who left, not Jayce, albeit Tiara hadn't had much choice in the matter at the time. Ultimately, it had been Angie's choice, but Tiara could have come back, and she hadn't. That simple fact alone had torn her apart—Slim, too, of course. If it hadn't been for Jayce's Aunt Edna, Slim would have fallen to pieces. So, why let Tiara get to her now? She'd gotten Tiara out of her system a long time ago. Well, kind of, and this wasn't about her.

She made a promise to Slim. Jayce's responsibilities were to watch the place in his absence and that included Tiara in the deal, whether Tiara liked it or not. Jayce hadn't expected such an adamant aversion from Tiara, though. Most people would like the idea of someone watching out for them, a sort of guardian angel ready in the wings.

"The chauvinist insult was cold blooded," Jayce grumbled. She brightened a tad, remembering Tiara had also used sexy and gorgeous in her diatribe.

Once in the house, Jayce poured coffee into her favorite mug. Tiara clearly wasn't going to make the job easy, so she'd have to be clever in handling her. Jayce gulped the hot coffee. In the end, Tiara would appreciate her decision to look after her.

BY SIX O'CLOCK, Tiara had finished the rebuild of about 100 feet of fence. Half an hour later, after a refreshing shower, she was ready to begin her usual routine. She'd made tuna salad and put two sandwiches together, grabbed two cans of soda and the bag of chips off the table from the night before and carried it all to the living room. She found a television station playing an old movie. She propped her feet up on the coffee table and arranged her meal around her, ready to relax. She'd taken a large bite of sandwich when the phone rang.

Jayce calling to apologize, Tiara thought with glee. She'd accept it graciously, of course. Tomorrow, she'd make an appointment to have phone lines put in other rooms, since the only phone jack was in the kitchen. Chewing quickly, Tiara swallowed and grabbed the receiver on the third ring. "Hello," she said sweetly.

"Let me talk to Slim." The nasal voice wasn't Jayce's. An image flashed in her mind and Tiara barely managed to contain the laughter. This guy sounded like Squiggy on *Laverne and Shirley*.

Tiara sobered. "He's not here at the moment. This is his daughter. May I help you?"

The man snorted. "Give him a message. Tell him I'm coming for Majestic. No one steals from Sparretti."

Any residual humor quickly drained and Tiara became defensive on her father's behalf. "Mr. Spaghetti, my father is not a thief."

"Sparretti," he corrected in a shrill tone. "I'll give him two days to return my property. Then I come for Majestic myself."

Tiara tensed. This man sounded serious, even with the ridiculous voice. Was this her father's trouble? She decided it best not to antagonize. Voices could be deceptive and he might be seven-feet tall and built like a linebacker. What if he followed through with his threat? "Maybe if you explained the situation, I could be of assistance."

"Two days," he whined nasally, and then hung up.

Tiara replaced the receiver on the cradle. "All right, Dad, call." She hoped the plea would make the phone ring. "This time I'll get answers if I have to track you down to do it." Tiara stared at the phone for five minutes, but nothing happened. "Okay, I'll give you a little more time," she said, then went back to her supper.

The old movie playing was a James Cagney gangster film. A cool breeze blew through the open window and she shivered; whether from an omen or the wind, Tiara wasn't sure. Was her father involved with gangsters? Did gangsters still exist like in the old movies? Killing whoever got in their way or had allegedly stole from them? She knew street thugs and gangs existed, but did the mafia-types?

The soggy sandwiches made her appetite disappear. So did the mood for old movies. Flipping the top on the soda can, Tiara guzzled half the contents, her form of liquid courage, before she rose, locking the house up as nice and tight as possible. She felt ridiculous when she had finished. It was still light outside and she sat locked inside like a paranoid spinster.

Better paranoid than dead, she reasoned.

Tiara shook her head. What was she worried about? Hadn't the spaghetti man given her two days? Nevertheless, gangsters lied. She went back to the couch, opened the bag of chips and stuffed three large ones into her mouth. Then she groaned. Between a missing father, Jayce Mansfield, the horse and the gangster—not to mention the wicked goose—her life had quickly become reminiscent of a bad B-movie.

This better not all turn out to be a joke, Dad.

Chapter Five

TIARA FELT SO bone-weary the following morning that even her steamy shower hadn't helped. Used to hard work, she hadn't expected the fence repairs to make her so tired. Of course, she admitted, nightmares of gangsters with Tommy-guns hadn't made for restful slumber.

"You're probably blowing all this out of proportion," she mumbled into her coffee.

"Blowing what out of proportion?"

Startled she set down her mug and turned to see Jayce leaning against the frame of the kitchen door she'd opened before starting coffee. Jayce's hands were behind her back and one booted foot casually crossed the other at the ankles. Her hair was damp and neatly combed. Evidence she had recently finished a shower; or dunked her head in the horse trough, Tiara quickly amended. The image of Jayce doing just that made her want to smirk.

She groaned instead, wondering if it was because she hadn't expected to see Jayce so early, or because the woman looked so darn good after her own rough evening of almost nonexistent sleep. Truth being told, Tiara realized sullenly, Jayce looked good to her no matter how the night had gone or what her present mood happened to be.

"I brought a peace offering," Jayce said softly.

"Unless it's your head on a plate, I won't accept it," Tiara replied. She wanted to demand Jayce leave her alone, leave her house—okay, Slim's house—but Tiara couldn't afford to expend more energy. She would need every ounce to finish the worst of the fencing before dark today.

"Will Danish do?" Jayce asked, moving into the kitchen and dropping the white paper sack onto the table. "Blueberry's still your favorite, isn't it?" She moved to the cabinets, pulled down two small plates and poured herself a mug of coffee, before sitting opposite her. Tiara was surprised Jayce had remembered something as personal as her favorite fruit filling. More surprised by how much it pleased her. "Eat up," Jayce ordered, putting one on a small plate before each of them.

Tiara stared at the peace offering as if it would jump up and bite her. What was Jayce up to now?

"Pastry won't bite back," Jayce said with a chuckle.

"Don't do that." Tiara glared at her. How did Jayce always manage to read what was inside Tiara's head? Like not knowing where plates were, or her trepidation in retrieving a mug or that Tiara wanted to bolt whenever they got close.

"Do what?"

"Know what I'm thinking, almost before I do." She should have known Jayce would laugh, but was unprepared for her own hurt response. "Glad I can bring amusement to your day," Tiara said. Taking her anger out on the Danish, she tore a section, shoved it in her mouth and chewed vigorously.

As quick as Jayce's laughter started, she stopped. "Come on, Red." Jayce shifted in her chair. "Okay, I'm sorry for upsetting you and for laughing."

"Who says I'm upset?"

"It's only obvious what goes on in that pretty little head of yours, since it's written all over your face. Not hard to figure out."
Tiara felt her face grow warm. Jayce thought her pretty? No, she chided herself silently, only a figure of speech. "Well, try to refrain from doing it altogether," Tiara mumbled grumpily around another mouthful.

"I'll do my best," Jayce promised, giving the pouting expression she'd used yesterday morning. Tiara still had the urge to tug at the extended lower lip—with her teeth.

"You had better quit that, too."

"What?" Jayce asked, taking a large bite of Danish.

"Pouting," she said. "Some bird may think it's a perch and land on it." Tiara giggled at the image flashing in her head. "You know how unpredictable birds are with their droppings."

Jayce laughed around the mouthful of food, nearly choking in her hurry to swallow. When she'd swallowed, she presented Tiara a quick flash of straight white teeth. "A sight you would pay dearly to see, I'm sure."

"As a matter of fact, I would."

"No offense, but I'd rather not accommodate you in that direction. Certainly, if you want me to indulge you in any other direction..." Jayce glanced toward the stove, then back with a mischievous grin. "Want to pick up where we left off yesterday?"

"No." Tiara felt her face go warm again, and decided to give breakfast her total attention. She lowered her head and let her hair fall forward, hoping it would shadow the blushing, if not hide it completely.

"Too bad," Jayce whispered huskily. "I was looking forward to seeing just what we could cook up together."

She knew Jayce wasn't referring to food. It bothered Tiara when her body grew warm at the suggestion and the tempo of her heartbeat increased. She clenched her hands to curb the impulse to reach out and pull Jayce closer. Tiara's gaze hypnotically pulled in the direction of Jayce's lips as her own mind conjured an image of...Jayce's lower lip caught between Tiara's own teeth before her tongue ran—

A hand passed before her face and startled Tiara.

"Hello?" Jayce's voice sounded filled with mirth.

Tiara blinked to clear the last remnants of...daydreaming? More like a sensual fantasy. If Jayce hadn't regained her attention, how far would Tiara's mind have gone? She shuddered. Too far, that's where. "Sorry," Tiara whispered, surprised and embarrassed by the huskiness of her own voice.

Jayce grinned at her like a kid who just pulled off a successful prank as she leaned back in her chair. "Nice little trip, I hope? Your body was here, but the rest of you went all *Star Wars*."

"Huh?"

"Red, you went far, far away."

Tiara cleared her throat. "Sorry," she repeated, relieved her voice sounded normal.

"Let me ask again, since you apparently weren't listening the first time," Jayce said, getting up and pouring another cup of coffee. She brought the pot over to the table and topped Tiara's mug off. "What'd you blow out of proportion?"

Tiara's heartbeat quickened, in panic. Did her expression reveal her internal vision? Did Jayce refer to her fantasy as blown out of proportion? She started it, Tiara's mind screamed. Damn her anyway. Jayce could have been more tactful in letting Tiara know her teasing was one-sided.

"If you'd kept your promise, you wouldn't be included or bothered by what I do or do not blow out of proportion," Tiara said.

"Come again?" Jayce looked bewildered.

How long would they play this particular game? "Knock it off, Jayce. You know what I'm talking about."

Jayce crossed her arms over her chest, drawing Tiara's attention from her face. Down, to...full, rounded breasts, strong and still sexy, such...

"No, I don't know," Jayce said.

"If you hadn't been reading my expressions, you wouldn't have known I'd blown the imagery out of proportion." Tiara finished, shaking her head and meeting Jayce's stunned gaze.

The corners of Jayce's mouth twitched. Her sky blue—no, cornflower-blue—eyes sparkled with the restrained mirth. "What imagery would that be exactly?" Jayce asked, her voice nearly bubbling with humor. "I was referring to what you said when I first walked in."

Tiara groaned at her own stupidity, not able to face Jayce. Tiara turned away, managing an awkward, "Oh."

JAYCE COULDN'T HOLD back any longer, the laugh burst out of her throat. Whatever imagery had gone on, she didn't need it voiced to visualize it, as Tiara's red cheeks and downcast eyes told her all she needed to know. Just picturing what Tiara was probably imagining had Jayce positively delighted. Until she realized Tiara could be envisioning anyone's lips while staring at hers.

Reaching forward, Jayce touched the loose hair that had fallen around Tiara's face and tucked it behind her small ear. She then cupped Tiara's chin and raised it. "When I came in," Jayce began slowly, "you said you were probably blowing something out of proportion. Should I worry? What happened, and is it something you need to talk about? I'm ready to listen."

Tiara carefully pulled away from Jayce's grasp, gaze darting around the kitchen, landing on everything and anything, but Jayce. Tiara appeared hesitant to explain. "I got a call last night, about Majestic."

"Slim called?" Jayce asked, relatively certain that wasn't the answer.

"No, some guy claiming Dad stole his horse and that he'd be coming for it in two days. Since I watched an old gangster movie afterward, I kinda had nightmares. That's what I meant. I blew the call out of proportion."

Jayce scowled. "Did he threaten you?" The question came out sounding harsher than intended. She didn't want Tiara hurt, her safety was Jayce's responsibility. For Slim's sake, she reminded herself. Tiara shook her head. "What's this guy's name?" Would Jayce know him? Probably not.

Tiara shrugged. "It sounded like food."

"A food name?" Wow. For a petite woman, meals seemed to be the one thing Tiara could relate to with any seriousness. "Can you be more specific?"

"Spaghetti," Tiara said, paused, and repeated with a nod, "Yeah, sounds like spaghetti."

Jayce chuckled at the declaration. "Okay. Mr. Sounds-like-spaghetti called and told you Slim stole his horse. Then said he, or Slim, was coming in two days?"

"Mr. Spaghetti was coming here," Tiara confirmed. "Dad never stated an arrival time when he called."

"Slim called? What did he say about the guy?"

"He didn't say anything," she explained. "Dad called the night I arrived, and told me to expect to see the brute. This other call came last night to announce Mr. Spaghetti was coming to get the horse."

Brute? Ah, Majestic, Jayce thought, trying to piece the information together without revealing how humorous, albeit frustrating, she found the situation. Apparently, from the way Tiara referred to the horse, she had little love for the animal, especially after their little "walk" together yesterday morning. If only Jayce had a camera. The picture would have been priceless, at least to Jayce.

"So Slim never told you when he was coming home?" Tiara shook her head. "The other guy's coming in two days to reclaim a horse he says Slim stole from him?" Tiara nodded. "Slim wouldn't steal, so this guy's lying," Jayce concluded.

"Ha." Tiara pursed her lips and rolled her eyes.

"What 'ha'?" Jayce couldn't believe that little outburst. Not from the sweet kid she remembered. Tiara wasn't a kid anymore. Maybe sweet had gone terribly sour.

"The guy gambled with Dad and got suckered," Tiara stated with bitterness.

This was too much. From the tone, Tiara sounded like she believed Slim capable of cheating. What was with the gambling remark? She knew little about her own father. Part of the guilt rested on the older man's shoulders, for maintaining the separation; but Tiara could have — should have — more faith in her own dad, not convicting him without any actual evidence.

Jayce's exasperation flashed so quickly she acted without thinking. Leaping from her seat and around the table, she loomed over Tiara for half a second, grabbed her by the shoulders and tugged her from the chair.

"You spoiled brat," Jayce ground through clenched teeth. "Your father hasn't gambled since you and Angie left. Not that it was ever the issue Angie made it out to be, either. You'd have known that, if you cared enough to ask."

"He admitted as much in his call." Tears gathered in Tiara's eyes, her lips trembling when she replied, "I wasn't given a choice in leaving."

Jayce suddenly felt like a raving lunatic. She was holding Tiara off the floor with her feet dangling, and she'd caused further emotional pain by dredging up the past. Tiara was right. Angie hadn't given Tiara or Slim a choice in the matter. Softening her voice, Jayce replied, "You could have, should have, come back."

"Why?" Tiara asked.

The gold flecks in her eyes sparkled through her tears, the gray blending with the watery haze. How could Tiara not know the answer? Jayce swallowed hard. "You had people here who loved you, needed you, cared about what happened to you."

"People?" The disbelief she must be experiencing, strengthened with the one word, as a smirk twisted Tiara's lips.

"Yes, Slim, Aunt Edna..." Jayce hesitated, wondering if she should be completely honest. When Tiara rolled her eyes, she didn't debate the pros and cons of her next action. Jayce pulled Tiara up at her own eye level. Her gaze drawn to slightly tremulous lips, Jayce whispered, "I needed you, Red," before she brought her lips to Tiara's in a hungry kiss.

Jayce felt Tiara lean into the kiss and answer with her own need. She gently thrust her tongue into Tiara's mouth, rewarded with the return thrust dancing against her teeth and the roof of her mouth. The sensations stirred had Jayce blocking out all else.

Until she felt a sharp jab to her shin as Tiara kicked her.

Jayce jerked back with a mumbled curse and reached for her injured limb as Tiara dropped onto her backside with a thud. "What the..." Then Jayce heard the frantic beeping of car horns from outside.

Tiara stood and massaged the abused area. Jayce thought to offer assistance, but decided to leave well enough alone.

"I have company," Tiara informed her coldly, spinning on her heels toward the hallway. She turned and flashed Jayce an angry glare. Tilting her head and looking to a point behind Jayce's shoulder, Tiara said, "The road traveled both ways, Jayce. I don't remember anyone driving to see me, either."

Jayce stood statue-still in Tiara's kitchen and monitored the woman's retreat, not missing Tiara's hand rubbing an injured backside, knowing she should go after her, but unable to do so. Jayce didn't chase women, even when she owed them an apology. Tiara had hit the nail on the head, though. Both she and Slim could have brought Tiara back, ignored Angie's directives otherwise, and explained Tiara had a place here. Neither of them had done so, not after all Jayce's letters returned with hateful remarks scrawled on the unopened envelopes; or, after Angie managed to put a restraining order against her and Slim. Regardless, Slim kept track of Tiara during her absence: her accomplishments and her career; and, subsequently, shared them with Jayce and Edna. All of them had believed it enough, at the time. Could they have been wrong? Had leaving Tiara to make the decision, the effort, only increased the problem of her thinking that she didn't belong?

No, it needed to be Tiara's choice. Had Tiara chosen to believe her father, Aunt Edna and Jayce had abandoned her? Apparently, yes. That's why her sorrow had never disappeared. Jayce had to explain, let Tiara know the truth. Maybe chasing someone wasn't a bad thing.

Jayce charged down the hallway and out the front door, then stopped short. One car and two vehicles loaded with building material and other supplies had parked behind Tiara's truck. Jayce paid them a cursory glance. What had stopped her was the scene enacting on the concrete slab. A homely pregnant woman stood behind Tiara, a huge man beside her and both watched a young blonde boy give Tiara a more than friendly bear hug, and followed with spinning her in a circle and a loud kiss directly on Tiara's lips.

Those being the same lips Jayce had tasted only a moment ago.

Jayce recognized her inner rage to be jealousy. She hated that it was because of a kid probably barely out of high school. How could I have read Tiara so wrong? Had she misinterpreted Tiara's return kiss in the kitchen? Who was playing games now?

"She felt abandoned, my Aunt Fan...Edna," Jayce mumbled.

Quietly, so not to draw attention, Jayce retraced her steps and left out the back door, carefully closing the screen behind her. She'd just go around the back and head home. Obviously, not needed anymore, Jayce didn't intend to watch some kid manhandle Red.

As Jayce crossed the back fence, Majestic whinnied loudly. For the first time in her life, she felt betrayed by a horse. The goose honked its own discordant broadcast.

The cacophony caught Tiara's attention, "Jayce, where are you going?"

Chapter Six

TIARA COULDN'T BELIEVE Jayce tried to scurry away like the rat she'd been in the kitchen. "Come meet my friends," she ordered, waving Jayce over. She hoped Jayce felt horrible for the things she'd said, but Tiara doubted it, especially when she noticed what she supposed was ill humor emanating from Jayce's eyes and directed toward the group. Tiara's own aggravation billowed around her like a tarp caught in a strong wind. She wanted to fling it back at Jayce, but held it under control. Did Jayce feel guilty for what had transpired in the kitchen? That's what it had to be, slinking away because of guilt. Maybe a little constructive time with real people would level Jayce's attitude, not to mention cement the understanding that Tiara had done just fine on her own, and didn't need Jayce or her kisses.

Tiara shuddered. Gosh, I even think in building terms. "Everyone," she started when Jayce joined them. "This is Jayce Mansfield. She lives on the property joining Dad's and is helping with the horse."

"Horse?" Darla exclaimed. "I didn't know your dad had a working farm."

"He doesn't. Long story." Tiara assured her. "Jayce, Darla," then she pointed to the towering behemoth pussycat of a man, "and Mark Chester. They're expecting baby Chester soon."

"Not too soon." Mark gave his haw-haw-haw and extended his hand in Jayce's direction. "Pleasure. Hope we won't disturb you too much with all the fixing Boss Lady's got in mind."

"Nice to meet you, Mark, Darla," Jayce said. "It'll be nice to see some changes around here. If they're too good, though, we'll–she'll–have to change the name of the place."

"And this," Tiara said, indicating the youngest of her crew, "is Craig Walters."

"Pleased to meet you, Jayce." Craig vigorously shook hands with Jayce and beamed an ear-to-ear smile. "Tiara's doing the fixing, so you'd better work on new names now," he stated, draping an arm across Tiara's shoulder.

"Really?" Jayce sounded unconvinced.

Tiara wanted to slap Jayce upside the head, would have if she could easily reach the eight-inch difference. Instead, she planted herself directly in front of Jayce and snapped, "Yes, really."

Jayce gave a quizzical expression. "I never meant—"

"You did. I can... Oh, never mind. We've covered this ground before."

Jayce crossed her arms. "If memory serves, you had a closer acquaintance than I did, with the ground that is."

Tiara's face fused with heat, whether with anger or embarrassment that the incident with the brute was brought up at all, she couldn't be sure. Either way, Tiara fumed. "That was low."

"Then we're even," Jayce stated while glaring at Craig.

"For what?" Tiara demanded. She wanted to demand a reason from Jayce just what Craig had done to warrant her obvious disfavor.

"The chauvinistic crack, okay?"

"Geez!" Tiara groaned, poking Jayce in the stomach with her finger. "I was talking about handling the repairs, not that—that—"

"Horse," Jayce supplied through gritted teeth. "That's the second time you've poked me. Don't do it again. And Majestic is a horse."

"It's a beast—just like you."

Jayce's eyes darkened. "Better a beast than a foolish, heartless, munchkin female without a clue."

Tiara gasped at the words. She felt the verbal blow as keen and biting as any physical assault. Words she'd told herself often enough, but it hurt painfully that Jayce would declare them to her face. "I guess you're right, Jayce," Tiara mumbled, turning to find three pairs of shocked eyes glaring at Jayce, then back toward her.

"Who the hell does she think she is?" Craig spat. "Woman or not, she has—"

"Whoa, pup," Mark grabbed Craig by his shirt collar. Mark stared at Jayce. "Tiara, I'd like to get my wife inside and settled outta the heat and all."

The sting of Jayce's words drained her emotionally and physically, and Tiara willed her feet to move toward Darla. "I'm sorry. Let me show you inside."

From behind, she heard Jayce's whispered plea, "Red, wait. Let me—"

When her words cut off abruptly, Tiara twisted her head to find Craig and Mark blocked Jayce's path, Mark's huge hand on her shoulder. "I think you've said enough for now, Ms. Mansfield. Go on home and lick your wounds. Darla will tend to Boss Lady's."

"Yeah, but—" Jayce, a tall woman in her own right, had to look up at the towering man.

Tiara knew Jayce had no way of knowing Mark's true nature. At this moment, she was uncertain she knew it very well, having never encountered this situation before. Mark shook his head, "But nothing, Ma'am." Tiara felt the urge to intervene. She stanched the impulse when Mark's voice dropped menacingly, as he told Jayce, "Don't ever talk to her like that again, in or out of my presence, being a lady or not... Understood?"

Tiara winced at the antagonism lacing the words. She glanced at Jayce and saw what appeared to be frustration broadcasting from her eyes. Jayce met her gaze and the emotion softened for half a second, before she spun on her boot heels and stomped off in the direction of her home. Without completely understanding why, Tiara started after Jayce, but Darla halted her with a gentle hand on her arm.

"Give her a chance to cool down," Darla said with gentleness.

Tiara gave a wry smile. "No, she isn't wrong."

Darla stared at her for a long moment, as if gauging adequate words by gleaning hints from Tiara's features. "Then you both need to let it all sink in and cool off." Tiara gaped, disconcerted that Darla read too much. Darla laughed pleasantly and nudged her up the porch steps. "Come on, show me around. If I know those two," she said, inclining her head in Craig and Mark's direction, "they want to see how much can be unloaded before lunch."

Tiara paused. "Oh, lunch." Honesty being best from the get-go, she explained, "Junk food is about all you're going to find in the kitchen, right now. Dad doesn't appear to be much into culinary arts." After her argument with Jayce, not being straightforward seemed to have consequences of their own. Well, they'd learn soon enough. "Darla, I...I can't–"

"I need to ask a favor," Darla interrupted, her brow puckered. "I appreciate you allowing me to join Mark and this invasion on your home."

"I didn't give you much time to give the decision any thought. And I don't mind. It'll be nice to have another woman...um...have you here."

Darla continued, "It's nice to get out of the apartment, sort of a vacation in the country. But I wouldn't feel right if I didn't contribute in some way, and since you'll be working, I'd like to do the cooking."

Tiara laughed nervously and cast a glance at the two men unloading the trucks, hoping they weren't listening. "I appreciate the offer, Darla, but I certainly don't want you overdoing it, either, not in your condition. Cooking isn't exactly my strong suit." She hoped glossing over the topic didn't constitute lying.

Pushing the front door open, Darla stepped inside. While giving a quick look around, she said, "Actually, I believe you've forgotten your bad case of flu last winter. I stopped by with homemade chicken soup."

Tiara remembered, but didn't understand the correlation. "I've seen your refrigerator and cupboards." Darla caught sight of the couch. Sitting down, she patted a spot and Tiara joined her. "Except for munchies, you had the *Old Mother Hubbard* look going on."

"I eat a lot of take-out," Tiara explained.

"Maybe, if you have a bit of time while I'm here, I can work with you on easy recipes that don't take much longer than nuking something in the microwave."

"I'd like that."

"Well, it's the least I can do, seeing what a great boss you are to Mark, and the others. The barbecues, the Christmas parties, and never forgetting anniversaries—"

"Gotta keep up morale." Tiara shook her head. "Besides, I'm

simply assuring my company does well. It's good business."

Darla frowned. "You don't recognize your place in this 'family', do you?" Tiara must have made an expression she was unaware of. "I didn't mean to upset you," Darla said.

"You didn't."

"Yes, I probably did, but we'll move on. For now."

Darla hit the proverbial nail squarely. Tiara didn't know how to behave or react. With Angie, she was a sounding board for drunken rage, depression and disapproval. With Slim, the early years, anyway, she was the clumsy child who couldn't do anything right, though he patiently looked on. With Jayce, she wasn't a strong enough woman. Jayce may have kissed her less than an hour ago, but, similar to the summer ten years ago, found Tiara lacking. Jayce proved it by not returning to the antics she played, or spending time alone with her while she lived in Silver Waters. Something about those memories felt wrong, but would have to wait until later to give more thought. The part she played in people's lives had her feeling like...well, like the redheaded stepchild. When it came to family, Tiara didn't belong, didn't fit into any picture of the average expectations.

Unable to meet the disappointed stare in Darla's eyes, Tiara stood and tugged her hands free. "You're probably tired after the ride down. I'll show you to a room. All the bedrooms are upstairs," she explained, "but there's a den. I could bring down a bed and make it more comfortable and convenient for you not to have to climb."

Darla sighed wearily. Tiara wasn't sure if it were exhaustion or acceptance at the change of topic. Either way, it would be best to get the woman settled and herself outside and working, as work was the only cure for her bad mood.

"Upstairs is fine, I can use the exercise. If we need to adjust rooms later, we will."

Half an hour later, Darla set up in Slim's room for a nap, Tiara made her way to the side of the house and the rhythmic pounding of hammers. They'd started on the obvious points of neglect and Tiara pulled Mark aside to explain the ideas she had and to formulate a plan for basic time scheduling. When they'd finished their conversation, she began to fret they hadn't made adequate accommodations for Darla's condition and nap time, and brought it up to him.

Mark relieved her worries. "Boss Lady, she'll sleep through anything. Any noise we make will be a lullaby to her."

"Then I'll finish the corral." Tiara realized she hadn't thanked him for earlier. Whether she deserved his concern or not, she appreciated the protective gesture; and wondered if the mixed elation and discomfort was how sisters felt when brothers defended their honor. "About Jayce — um..." Tiara wasn't sure how to begin or exactly what to say.

Mark smiled and bowed his head closer to her. "She probably could have whipped me. I may be a lot taller than most, but I can't fight a lick. My size usually scares most folks off. Besides, I couldn't hurt a woman."

"Thanks," she said. "Jayce wouldn't hurt me." Not physically at least.

"My pleasure. Now get to work, slacker," Mark said.

"Yes, sir, Boss Gentleman." She gave a mock salute and hustled toward the fence.

The brute greeted Tiara by trotting closer and stomping a hoof soundly against the sun-dried dirt, his tail swishing. "What?" she barked, releasing a bit of tension. He replied by craning his neck over the wood rail, mere inches from her face, and exhaled a warm breathy snort. "I hope that's an apology." The horse whickered. "Don't play dumb," she said, placing her hands on her hips. "If you had let Jayce sneak out, I wouldn't have introduced her to my, well, my friends, I guess. You're at fault, too, you know. Not to mention your peanut gallery." Majestic tossed his head. "All right, we're all at fault, but you're not totally forgiven."

Majestic's snout was close to her face. Hesitant and slow, she raised a flattened hand toward his nose so he could sniff her. She'd seen it done in the movies, but didn't remember the actors trembling like she was. The horse sniffed with flared nostrils and Tiara brought the hand under his jaw and rubbed. He was soft and coarse at the same time and he seemed to like the attention, staring at her sideways with a huge and very dark-brown eye. "I wonder if this would work on Jayce?"

With a nudge of his long face into her chest, Majestic applied enough force to send her back a step. "Okay, bad idea." Tiara shook her head and continued to rub. "Don't know what I was thinking, either." The horse stared at her, so she stared back and the realization of the last few minutes hit home. She dropped her hand and slapped it against her leg. "What am I doing? I'm talking to you as if you understand every word. You're just a dumb animal."

The horse didn't take the insult well. Neither did his commando goose. Tiara knew she should prepare herself for their rebuttal, but stood watching, like a dope. Majestic stomped his hoof as he leaned a shoulder...or were they flanks...whatever, into the wood rail and, with entirely more force than necessary, head-butted her solidly in the chest. For the second time in one day, she landed with a hard thud on her buttocks. The goose took advantage of the opportunity, and bit her thigh. "Geez!" Tiara scowled at the massive animal and then at the fowl. "Jayce teach you that move?" she growled. "You could just as easily be someone's supper," she cautioned the goose when he came in for a second nip.

Being short, Tiara hadn't had far to fall, but it still hurt. She got to her feet and slapped at the dirt coating her jeans. "I suppose when Jayce comes to feed you, you'll all have a good laugh over this. Now, if you don't mind, I'll finish your fence. I hope the spaghetti guy does come and that he makes you into a plow horse. You're a pain in my..." she groaned, both instances too vivid in the throbbing of her backside.

Not only was she still talking to them, she'd threatened both animals. "Congratulations. Now I'm a raving lunatic."

Chapter Seven

JAYCE POKED TESTILY at the baked potato on her plate. She wasn't hungry. The usual satisfaction she received from the succulent aroma of Aunt Edna's pot roast only made her nauseous tonight. Eating seemed to be out of the question.

"Something wrong with supper?" Edna asked. Her tone implied it more for dialogue than any actual concern. Of course, there was never a thing wrong with the meal and her aunt knew it, having almost cleared her own plate, and Edna's palate being more culinary sensitive.

Jayce expressed the expected compliment. "No, it's great."

"Don't know how you can say that. You've hardly taken a bite." Edna pushed her chair back with a loud scrape against the hardwood floor. Jayce understood that Edna was peeved at the inattention. "Work my fingers off, cleaning and cooking, and what do I get? Heartache, that's what," Edna sobbed in mock misery.

"You don't have to be so dramatic," Jayce grumbled.

Pointedly ignoring her, Edna squirted dish soap in the sink, ran the hot water and stacked the soiled plates so they clanked in a noisy chorus of disgruntlement. "Never appreciated, don't know why I stay for the abuse."

"I hardly think you're abused." The statement sounded flat, even to Jayce's ears. She couldn't work up enough energy to argue, let alone put any conviction in her words.

Edna jerked Jayce's plate off the table, the potato rolling precariously close to the edge of the plate until she clamped a thumb on it. She thrust her bony hip at an angle and gave Jayce her you-don't-understand look. She loved her aunt, but at moments like this, she didn't like her much. For a woman of average height, too skinny, dark haired, with Mansfield-blue-eyes, Edna had more gall than should fit into any one body. They both knew she didn't stick around for Jayce, but was waiting for Slim to make his move and seriously court her.

"There are different forms of abuse, Jayce." She flung her gaze to the ceiling, set her bottom lip to quivering, and added just the right touch of hurt, "This is emotional abuse."

Jayce groaned at her melodramatics. "If this is about supper, give it back and I'll eat every last morsel."

"No, it's not about supper. I doubt you'll wither away from one missed meal," then Edna picked up a fork and hit the tines on the top of Jayce's head.

"Ouch." Jayce rubbed her injured skull. "Then what is it about?"

Moving to the sink, her aunt scrubbed at a plate hard enough to take the porcelain design off it. Jayce got her first clue about what–who–

the charade really referred. In a wistful voice, Edna said, "Little Tiara is working so hard next door. Slim will like having her home, as do I." Her aunt had spoken tenderly and often of Red after she left with Angie, and asking questions that Jayce never had answers for.

The comment brought back so many memories, reminding Jayce of the history between Edna and Tiara. Any time Jayce had played a prank on Red, Edna washed Tiara up. Most times, Jayce would get her messy just so Edna would have more time with Tiara. Scraped knees and elbows cleaned and kissed; milk and cookies supplied to balm the heart, all courtesy of dear Aunt Edna — never Angie Summers. After the kiss in the barn, the friendship between her and Tiara grew strained, but Tiara still sought Edna's company. Jayce forced herself to think back to the specific time when that all stopped.

When Tiara had left with her mother? No, a little bit before then, Jayce remembered with clarity. It was in the beginning of that year; after a heavy snowfall, that Jayce had seen the real extent of Red's unhappiness, while they were sledding. Tiara had been unusually despondent after asking Jayce about Christmas. Jayce had teased, "Pouting over lousy gifts?" That had been Jayce's first mistake.

Tiara's eyes had filled with tears. "Am I that immature to you?"

Jayce had already recognized that Red didn't act like a typical "nuisance" kid for her age. Before she could muster a reply, or even shrug, Tiara had asked the whammy question. "Jayce, did your parents love you, before the car accident, I mean?"

She had discounted the question. "Yeah, why wouldn't they?" That had been her second mistake. Red had silently walked away; and, except for glimpses at school, she hardly saw Tiara after that — except for the kiss in the barn. The visits to Edna had completely stopped that winter.

Did Aunt Edna know the true cause of the abandonment of their relationship? Edna never questioned; at least not openly in Jayce's presence. Jayce propped her elbows on the table and dropped her head in her hands. She decided to set Edna straight before she got her hopes up. "She's only staying until Slim gets back. Whenever that is," she grumbled under her breath.

"Soon, dear," Edna stated matter-of-factly.

Jayce twisted her head and stared in shock at Edna's back. "You know when?"

Edna shook her head and the long braid swung like a pendulum. "Not specifically." Edna rinsed a plate, never turning to face her. "Maybe we could invite Tiara to dinner one night this week. Do you think she'd come?"

"With her friends staying there, I don't know." Her angry words this afternoon would assure a negative response to an invitation from her. Jayce still couldn't believe she'd said them, certainly never meant them; but after seeing that blonde kid kissing her, she'd wanted to hurt

Tiara as badly as the double defection had wounded her. Not to mention, Jayce couldn't get a hold on the mood swings Tiara went through; and wondered if she was bi-polar. "You'd better do the asking. After today, I don't think I should show my face over there."

Edna spun around and flashed an antagonistic glare, but Jayce thought she recognized the real emotion behind the wet sparkle of the light blue eyes. "What did you say this time?"

The words confirmed her earlier question. Edna had probably blamed Jayce when Red never came back. She could tell a little lie, if the need suited her, to anyone but her aunt. Would Edna see through Jayce's attempt if she tried now?

"Don't even," Edna snapped. "The truth."

Honesty was a pain in the derrière. "Um...I told her she was a munchkin female without a clue, in front of her friends," she admitted grudgingly.

Wiping her hands on a towel, Edna sat at the table. "You can be so stupid sometimes. You're such a beast, Jayce."

Though Edna said the words lovingly, it irked Jayce that they were the very words Red had used to describe her. "That's what she said, too."

"Serves you right," Edna scolded. Then in a gentler tone, "Did she accept your apology?"

Jayce smirked. "Frankenstein wouldn't let me apologize."

"I beg your pardon?"

"One of her guys over there, he must be seven feet tall." Jayce released a sigh. "I wanted to apologize, really." The humiliation, not at being ordered home, but that she'd acted as she had toward Red, had forced Jayce to comply with the giant's demand.

"What provoked the argument this time?"

There was no way she'd tell Edna the truth. After all, Jayce had admitted that she needed Tiara, and then kissed her, only to be rejected for a male teenager. Jayce had her pride after all. "I don't really remember."

Edna nodded and then reached across the table and patted Jayce's hand. "Well, I'm sure it's for the best. Slim asked you to look after the property, not his daughter. Even he knows you have limitations." She returned to the dishes, the topic evidently closed with that harsh statement.

Jayce gawked at her aunt as Edna hummed and finished the clean up. She didn't know what to say or if she should attempt a vehement denial. *He knows I have limitations. Did Edna mean it as a taunt for action or as a statement of fact?*

THIS WAS AN uncomfortable situation to say the least--one entirely of Tiara's own making, so complaining wouldn't help. In her hasty decision to repair Slim's house, she'd failed to think about all the aspects of having her personal space invaded. Thank goodness this much change didn't riddle most construction projects, she thought dispiritedly. After her shower, she'd put on a fresh pair of jeans and a t-shirt. Tiara combed out her damp hair and twisted it into a hasty braid. "Now, to brave the folks downstairs," she whispered to her mirrored image. "I already miss my sweats."

The heavenly smell of fresh baked bread and frying chicken teased her nostrils the second she opened her bedroom door. Tiara skipped down the stairs and headed for the kitchen, quickly glancing into the living room to see Craig and Mark on the couch watching television. Had she forfeited remote control rights, too? It was doubtful the men would opt for old movies unless coerced. At least they weren't watching sports...yet. That would make the situation intolerable.

Darla stood by the stove with a pair of metal tongs in her hand, which she used to turn the chicken in the huge iron skillet. She looked so content, so happy. Tiara felt a pang of envy and wondered if Darla's mood was a natural side effect for expectant mothers or if she simply enjoyed cooking. She discounted cooking immediately — nobody could find that chore pleasurable, could they?

"Anything I can do to help?" Tiara asked, noting the table already set for four.

Darla giggled and faced her. "Are you silently chanting 'please say no'?"

Tiara nodded vigorously. "You will, won't you?" They both laughed.

"Can I get you a cup of coffee? Wait, maybe a cola with ice?" Darla pointed to the long cabinet as if needing an exhibit for her question. "Hope you don't mind I snooped around."

"Hardly snooping, Darla. How else were you to know what I had and where everything is located? And, by the way," Tiara inhaled the delicious aroma filling the kitchen, "I know the contents didn't include the essentials for the marvelous smell of chicken and homemade bread, I'm sure. Remember to bill me for this."

After lowering the heat under the frying pan, Darla waved her into a chair. "Coffee or cola? No, no, I'll get it," she stated firmly. Tiara accepted coffee, which Darla retrieved and set in front of her, before she lowered herself into a chair. "You don't need to reimburse me. Right now, I'm in my element and loving it. You can pay for the groceries going forward if it makes you feel better." Darla shifted in her chair. "We have a few minutes until dinner. I could use a chat."

"Oh," escaped Tiara's lips before she could bite it back.

"A chat, not a lecture," Darla giggled, again.

With any other person, giggling would seem immature, but it sounded sweet coming from Darla. They'd established, upon first meeting a few years back, their only commonality a five-month age difference, Tiara the younger. Yet, it hadn't mattered in their becoming friends. At least as much as Tiara had ever considered a personal friendship with another female — not after Jayce's rejection so long ago. Physically, she and Darla were opposites. Darla stood barn pole straight at five-ten, had thin black hair, nutmeg colored eyes, and a pinched appearance to her long nose. Her long fingered hands, which looked to have seen their fair share of hard work, maintained an elegant flair when she gestured. Her rounded jutting chin had the look of clay pinched by the artist. To most people, Darla was homely; yet her gentle nature and caring heart had Tiara admitting beauty really did come from inside. Little wonder Mark was so in love with his wife. Moreover, Darla had the essential quality men loved in women — she could cook.

"So how did you manage to find food for supper? Or for the marvelous lunch today, for that matter?" Tiara asked.

Darla dropped her gaze to the table. "I knew it would be the last thing on Mother Hubbard's mind, so I brought a few groceries. Your father did have some basic staples, other than canned goods. Should I have whipped up a tuna casserole? Opened some canned spaghetti?"

"Heavens, no!" Tiara rolled her eyes. "Mark and Craig would waste away with canned food. I need the guys in peak condition to fix this place, and quickly."

"So this is a short stay?"

"An unexpected visit." Darla had a quizzical wrinkling on her forehead. Tiara smiled as she explained. "My father sent a box with a key and note saying he needed my help since he had a little trouble. Part of the trouble is the horse."

Darla nodded as if it clarified everything. "The loving daughter races to her father's rescue."

Staring into her coffee, Tiara grimaced. "Not exactly."

"You didn't race?'

"Not the loving daughter."

"He's your...stepfather...or something?" Darla's eyes appeared to convey confusion.

"No, he's my biological father. I'm not exactly a loving daughter as I haven't seen him in ten years."

"Oh, I see." Darla's tone suggested otherwise.

Tiara sipped her coffee. "I'd been a major disappointment, always proving he'd fathered a clumsy child. He never put up a fight when Angie took me away. Never came to see me. We aren't close, I guess."

"Still you came here for him, willing to help."

"Yeah, well," Tiara raised her hands and gestured outward, "he never showed. What's that tell you?"

"You love him."

The stove timer buzzed and Tiara controlled the urge to shout, "Saved by the bell." It halted any nudging of the dialogue along its current course, as had the entrance of Mark and Craig at a near run.

They consumed the meal in pleasant comfort, the focal topic of conversation being Mark's excitement and long-range prospects for Baby Chester. Having delved generously into the food portions provided, Tiara hadn't been surprised to find every edible morsel devoured. With nothing left to eat at the table, the men hastily returned to the living room couch and television. Tiara had commanded Darla to rest, and she did dishes and clean up duty. Tiara rinsed the dishcloth when she finished washing, and draped it over the faucet to dry. "That's all done," she proclaimed, swiping the damp hair from her forehead.

Darla presented her with a teasing grin and applause. "I could get used to this. I love cooking, hate cleaning."

"Well, don't worry—"

A knock at the back door filled Tiara with dread. She glanced at Darla, then at the door expecting to find Jayce casually standing as she had this morning. She wasn't. Slowly, Tiara walked forward, preparing for another verbal confrontation instead.

Tiara opened the screen door, looked left then right, and found no one. A mixture of elation and disappointment played tag in her stomach. Halfway through closing the screen door, Tiara stopped. A large purple plastic container lay on the back porch, a piece of paper taped to the lid. Tiara bent and picked it up, the plastic warm from the contents.

"What is it?" Darla asked excitedly.

Tiara let the screen door slam closed behind her and joined Darla at the table, almost giddy with bewilderment. She pulled the lid free and the enticing aroma of fresh chocolate chip cookies assailed her.

"What's the note say?" Darla inquired impatiently.

"Gosh. I bet you're truly fun to watch at Christmas." With a smile and shake of her head, Tiara tugged the paper free. "Hold on," she admonished when Darla tried to sneak a peek. She read the note in silence, then reluctantly aloud for Darla's benefit. "I hope these satisfy your appetite in a way my apology could never be enough to soften the hurt I've caused you. I'm truly sorry." Tiara blinked back the unexpected tears suddenly clouding her vision. "It's signed, J.M."

"Jayce Mansfield," Darla said with a blissful sigh.

"More like Jackass Monster."

Darla grunted her disapproval over Tiara's remark. "Just Misunderstood is more like it." Tiara stared at her. Darla waved a hand in a dismissive gesture. "Later, we'll talk. Now, eat quickly, before the guys get a whiff of your apology."

Chapter Eight

TIARA HAMMERED THE last nail of the replacement piece of wood. She couldn't believe how neglected the outside of the house had become over the years. It had been an old house during her childhood, but that had been part of the charm: old, big, and real wood.

Already well into the second full day of work, Tiara had little chance to agonize over her decisions. She'd also had little chance to wrestle with Jayce's apology, tasty as it was. With the zealous help of Craig and Mark, they'd managed to consume the entire bowl of cookies last night. All morning Tiara had wondered what to say to Jayce or if she should say anything at all. Tiara even had dreams — nightmares — keeping her from another night of much needed sleep. Dreams of lying entwined on a warm bed of chocolate chip cookies, Jayce hungrily devouring her. When she finally did wake, Tiara felt both flustered and famished.

Tiara had been disheartened to come to the kitchen this morning, the hearty smells of breakfast dished out by Darla and no sign of Jayce. Not that Tiara didn't appreciate all the effort Darla put into making breakfast. She did. However, a huge part of her wanted to find Jayce standing beside the sink, or the back door, the sun casting shadows of her tall, beautiful body across the kitchen floor, a bag of Danish clutched temptingly in her hand. A hand she wanted to feel once again.

A shiver raced through Tiara's body. She spun around on the ladder and was precariously close to tottering over with the sudden movement. Someone was watching her. True to her clumsy nature, the hammer slipped and slammed into her shin before tumbling to the ground with a thud. Tiara pinched her lips tight to hold back the curse. She scanned the area with a scowl. No one appeared to be looking her way.

No one she could see, anyway.

The sudden image of gangsters filled her mind. This was the second day; the day the nasally voiced man warned he would come to take possession of Majestic. With all the work on the house, she'd forgotten about him. Had this Mister — she still couldn't remember his correct name — sent his goons to survey the area before making his appearance, see if she'd disposed of the horse?

Well, he'd find the horse where it had been since arriving that horrible morning. Tiara glanced toward the corral. Majestic munched on a patch of grass oblivious, so it seemed, to the noisy work going on nearby, the goose watched from the trough's corner where it had perched itself. She should probably feel guilty for ignoring the animals, having relinquished all duties to Jayce since the morning of arrival, their daily care not a chore Tiara relished. She knew Jayce was feeding them because she'd caught glimpses of her riding away. If Tiara had fed them, Majestic would probably chomp on her hand, decide Tiara wasn't a scrumptious enough morsel, and give his evaluation as "don't bite the hand that feeds you, because it's not at all tasty." Tiara snorted. "If it came to pass, Majestic would have firsthand knowledge," she said, stepping down the ladder to retrieve her hammer.

"Majestic would have knowledge of what?"

The question came from behind her, startling her into missing one rung, her chin slamming into another. She clutched at the ladder in a frantic attempt to prevent a free-fall to the ground. Reestablishing her balance, Tiara finished her descent without further incident. "Jayce, I knew it."

"If you knew, how'd I startle you?"

"I'm not startled," Tiara said defensively.

"Could've fooled me," Jayce said with a glance at the ladder. "You okay?"

Tiara bent to pick up the hammer, barely curbing the impulse to hit Jayce with it. Why damage a perfectly good hammer on her hard head, anyway? "Fine. Is there something I can do for you?" she asked, barely able to keep the petulance from her tone.

Jayce smirked. "Not work related, certainly. I couldn't handle another argument where you intentionally misinterpret everything I say."

Reining in her temper, Tiara placed the hammer safely in the empty loop of her leather work belt, the temptation to use it on Jayce too great. "Wonderful, then, because I can't do anything for you right now. We munchkins have our meeting of the lollipop guild in a little while." She crossed her arms over her chest. Jayce reached over and swiped a thumb across her lower lip. Tiara noticed the spot of blood staining the tip. She also noticed the increase in her heart rate, just now realizing she must have bit the side of her mouth when her chin hit the ladder rung. "What'd you want?"

With a strange look that Tiara couldn't immediately associate with a specific emotion, Jayce stared at her, a barely audible, "I...uh...uh..." Had Jayce forgotten what she came here for? It didn't matter, Tiara wasn't about to stand around and wait for her to finally say something.

Tiara walked away.

JAYCE HADN'T BEEN aware of the weird enchantment that overcame her from one simple touch. At least not until Tiara wasn't in front of her anymore. When had that petite, freckle-faced girl become so beautiful? The question puzzled her, since she had always been attracted to Tiara. With Tiara wrenched from her life, it had torn a piece of her heart. Her dreams, *poof*, evaporated in a puff of smoke.

A moment ago, Jayce had been watching Tiara from beside the house, she thought unobserved. She'd witnessed the different aspects of Tiara, from confident worker to klutz. Not to mention a wonderful view of the cutest little bottom Jayce had ever laid eyes on. Her palm itched with a desire to caress what her eyes were inspecting. And given a chance to say something, she'd been speechless, driving Tiara away.

"Wait," Jayce called out, lengthening her stride to catch up.

Tiara whirled on a small booted feet and flashed a molten glare that made Jayce flinch. Why was she always so angry? Immediately entranced by the damp lock of hair plastered to Tiara's forehead, worried by her earlier awkward descent from the ladder, Jayce had forgotten to finish her request, ask the question for which she sought an answer. Heck, Jayce had been so distracted she could barely remember the conversation.

"Jayce, I have things to do," Tiara said in a clearly annoyed tone.

Now Jayce remembered. Too bad that she couldn't take back words or exchange them for the right ones. She'd need to think long and deliberately before speaking with Tiara. "I'm sorry," Jayce said, stepping closer.

"Not like I haven't heard that from you before," Tiara said.

She gaped at Tiara a moment. "Geez, give me a break, Red. I swear—"

"Oh, goody-goody for you, now you're a big girl. Swearing is adult?"

Jayce recognized Tiara was too angry for a civil exchange. When mad, the gold flakes in Tiara's eyes sparkled so alluringly as if beckoning Jayce to gaze deep into the depths. Her golden-red hair shimmered in the sunlight, sweat dampened and made a touch inviting. As when gazing at Tiara's derrière, now Jayce's palm tingled for one touch, one more stroke of Tiara's face.

She reached a hand forward, saw Tiara's eyes widen though she didn't budge. Gently, Jayce brushed the tips of her fingers under the loose hair on Tiara's forehead and tucked it behind an ear. Instantly, reminding Jayce of corn silk and satin softness.

Tiara's eyes closed for the briefest instant. "Jayce, please."

Stepping closer had Tiara's breasts making the slightest contact with Jayce's abdomen and sent waves of heat through her, as she whispered, "Please, what?" She bent slightly, placing a kiss behind Tiara's ear, and felt her tremble. "Kiss me senseless?" Jayce whispered huskily.

"Please stop," Tiara said, giving a gentle push to Jayce's stomach. "Someone could be watching." Tiara glanced around hastily. "Craig—"

Jayce took an awkward step back, a chill coursing through her. She shuddered and acknowledged, "So I did read you wrong." She tried to laugh, but it came out a nervous twitter. "I'm sorry, Tiara. I thought... Doesn't matter." Taking a deep breath and hoping to steady her jumbled nerves, Jayce shoved her hands into her back pockets. "I hope you two are happy." Not usually a terribly emotional person, Jayce felt irritated by an urge to weep. "I never meant to shame or disgust you. Guess Angie was right about me, after all. I'll stay out of your way from now on." Jayce retreated.

Maybe there *was* a time to run from a woman.

There weren't many things that could make Jayce cry, normally having a too-positive nature; however, that's what she wanted to do the whole hike home. She needed to get inside her room before she released the waterworks building behind her eyes. She sidestepped a dark blue Ford Mustang she hadn't expected to be in front of the porch steps, let the screen door slam behind her and started up the hall stairs when Edna called out her name.

"Jayce," Edna repeated from the foot of the stairs. "What's wrong with you?"

Not facing her, Jayce barked, "Nothing."

"Did you talk to Tiara?"

"Yeah, and you can forget—"

"What did you say this time?" Edna stomped a foot. "Turn around and talk to me." Straining to hold back the tears, Jayce complied. "Oh, honey, what happened?" Edna asked more solicitously.

"Nothing. I'll be in my room for a while." Jayce turned to finish the trek upstairs.

"But Jayce—" Edna started.

"I don't want to talk right now."

"You may be sorry you're not listening," her aunt shouted after her.

The comment barely registered as Jayce slammed the bedroom door behind her and instantly collided with the naked woman exiting her bathroom. She vigorously rubbed a towel against long, black, wet hair. Jayce would recognize that curvaceous body anywhere. "Sarah," she managed to whisper, just before the woman dropped the towel, wrapped arms around Jayce's neck and placed a firm, more than friendly kiss on her mouth.

Pulling away only slightly, Sarah purred, "Ooh, missed those yummy lips, babe."

"Sarah," she repeated, though difficult with the woman tracing a finger across Jayce's bottom lip. "What are doing here?"

Exaggerating the pout by puckering her full red lips, Sarah said, "I wanted you to be happy to see me." Sarah draped herself languorously across the comforter on the bed and raised her arms invitingly. "Come to Juanita, *Mi Corazón*. Tell me what has you so upset."

Jayce grimaced as she plopped down on the corner of the bed. "One, I won't call you by your made-for-cable TV star name. Two, you left my heart behind when you ran off with Johnny. Three, well, I'm not upset really."

Sarah sat up and scooted directly behind Jayce. Resting her chin on Jayce's shoulder, arms encircling her waist, Sarah asked, "You don't think I can still sense when you're upset, even if you hadn't slammed the door closed with tears in your eyes? A lot has changed between us, but I never thought our friendship was affected."

Closing her eyes and leaning into Sarah's embrace, Jayce sighed. "I'd rather not talk about it, to you or Aunt Edna. Why are you here so early, anyway? You aren't supposed to pick up Arabelle for another month."

Groaning, Sarah said, "Johnny and I broke it off. The tabloids are ecstatic."

"Well, you always have a place to hide here." Sarah clutched an earlobe between her teeth and nipped. Jayce shivered involuntarily. "I won't, however, be your rebound until you find another lover, Sarah."

"Was I asking that of you?" Sarah smiled wickedly. "You know you're the only woman to have ever turned me on. So, I wouldn't discourage any impulse you may have in that direction."

Jayce broke their contact and stared sternly at her, which wasn't an easy task with Sarah still naked and looking wonderful, as usual. "Juanita never asks." Jayce growled playfully. "Juanita takes." Both laughed then.

"Thought you weren't gonna use that name?" Sarah got off the bed and began dressing.

"I was teasing and making a point," Jayce said. "Don't know how you get away with it. You're too down to earth for a fancy-shmancy name like Juanita Juarez." Sarah glared at her. "Okay, maybe I should use the word exotic and not fancy. What was wrong with just being you, plain ole Sarah Marsh from Silver Waters, Colorado?"

Sarah buttoned her silver colored blouse, as she said, "Mom's genes gave me the Latin features and coloring for a reason, might as well use it. Besides, I save Sarah for when I want to be ordinary." Jayce gave a snort. "As long as that's what Hollywood wants from me, 'cause that's all they're gonna get, and it keeps food on the table—"

"And a Mustang in the drive," Jayce interjected lightheartedly, remembering the car in front of the house.

"Hey, I'm famous for playing a lady gunslinger. Fans expect my personal life to reflect my professional life, all equine related in one way or another."

Jayce gave her friend a serious expression. "Did Johnny get wrapped up in the hype, too? You okay?"

Now fully dressed, Sarah shrugged and sat beside Jayce. "I'm fine. Johnny thought he should prove himself a stud, so he jumped in the sack with anyone who'd have him. There was a long line it seems." Sarah shook her head. "Really, Jayce, I never wanted to hurt you, you gotta know that. This emptiness is too awful to dump on someone intentionally. And I don't think I ever really loved Johnny. I did and do love you." A pained expression crossed Sarah's face. "If I had realized about your nesting gene—"

Squeezing her hand gently, Jayce said, "I know. You just weren't in love with me. Home sweet home was out of the question for you."

"You were right about Johnny's attention being on my career, the notoriety, and not the real me holding his interest. He wanted Juanita Juarez, not Sarah Marsh. I'm just glad I never got around to telling him the truth, not that he ever asked about my childhood. So I don't have to worry he'll track me down and try to make up."

"He's a big fool," Jayce said, then kissed Sarah's forehead. "Hang in there, because someday someone will fall for the real you, not the TV star you."

"I hope you're right." With a heavy sigh, Sarah asked, "You gonna tell me your love trouble?"

Jayce felt the heat of her embarrassment suffuse her face. "It's not love trouble, not anymore. I misread somebody and was promptly put in my place."

Sarah frowned at her explanation.

How could Jayce have misunderstood Tiara so thoroughly? They had shared kisses. Was Tiara more like Sarah, curious only? "Honest, I'm over it, over her. By supper, I'll be right as rain. Let's go check on Arabelle. You're going to be amazed by how many stunts she'll do for you, and your *Deadly Aimes'* character."

They stood. Sarah moved to the dresser and picked up a brush, and Jayce couldn't resist a quick—and final, she told herself—glance toward Tiara's place. Though she couldn't see from the window, Jayce knew Tiara was over there working alongside her boyfriend. She could feel the tears begin to well up behind her eyes and quickly tried to blink them away. Jayce had just about managed it when she felt Sarah's arms encircle her waist again.

"She must be pretty remarkable," Sarah whispered next to her ear. "She's hurt you deeper than I ever did. You're in love with her."

Jayce had never stopped loving Tiara. She had anxiously looked forward to the day Tiara came home. But she never planned for the reality in her daydreams. Letting the tears fall, Jayce spun around and clutched Sarah in a fierce hug. "Totally," Jayce acknowledged.

Chapter Nine

TIARA CLEANED THE work area, picking up the electrical equipment she now stored overnight in the old barn, in case of inclement weather. Once done, she walked to the back porch and stared toward Jayce's place. She wondered if she should call, make sure Jayce was okay, but hesitated when trying to think of a plausible reason to do so that wouldn't be transparent and needy. Tiara couldn't very well say, "I want you, Jayce, always have, and that's why I get so angry, angry with myself." No, better she stick with her earlier resolution that the distance and misunderstandings were best for them both. Although Tiara hadn't understood what Jayce meant by Angie's opinion, knowing it was probably a question best saved for later.

Oh, but that was going to be more difficult after seeing the unshed tears in Jayce's magnificent eyes. Their shared kisses had produced passion Tiara had long since believed controlled and contained, unnecessary in her life. She'd been wrong, and knew it deep down, since each time Jayce was near, Tiara wanted to devour the woman. When she witnessed pain in eyes usually alight with laughter and mischief, correcting Jayce's misconceptions seemed vital. On the one hand, Tiara wouldn't have to worry about her own feelings if she let Jayce believe a romance existed with Craig. However, for the same reason, Tiara did feel a renewal of attraction and didn't want to lose Jayce before she could sort out her level of desire and want.

Right now, Jayce was a distraction that Tiara didn't think she needed.

As Tiara walked through the back door, Darla warmly greeted her. "Hello there. You look tired." Tiara merely grunted. "Go clean up and relax a bit," Darla said, "dinner will be ready whenever you are."

"Thanks. I'll just be a few minutes."

"No hurry. The boys finished washing up, and promptly dropped in front of the television. I put some chips and dip out for them, so they won't notice any delay in dinner, for a little while, anyway." Darla pointed toward the hallway, "So skedaddle and take as much time as you need."

Another warm, gushy feeling coursed through Tiara when she noticed the neat pile of clean, folded jeans, T-shirts and other clothing items on the bed. She couldn't remember the last time someone had done her laundry. Also unexpected was the short note resting atop the clothes.

Hope you aren't the type to get weirded-out by someone doing your laundry, but what else are "sisters" for? Let me know if I should discontinue this chore while I'm here.
      The Bigger Sister

The sentiment, though unexpected, gave Tiara pause. Friendship and sisterhood had never existed for her after leaving Silver Waters. She had always kept her distance from people. Why were all these changes happening at this point in her life? Tiara shook the questions out of her head. She could think on it later.

After a lengthy and very steamy shower, feeling more relaxed, though only physically so, Tiara got dressed and made her way back to the kitchen and the meal Darla had prepared. The group had barely finished eating when two, long bursts of a vehicle horn sounded.

"I'll take a look," Craig volunteered, rushing toward the front room. Darla and Tiara started clearing the table, until they heard his exclamation, "Wow, Boss. Who do you know owns the huge purple limo?"

Tiara could feel the color drain from her face, as she whispered hoarsely, "The spaghetti-guy gangster."

Simultaneously, Darla and Mark asked, "Are you okay?" Tiara barely nodded.

Mark straightened. "Want me to go check it out, send the guy away?"

"No," Tiara said, squaring her own shoulders. "I need to take care of this." An extreme sense of relief filled her, though, realizing Mark and Darla followed behind with Craig taking up the rear of the group as they passed him.

Had Tiara not already frightened herself in expectation of this visit, she would have laughed at the sight of the limousine in her driveway. It resembled a giant plum. However, the behemoth of a man unfolding himself from the front passenger seat was no laughing matter. He stood at nearly seven-feet, bald, and was dressed entirely in black from pressed cargo pants, leather dress shoes, a T-shirt stretched over huge biceps, that to Tiara's estimation, had to be the width of her waist. Tiara didn't know if it portended good or bad that the man was the hired muscle and not the Spaghetti-guy. She knew she'd get her answer soon enough when the limousine's back door slowly opened.

FEELING SOMEWHAT BETTER, physically at least, after a long ride on Arabelle and Buster, Jayce suggested she and Sarah go to town for dinner and maybe a drink. They were about to turn the horses over to one of her assistants, Charlie, for care; but Sarah's question halted Jayce mid-dismount. "Is your not-now-or-ever-a-girlfriend some kind of celebrity?"

Jayce gazed toward Slim's place, and then hastily prodded Buster in that direction. Her heart raced faster than the horse was running, and she silently chastised herself for getting ready to burst in where no longer wanted. Reining Buster to a halt at the corral, Jayce was able to ascertain the scene before her. A ghastly purple limo had parked behind Tiara's truck, a guy the size of a military tank stood on the passenger side, and the back door stood open, but apparently the occupant hadn't exited yet. Tiara and friends were in an expectant cluster at the bottom stair of the front porch.

Jayce recognized the surprise crossing Tiara's features at her approach; and for a split second, she considered abandoning her impulsive reaction to Tiara's possibly being in danger. She held her position. Tiara, after all, had men to protect her now. Jayce figured this had to be the man Tiara expected to come for Majestic. At least there weren't any weapons visible. If Tank had a gun he had it hidden exceptionally well. And Jayce didn't want to speculate as to where any hidden placement could possibly be on the man in those tight clothes.

As if the spectacle of his appearance had extended as far as prudent while maintaining an audience, a figure exited the limousine. He was barely five-feet and wearing a 1940s-styled pinstriped suit with a gold chain swinging from the vest pocket, a salmon colored shirt, thick black tie, a Fedora, and spats over patent leather black shoes. A fresh carnation matching the shade of his shirt was pinned on the left side of the wide lapel. Jayce's first instinct was to believe Slim was kidding around and sent this person as part of an elaborate charade to win his daughter's favor by arriving just in time to save the day. But this seemed too far fetched to be an attention gimmick, even for Slim. Either way, to hide her sudden bark of laughter, Jayce pulled on the reins in such a way that Buster reared back, punching the air as he whinnied. From the corner of her eye, Jayce caught the quick grin on Tiara's lips, before bringing the horse down in a small cloud of dust.

The man walked forward until alongside Tank, whispered something only the big man could hear, and then put his hands in his pockets. Tank glanced at Jayce, then to the group by the porch, before asking in a gravelly tone, "Which 'o yuze iz the Summers kid?"

Hesitantly, Tiara raised her hand and Jayce heard the nervous tremble in her voice when she answered, "That would be me." She pointed to the short man. "Are you Mr. Spag... Mr. Span...?"

"Sparretti," Tank supplied helpfully. "We don't see Slim." He stated the obvious with a frown. "Mr. Sparretti demands you turn over hiz prop'ty, bein' one hoss by da name 'a Majestic."

Tiara took a step in their direction. "As my father is unavailable, I have to decline your request until I can ascertain all aspects of it."

Jayce wasn't surprised to see Tank's disorientation from Tiara's reply. He bent toward his boss, who whispered into his ear once again.

Awkwardly, the man nodded before straightening and slamming a beefy fist on the limo's hood. The driver immediately exited the vehicle, though he continued to stand by the opened door. Expecting trouble to erupt, Jayce nudged Buster closer to Tiara and her group without actually becoming part of it.

"The horse is mine," Mr. Sparretti said in a nasally whine of a voice. "If you won't hand him over, we'll rightly take him into possession. Your father had no right to bring him here." He puffed out his chest. "No one steals from me and gets away with it."

"That's not the first time you insinuated Mr. Summers is a thief." Jayce shifted in the saddle. "Can you provide documented proof that Majestic is owned by you?"

"Calling me a liar, sister?" Sparretti asked, his voice raising an octave. "Who are you, anyway?"

Prepared to give an annoyed yet wonderfully clever retort, Jayce held her response when the sound of racing hooves drew closer and all eyes turned to watch Sarah's approach on Arabelle. Sarah's long black hair whipped in the air behind her, an expression of barely controlled ire had her eyes darkening, and Jayce instantly recognized "Juanita's" gunslinger character. The way Sarah sat in the saddle had her looking like a picture of royalty from a long forgotten Spanish Court.

Pulling back on the reins so Arabelle stopped mere inches from the men and casting a glance in Jayce's direction, she asked in a heavily accented and decidedly sexy voice, "What is happening here, *Señorita* Mansfield?" From the look on the men's faces, they recognized Sarah's television personality; and, like most fans, were finding it difficult to separate film character from the human actor.

"Ms. Juarez," Jayce acknowledged and joined Sarah's charade. She pointed to the little man in the Fedora, and shook her head sadly. "Mr. Sparretti has threatened our friends by calling them liars and thieves. He's claiming ownership of a horse without supporting documentation."

Arching a dark, delicate eyebrow, Sarah said in feigned shock, "Say this is not true, *Señor* Sparretti. You believe my friends to be *banditos*?"

He removed his hat and bowed elegantly in her direction. "It's a pleasure to meet you, Miss Juarez. I have always found you to be a remarkable woman," he declared in a gentled whiny pitch full of obvious awe. "And I never said they stole my horse, exactly."

Sarah raised the corner of her lip. "Ah, but guilt by association can be just as hurtful and character demeaning. They have taken insult, though you may not have intended it. *¿Ah, sí?*"

Sparretti shrugged. "I just want Majestic returned."

Nodding, as if sympathetic with his situation, Sarah tossed a leg over the saddle horn. Jayce knew she would dismount, and jumped off her own horse to assist, and play bodyguard. However, Mr. Sparretti rushed forward to position himself beside the horse to assist Sarah.

Tank moved to block Jayce's own advancement. Sparretti reached up and wrapped his small hands at Sarah's waist gently guiding her to the ground. Her descent was less than graceful due to their size difference, and Sarah just about knocked him to the ground. "*Gracias, Señor*," Sarah cooed as she kept him from stumbling in such a manner as not to wound his dignity in front of the others. "It is always wonderful to witness gallantry in this day and age." He blushed profusely. She looped an arm in his and leaned into him. "Now, Mr. Sparretti—"

"Elmo, please," he told her.

Jayce rolled her eyes when she noted Sarah flutter her eyelashes, as if *he* had just proffered a wondrous honor upon her. Sarah slowly, yet effectively, tugged him closer to Tiara. So occupied with preventing her own advancement Jayce didn't believe Tank even noticed the maneuver. She hoped Elmo thoroughly chewed Tank out for dereliction of duty, as it would serve him right. Peering around the behemoth, Jayce tried to watch Sarah in action.

"Thank you, Elmo." Sarah nearly purred. "I understand how you believe yourself taken advantage of. Fine men are always so abused. But we would all," she indicated Tiara and her group with a nod in their direction, "like to see this resolved amicably. You must understand that *Señorita* Summers is only attempting to protect her Papa." Sarah linked her free arm with Tiara's and gradually edged her and Elmo toward the limousine's back door.

Watching her progress, Jayce silently admitted that sometimes the Juanita persona was a remarkable, and useful, piece of work. Slowly twisting to watch the three must have alerted and reminded Tank of his duties. He darted toward his boss, who didn't seem to notice the large man hadn't been at his side. "I understand, of course," Sparretti agreed. "I will give your friend, Ms. Summers, another week." He glanced at Tiara. "If you haven't contacted your father by then, I will have no other choice than taking Majestic, forcibly, if I must."

"*Sí*, you must do what is right by the horse," Sarah said with a nod. "One week, all will be resolved. You are a great and kind man. ¡*Gracias!*" With the last comment, Sarah leaned down and kissed his cheek.

Sparretti, his face bright red, pulled the flower from his lapel and stammered, "Miss Juarez, it has been an honor. Until next we meet." He handed her the small carnation, snapped his fingers, which immediately had the driver and Tank getting in the vehicle, and then moved to the limo's back door. He blew Sarah an air kiss, wriggling his fingers in a childish good-bye gesture, closing the door himself after entering.

As they drove away in the limousine, Jayce waved and shouted, "Bye, Spaghetti-man and Tank," and then moved to Sarah's side and put her arm around her waist, presenting a relieved and thankful smile. Still in Juanita mode, Sarah leaned into Jayce and said to Tiara, "So, one week to find your missing Papa and make this go away, *sí*?"

Tiara frowned as she gazed at the closeness of Jayce and Sarah. "I appreciate your assistance, Miss Juarez, and only wish contacting my father were that simple." Directing her attention to Jayce, she said, "Thank you. I appreciate—"

"Hey, no worries, Tiara," Jayce interrupted. "We didn't mean to intrude, you able to take care of yourself and all." She pulled Sarah closer. If Sarah were making more of their friendly embrace, Jayce decided to go with it. "Juanita, we should be going. You've promised to join me for dinner and drinks, remember?"

Sarah raised a hand and caressed Jayce's cheek. "True, *mí amor*. I will allow no further intrusions," she said, sealing the statement with a tender peck to Jayce's lips. She quickly turned her head toward Tiara. "I hope you and your friends have a wonderful evening." A devious smiled played across Sarah's lips, "I plan on one," she said huskily before moving to Arabelle and fluidly hopping into the saddle. "I will await you at home, Jayce, darling."

Jayce started toward Buster, but stopped when Tiara placed a halting hand on her arm. She turned to find Red staring at her with a mixed expression of surprise and hurt. Tiara asked in a whisper, "You're dating a famous star?"

She shrugged. "I wouldn't want to disgust you with particulars, Tiara. However, I was training Arabelle for her, and Juanita has wanted more than a business relationship for quite some time. You've made me realize that I have no reason to continue putting her off. So, if you'll excuse me, I have a date." Tiara dropped her hand, and Jayce got back on Buster, yanked the reins to turn him toward home. From over her shoulder, she said, "Evening, folks," to the rest of Tiara's crew as she kicked Buster into a gallop.

Part of her hated misleading Tiara into believing there was more than a friendship between her and Sarah. When she saw Tiara's response to the feigned romantic touching between her and Sarah, part of Jayce clutched at the hope that maybe Tiara, even if just a little tiny bit, did care for her a smidgen more than the she cared for the boy-toy.

Chapter Ten

JAYCE TURNED BUSTER'S care over to Charlie at the barn and caught up with Sarah, who was sitting on the porch. "Thanks for your help with the little gangster," she said.

Sarah asked as she patted the empty spot next to her. "Just with the gangster?"

Jayce shrugged. "Mostly, but no, not just with the puny guy, who is more of an admirer after you bestowed a kiss on him. Also, for helping misrepresent our relationship. For half a second, I actually thought Tiara was jealous. Strange, huh?" With a quick smile that held no warmth, Jayce said, "I'm not going to back out of dinner, either. You want the shower first?"

Sarah grinned. "We could share, that way Aunt Edna is aware and helps perpetuate the return of our tumultuous relationship."

Blushing, Jayce corrected her. "I told Tiara I'd held you at bay for quite some time and that I'd finally given into your magnetism."

"Ah, *me siento honrado*. Then I gallantly fight for your affections. Melt each time we touch or gaze into one another's eyes." More seriously, Sarah dropped the accent and added, "Not a difficult role to play, babe. You are, after all, the only one to treat me like a woman, not a conquest or a rung upward on the Hollywood ladder."

Jayce wrapped an arm around Sarah's waist and pulled her close, kissing the top of her head as it leaned against her shoulder. "Honey, I never understood the TV star stuff. Guess I'm a dolt. I see the sweet woman that lives inside that hot body of yours."

"Are you sure you want to keep the charade going? Tiara seemed like a nice kid, even from a first impression."

Biting her lower lip, Jayce swallowed the lump in her throat, "She was—once. You probably won't need to do more than you just did. I'll have a talk with Edna, tell her about Sparretti and get her to talk to Slim. I'm almost certain she knows more about his whereabouts than she's telling me. I wish I knew all the details of what they had concocted to get Red here."

Sarah sat up. "You think that man was part of a plan?" Jayce nodded. "We have a fairly good idea where everything is leading, so I say we just continue this course and see who we drag out of the woodwork." Jayce flinched at the last word. "Sorry," Sarah said. "I'll leave carpentry words and phrases alone. Maybe a little jealousy will get you those answers you crave."

"Either way, I'm famished. Let me tell Edna not to hold supper for us, while you take a shower. Make sure to save me some hot water." Jayce stood and started for the door.

"Aren't you in enough hot water now?" Sarah slapped Jayce playfully on her rear-end as she rushed passed her and jogged up the stairs. Jayce smiled as Sarah's laughter filled the house.

"TIARA, SWEETIE, ARE you okay?" Darla asked with concern.

The question broke Tiara from the spell of watching Jayce ride away. She wasn't exactly stunned that someone as beautiful and full of life as Jayce had women, even one as famous as Juanita Juarez, waiting in line for her attention, her affection. Tiara had personal experience of just how affectionate Jayce could be. Automatically, Tiara touched a finger to her lips in memory. "Yeah, fine," she said, dropping her hand and turning to face Darla.

Not certain what emotion Darla saw on her face, Tiara heard Darla say, "Oh dear, let's get you in the house." Then, as if realizing Mark and Craig were still there, Darla added, "Can't you find somewhere else to be? Shoo. Go sit in front of the brain drain." When Mark started to protest she scowled up at him, "I'm not kidding. Go," she said, while dragging Tiara toward the back porch.

Amazed to see Darla seriously bossing the guys around, Tiara allowed herself to be pulled along by Darla who opened the screen for her to enter the kitchen, and then pushed her gently into a chair. Tiara protested and stated she was fine, but Darla silenced her with a glare the second she opened her mouth. It wasn't until Darla had the kettle heating, two mugs ready with the teabags inserted, and then sitting in the chair to Tiara's right that Darla finally spoke. "Okay, spill it. And don't leave anything out."

"Well," Tiara said, "you know I got the key and note to come down here? In his note, Dad mentioned the horse and that he was in trouble."

"No, Tiara." Darla sighed. "Tell me about Jayce."

"I don't know—"

"Tiara Summers." The kettle's whistle punctuated Darla's use of her nearly full name. As Darla stood up to turn the heat off, Tiara tried to decipher what the other woman expected to hear and what she already may have figured out about the relationship between her and Jayce. She hadn't come up with any ready response before Darla had a mug in front of her and took her seat again. Darla sighed, again, more heavily than a moment ago. "I may look like an ugly country bumpkin who doesn't know a thing, but anyone has only to be within a few feet of you two to feel the energy."

"You are *not* ugly. And, there isn't energy," Tiara said, "mutual irritation is what you feel."

"Are you that far into denial, or don't you truly understand what's going on?" Darla asked. "Never mind, it doesn't matter. Talk to me, please. Tell me about Jayce. How old were you?"

Dunking the teabag into the hot water, Tiara decided to answer in as short a reply as she could get away with giving. "Twelve."

"So about twelve years?" Tiara nodded. "You were good friends back then?" Darla asked, causing Tiara to glance away. "This would go much quicker if I didn't have to get the information playing twenty questions. Have you any idea how ticked off Mark is going to be if I don't get my baby sleep?"

"Darla, it's just—"

"Sweetie, don't you think I recognize love comes in different packages, or that it has no boundaries, can even be unconventional?" Darla lowered her voice and reached across the table, taking one of Tiara's hands in her own and squeezed reassuringly. "You think I haven't noticed how sexy your neighbor is? Let's not get started on Ms. Juarez. Wow." She laughed at Tiara's shocked expression. "Admiring a woman isn't exclusively lesbian, you know. Besides, what kind of woman would I be if I hadn't learned to appreciate what might catch my husband's eye?"

Tiara raised one shoulder in a quick shrug. "I wouldn't think you'd have to worry about that with Mark."

Blushing, Darla smiled. "Actually, I don't worry anymore, but let's get back to you. I know you feel something or you wouldn't have released the green jealousy monster from your eyes. Don't you return Jayce's affection?"

"It's complicated, Darla."

"Is it? Or are you making it more so because we're here as witnesses to your personal life, let alone your love life? I can't answer for Craig, but neither Mark nor I are homophobic." Darla squeezed her hand once more before releasing it, then picked up her own cup and took a sip. "More importantly, I'm a sucker for a truly mushy romance, you know."

Tiara grinned. "I bet you are, however, this isn't a romance, most certainly not a mushy one." She took a deep breath. "Okay, you asked for it. When I lived here as a kid, I had a huge crush on Jayce. She's wonderful, so full of life, so who wouldn't fall for her, right? I didn't think she returned my interest because she was always pulling pranks on me. After a while I didn't care because I wanted any of her attention, good or bad. One day she found me hiding away in our old barn." Tiara hesitated, not wanting to mention she was whittling. "Well, anyway, she kissed me."

Nodding, Darla sighed. "It was wonderful and you realized Jayce cared for you too."

"No. She literally ran off," Tiara said. "Guess kissing me scared her. Or made her realize I wasn't worth her time."

"Maybe there's another explanation. Did you ask?"

Shrugging, Tiara said, "Seeing her with Juanita, I know it was me not fitting her type. Things grew a little more distant between us after that, but I admit she was always there for me. Up until just after

Christmas, when my mother took me away."

"I've seen the way she looks at you, Tiara," Darla said. "This is not a woman who has in any way discounted you from 'her type', even if she has one. If you weren't back then, you most certainly are now. I can't believe you two have dissociated yourselves over what may very well be a misunderstanding. What you need to do is talk to her."

"Not gonna happen, Darla. There's a wedge between us now. I think she's a bonehead, and Jayce can't accept that I'm capable of actually handling myself." Tiara raised an arm and flourished it in an arc. "I tell her I'm going to fix the place, and she tells me not to hurt myself. Damn it, I'm not an incompetent child."

"Just a petulant one," Darla stated. "Seriously, Tiara, have you considered now that you're back home, Jayce is worried about you for other reasons than hurting yourself because of incompetence?"

"Why care now? Why not back when I needed her and Slim, even Aunt Edna, while I dealt with Angie alone?"

Darla flinched at the fury heating the words. Quietly, she asked, "Is that what your alienation is really about? They abandoned you, and you want to return the favor, no matter the cost?"

"It's not like that," Tiara denied. But she realized that was a huge part of it, what she had believed as the best course of reaction. Was Jayce correct that Tiara twisted every word Jayce uttered into a negative disparagement? "Okay, maybe it is like that. Not that it matters. Jayce has apparently moved on. Let's not forget that Jayce thinks Craig is my boyfriend, which is why I'm surprised she even rode over here like Annie Oakley ready to save me from the bad guys."

Darla snorted a laugh. "You and Craig an item?"

"Yeah, I'm thinking that's what prompted her attitude the first day you got here. She probably saw Craig's greeting." Tiara blushed. "She was kissing me when you arrived. Needless to say, I haven't corrected her misunderstanding." Tiara shook her head, and then focused on Darla. "Did you see the way Jayce had the horse going all 'hi-ho-Silver' to cover wanting to laugh at Sparretti and his goons? That's what she does, you know, trains horses for TV and the movies. I assume with Juanita Juarez here, she's training a specific horse for the *Deadly Aimes* series."

"Never miss that show myself, and I'm not usually a western fan," Darla said gleefully. "Of course when I watch horses doing something incredible now, I'll actually know a person who trains them for that kind of stuff." Darla frowned. "Are you trying to change the subject so I won't ask about the kiss?"

Tiara flushed. "I thought Jayce was the subject?"

"Smart aleck," Darla said playfully. "So do you like her the same as you did as a kid?" Tiara nodded. "Okay, then you need to go talk to her."

Smirking, Tiara asked, "Before or after her date with the TV star?"

Darla glowered in annoyance, folded her arms across her belly and asked, "Who is Aunt Edna?"

"Jayce's aunt. She used to clean me up after a Jayce prank and she patched me up and comforted me with milk and cookies when I got hurt from other mishaps. I guess Edna used to feel guilty for all the harassment I endured at the hands of her niece."

"Would you consider her an ally or foe?"

"Definitely an ally ten years ago when I left, but I couldn't suppose about now. We had a couple years that were friendly. I haven't kept any contact with people from the past." Tiara wished she had, with Edna, at any rate. Maybe with the caring concern from her, dealing with Angie would have been more bearable. "All spilt milk though."

"I think you may be totally wrong about that." Darla stood and pointed to the back door. "In fact, I expect you to march yourself right over there and find out the answer."

"Yeah, but—"

"No, Tiara. You aren't going to clear any of this up until you talk to at least one of them. I gather it will be a heck of a lot easier to talk to Edna than Jayce." Darla followed a reluctant Tiara to the screen door and held it open. "And don't think you can avoid this and bamboozle me. I'll know." Darla nudged her through the opening. "Good luck, kiddo, you probably need it."

Tiara felt the color drain from her face as she swallowed hard. Darla's kind laughter followed her as she slowly made her way toward the Mansfield property. Why didn't she just toss Slim's box in the trash before opening it?

Chapter Eleven

TIARA COULDN'T CONTROL her racing heartbeat. She didn't know if the fear stemmed from possibly running into Jayce and her girlfriend, or from not knowing the type of reception she'd receive from Edna. Her nerves were so taut that Tiara thought she'd be physically sick.

Just as she gave serious consideration to turning around and running home, even though it meant disappointing Darla, a shadow passed across the inside of the screen door, her name loudly whispered in disbelief. As Tiara jumped in surprise, the door swung open, a basket of laundry flew across the porch, landing beneath the swing, and a tall, lean figure dashed down the stairs and clamped Tiara in a hug that had her feeling she'd burst apart, if she had seams.

"Oh, honey, I'm so happy to see you," Edna said, giving another squeeze before holding her at arm's length. "What a beautiful woman you are. Of course, you were always an enchanting and lovely child. I've missed you so much. When Jayce told me you were here, I wanted to fly over and see you—" Edna released her hold of Tiara, wiped tears from her eyes and took a deep breath. "I'm rambling. But when Jayce said you were mad at us, I didn't know what to do."

"If I'm mad at anyone, it's Jayce. Admittedly, I'm just as much at fault for not getting over here sooner, though."

"Please come inside and let me get you some iced tea, unless you'd prefer hot tea, maybe a snack? Cookies." Edna hooked an arm through Tiara's and tugged her toward the screen door. "You and your friends should come for supper when you have a few free moments. Or we could have an old fashioned cowboy barbeque." Edna carried on a non-stop barrage of dialogue, interspersed with questions she didn't allow Tiara to answer, until they'd reached the kitchen. Tiara figured Edna was afraid that allowing an opportunity to answer those questions would scare Tiara off. "Sit down, Tiara," she said, quickly moving to the sink and running water into a kettle, "and I'll have tea ready in just a bit."

It didn't take long for Tiara to notice that the kettle had filled a number of times over, the faucet still running, Edna seemed unaware and hadn't budged. Tiara was tempted to tease Edna, until she noticed Edna's shoulders trembled as she leaned into the sink edge with her shoulders trembling. Was she crying? Alarmed, Tiara jumped from the chair and turned the water off. Gently, she took the kettle from Edna's hand. When she looked up, Tiara experienced a jumble of her own emotions being overwhelmed and brokenhearted at seeing the steady stream of tears rushing down Edna's cheeks.

"I'm sorry my presence is making this into a bad time for you. Do you want me to leave?" Tiara asked, realizing she'd created the emotional turmoil, not wanting to hurt the dear woman any further.

Edna wiped ineffectively at the tears, shaking her head furiously. "No, heavens no, I never wanted you to leave in the first place." Her voice caught on a sob, which took a couple of deep breaths to settle somewhat. "Not that my opinion mattered then."

Tiara rubbed Edna's arm reassuringly. "It wouldn't have changed circumstances any, but your opinion has always mattered to me."

"Oh, honey," Edna said clasping Tiara in a bear hug before releasing the hold. Edna put the kettle on the burner but didn't start the heat. "I wish I had been stronger for you. That wretched woman—" Edna clamped her lips firmly together. "I'm so sorry. She was your mother and I have no right to speak ill of the dead."

Tiara shrugged and said, "I've had a few choice words of my own where Angie was concerned. Relax on that account." Tiara sat down again. "Tell me how you've been. It can't have been easy living with Jayce." Tiara remembered Edna's brother and wife, Jayce's parents, had been killed in an automobile accident just a couple of years after she had left for Colorado Springs. "I'm sorry about Dexter and Jeannie."

"They had a good life. Still miss him, my little Dex. Sometimes I'll be doing the most inconsequential thing and remember those precious moments with us as kids, or some funny thing he did while he was dating Jeannie." Edna smiled wistfully. "I know it's the same for Jayce, too."

"They—you—all of you were very close. I miss how everyone made me a part of this family when I was around." Tiara could feel the tears building at the truth the words invoked in her memory. "The Mansfields were truly a godsend for almost three years of my life."

"Even with Jayce at her demonic best?" Edna smiled with a watery laugh, wiping away fresh tears. "No, Jayce being a beast, wasn't it?"

She knew Edna was teasing, but couldn't stop the flush of embarrassment at hearing her own words repeated. "Yeah." Tiara gave a weary exhale of breath. "I just wish she wasn't always getting me so riled. I don't know what's wrong with me."

"Jayce can certainly have that effect on a person," Edna said, then laughed.

Tiara joined in until she felt the tears dampen her cheeks. "And Lord help me, I actually missed Jayce so—" She swallowed to stop the rush of words her useless brain wanted to spout. Shrugging, Tiara decided to speak her mind, as she used to do when she was younger. It seemed the natural thing to do. "I didn't realize just how much until she started pestering me the moment I stepped foot on Dad's property. Not that I didn't truly miss you, too, since you were more my mother than Angie ever was. But—"

"Oh, thank you for that." Edna bit her bottom lip and took a deep breath. "And you don't have to explain anything to me. I know how ornery Jayce can be. Also, how strong and supportive when truly needed." Edna got up and walked to the refrigerator, removed a large glass pitcher of iced tea and a tray of ice, and brought them to the counter. "She explained about your visitor earlier today," she said, taking two glasses from the cupboard, filling them with ice and pouring the tea into them. "Some of the information got a bit confusing, but the general idea was easy enough to figure out." Edna handed a glass of iced tea to Tiara. "I have to agree with her on one point, honey. No matter what you remember from your childhood, Slim would never involve you in anything illegal. I can't believe he had any idea those men would show up at the house."

"I don't know what to think anymore," Tiara said, as she placed a hand on the table beside her tea glass. "I just wish he'd come home so we can work this out."

"We'll get him home before long." Edna squeezed Tiara's hand. "He'll be so happy to see you again. He's missed you. We've all missed you."

"Thank you." Shaking her head, Tiara said, "I shouldn't take up any more of your time. I need to get back before Darla sends a search party for me. With the baby coming, I don't want her stressed more than she needs to be."

Edna raised an eyebrow. "Ah, no wonder Jayce has been acting strange. You're attached."

For a moment, Tiara didn't understand what she meant. Then it dawned on her what Edna probably thought. "No, Edna. Darla is the wife of one of my employees. Jayce is under the impression I'm dating Craig, another of my employees."

Face flushed, Edna said, "Oh, I'm sorry. This changes a lot. I didn't mean to imply anything to make you uncomfortable. I mean, all those years ago, I thought maybe you and Jayce—I don't know what I thought. Forgive me. I don't mean to insult you. What you must think of me, the old busybody."

"I think you're still adorable, Edna." Tiara stood up. "You didn't insult me. I did have a crush on Jayce then, still do actually. Nothing is, or ever will, go on between Craig and me, or any man for that matter. However, if the misunderstanding—"

"Keeps Jayce away, then you've created a safety zone." Edna stood and wrapped Tiara in a hug. "Are you certain that is the best course of action?" Edna asked gently as she released her.

"I have to believe it is. We have too much baggage now. Besides, even if I had the inclination to chase after Jayce, I could never compete against someone like Ms. Juarez."

Edna stared at her for so long, Tiara worried another emotionally charged breakdown was coming. Finally, with lips pursed, she patted Tiara's shoulder and said, "Maybe you're right." Tucking her arm through Tiara's, Edna tugged her toward the door. Once they were on the porch, Edna said, "Thank you for stopping by. Please don't be a stranger, sweetheart. You always were and always will be welcomed here." She let go of Tiara and began picking up the clothes she'd dropped earlier.

Tiara helped pick up the laundry and then said, "Thank you. And thanks for those wonderful cookies, by the way."

"Don't thank me. That was Jayce's doing." Edna shook her head. "Don't tell her, but I think she cooks better than I ever dreamed possible."

"Jayce? Really? Huh, who would have guessed that? Please, give her our thanks. Well, good-bye, we'll talk again later," Tiara said.

"You won't be able to keep me away." Edna flashed a smile that was a duplicate of Jayce's at her most mischievous moments. "And you're probably right. Not many women could compete with a woman like Juanita. Why even try?" Edna gave a wave, turned around and walked back into the house.

Tiara stood on the porch and stared at the screen door. What did that mean? She knew she didn't look exotic like the television star; however, she could compete against any woman if she truly wanted. Tiara could more than hold her own against Juanita, if she even remotely wanted to fight her for Jayce.

Couldn't she?

Chapter Twelve

DRIVING HOME WAS uneventful and, except for the gentle rumble of the truck's engine, quiet. Too quiet, obviously, from Sarah's heavy sigh before she said, "Okay, we need to think of a strategy. I don't think making Tiara jealous is going to work fast enough for you."

"What do you mean?" Jayce asked. "No contest, she's got a boyfriend."

"Sweetie, it's plain to see that you're lost in thought, probably about Tiara." Sarah held up a hand. "No, don't deny it. Just think about this. From what I've seen, Tiara isn't entirely opposed to your affections. I think you're wrong about that cute boy." She snorted. "Oh, wipe that scowl off your face."

Jayce continued glaring a moment before returning her attention to the road. "He kissed her, and she didn't stop it. I tried to kiss her after his arrival and she was worried he'd see us." Jayce shrugged. "I don't know, maybe she's jerking my chain. It doesn't matter, Sarah. More than five minutes in each other's company and all we do is argue about what she thinks I believe she can and cannot do, or what I did or didn't mean to say. Communication is impossible with her."

Sarah reached over and squeezed Jayce's thigh. "More proof that the situation isn't hopeless, and that we probably need try another tactic."

"Like what?"

"Maybe she needs an old fashioned wooing." They had reached the ranch and Jayce parked her truck near the Mustang, and shut down the engine. Sarah shifted in the seat and faced Jayce. "Better yet, maybe you both need a lesson in understanding the whole grass-is-greener concept. Seems to me that's what most of the bickering is about."

"So I should, what, send flowers and chocolates, take her to dinner?"

"Yeah, show her your courtly side." Sarah laughed, and then wriggled her eyebrows. "Come on, Jayce, when was the last time you showed a lady the ranch? Had a picnic lunch and just relaxed and stared at the clouds? For that matter, when was the last time Tiara saw your place? Take her horseback riding, just the two of you."

Jayce shook her head. "That won't work, I think Tiara's scared of horses."

"Even better," Sarah said. "Arabelle needs to work with the old buckboard, learn to follow behind with the dust kicking up. This way my horse is being trained, and you two have to sit side by side."

"So it will be easier to reach each other's throats," Jayce said with a smirk.

Sarah chuckled. "Try to refrain from that, will you."

"Yes, dear."

This time Sarah groaned. "You can be such a pain in the keister. Be serious, sweetie. I'm kinda thinking your gonna thank me later, when you both realize what dolts you've been by wasting time fighting. Unless, of course, it's the kiss-and-make-up kind of fight, which you two *aren't* doing, so what's the point."

Jayce raised an eyebrow. "Know a lot about that do you?"

"I've had my fair share, yes."

"Huh." Jayce rolled her eyes. "Okay, then what?"

"I know you know what to do next."

Chuckling, Jayce said, "That part I got. I meant what else is on the agenda with the green grass thing."

"I'm not sure, yet. Maybe while you're out sparking, and I'm changing the motor oil in my car, we'll think of something. Until then, try to avoid comments about her lack of height or ability to do manual labor. It's obvious the topics are too sensitive for her. You also have to admit that the work she's done so far is exceptional. I like Slim, wouldn't talk behind his back otherwise, but he certainly let the place go. Not that he spent much time there in the last few years."

They both got out of the truck and started up the front porch.

Jayce nodded. "Which is why I suspect Aunt Edna knows more about his whereabouts and whatever plan he's hatched than she lets on. Heck, she may have helped him arrange getting Tiara here."

Sarah grinned, opened the screen door and walked in, Jayce just steps behind her. "I agree. Let's just hope she spills the beans before something unexpected happens with that strange little Elmo."

"Strange Elmo is right," Edna said irritably from the living room's archway. She pointed behind her. "Twelve dozen roses for you, *Ms. Juarez*, some in colors I've never seen in a flower, too." Edna crossed her arms over her chest and tapped her foot in annoyance. "The smell's so strong I could hide a rotting corpse in there and no one would be the wiser. And I'm looking at a couple of candidates for the corpse."

SARAH AND JAYCE managed to get Edna calmed down about the flowers. After Sarah made a few phone calls to arrange the entire bunch be picked up for donation, Edna excused herself to make a call of her own.

"Slim's away, so Edna's gonna play?" Sarah asked.

Jayce sniffed. "My guess is she's got to update Slim."

"As it's none of your business, either of you," Edna said, pointing a finger at both Sarah and Jayce. "I don't intend to acknowledge either snotty comment."

"You hurt me, *Señorita*. I'm not snotty."

"Yeah, you'll give us both a fit of the vapors." Jayce said.

Edna smirked. "Oh, I'll give you both something, all right. And vapors won't have anything to do with it." She left them in the hallway and headed for her room.

Jayce shook her head. "Do you think she's in on this charade with Slim?"

Sarah placed a hand on Jayce's arm. "I believe she knows where Slim is hiding. I don't think she knew anything about Elmo or Majestic."

"Well, if she didn't, she will." Sarah nodded her agreement. "I'm gonna watch some TV. You coming?"

"No," Sarah said. "I'm gonna get some tea and sit on the back porch for a while."

As Sarah walked out the screen door onto the back porch, she noted light coming from Slim's barn. She hoped it was Tiara, and made her way over. With all the drama surrounding Elmo, she couldn't tell if Tiara remembered her or not. A little visit might help her get a better feel for Tiara, too.

Sarah expected someone to be working in the old barn, and was surprised to see Tiara leaning against the opened barn door. She didn't want to frighten Tiara with her presence, so she called out, "Hello in the barn." Tiara straightened up. "Enjoying the beautiful night?"

"Ms. Juarez?" Tiara asked, then frowned in puzzlement as Sarah stood beside her.

She grinned. "You think I'm familiar, but the television star name is messing with your memory." She extended her hand. "Sarah Marsh. I was a friend of Jayce's in school. Since you were younger, we didn't have much interaction back then." Sarah feigned hurt. "Guess I wasn't so memorable."

"So which of you is dating Jayce?" Tiara asked.

Sarah laughed, hoped it would dispel the hurt in Tiara's tone. "Neither, really."

"Is that what you came here to tell me?"

"No, actually, after this afternoon, I need a favor," Sarah said. "I'd like to keep Juanita and Sarah separate. It's a vacation for me, after all."

"Don't want anyone asking you about your recent breakup?"

"You read the gossip rags? Tiara, I'm shocked."

Sarah watched Tiara's face darken in embarrassment. "I may have seen something while standing in a checkout line recently."

Sarah shook her head. "That's why I need your help. There are certain expectations I can avoid as Sarah the stunt double. Most folks around here are aware and play along."

Tiara bit her bottom lip. "I understand. After all, I also got caught up in the Juanita character when you rode up today. Okay, I won't let on."

"Thank you, Tiara. Well, have a good night." Sarah turned and started to walk away.

"You answered, 'neither, really' a moment ago." Tiara said from behind her, barely audible.

She stopped and looked over her shoulder at Tiara. "I love Jayce, deeply. Would I turn her down if she were serious about a relationship other than what we have as dear friends? Probably not." Sarah started walking away, just a little louder added, "I'd have her as Sarah or as Juanita."

Though Sarah was curious about Tiara's reaction to the statement, she forced herself to keep her course and not look back. Yeah, Jayce is definitely under your skin too, she concluded with relief.

TIARA MOVED SLOWER than usual this morning. Sleep should have come easily, what with exhaustion from all the work in the Colorado heat; but, once again, she'd tossed and turned with dreams of gangsters and, now, the addition of gunslingers. She just hoped that today would go better than the last couple of days. When she got to the kitchen, Darla was drinking a cup of coffee at the table, grinning as if she was the cat that ate the canary. Tiara expected little yellow feathers to fly out of her mouth when Darla asked, "Fine morning, isn't it?"

"Did I miss something? Or is this one of those pregnancy moments?" Tiara grabbed a mug from the dish drainer, filled it with coffee, and brought it to the table. She plopped into a chair. "Okay, spill it."

"You're so suspicious," Darla said, putting her cup down and waddling over to the walk-in pantry. She opened the door with a *ta-da* expression. Sitting on the floor was a large bouquet of flowers: a mix of daisies, roses, and lilies all in whites, yellow, and oranges. Darla picked up the vase and brought it to the table. "It's such a sunshiny arrangement and there's a card, too. Please read it out loud."

Reluctantly, especially with an audience, Tiara opened the card, and read, "You're invited to a picnic supper with someone who wishes to make amends. The buckboard will arrive at four o'clock to pick you up. Hope you are waiting. Until later, and ever optimistic, Jayce."

Darla giggled. "First the cookies, and now this romantic gesture. Tiara, this woman's a keeper."

"There's too much to do. I can't go off willy-nilly, whether the mood strikes me or not. I'm the boss for goodness sake. What kind of example is that?"

"I know Mark would find it a fine thing, as do I. It'll be close to your usual quitting time anyway, and no one cares what Craig thinks. I ask you, when was the last time you did something fun like this, or had a date? And it's so wonderful—"

"Maybe *you* should go, then."

Darla said, "If I didn't think the ride might be uncomfortable for the baby, I'd go in a heartbeat."

"She got over her TV star girlfriend quick enough," Tiara said sarcastically. "Dinner must have been a bust. I don't fancy being the rebound."

"Arrgh, you're driving me crazy. I adore you, Tiara, but I'm getting a taste of Jayce's frustration with you. You've been rebuffing her since her first hello. Jayce is extending the olive branch. Take it, clear things up." Darla pointed at Tiara's face. "If nothing else you'll have a chance to relax after what appears to have been a rough night's sleep. Come on. Go. Please."

Tiara shook her head. "Okay, fine. But if this turns out badly I get to say I-told-you-so until Baby Chester is in college."

"Deal," Darla said excitedly. "Honest, Tiara, if I thought you'd regret this I would be the first one to talk you out of it."

"I better get to work before I have to meet the infamous cowgirl Jayce." Tiara gulped the now cold coffee. "By the way, smarty, any special outfit you think I should wear to this rendezvous will need to be laid out for me. Otherwise, she gets me all sweat-drenched in these very jeans and t-shirt."

KNOTS BUILT IN Jayce's stomach. She worried she'd pull up and find Tiara had turned her down. She felt a bit irrational over being so concerned, it wasn't as if no one had stood her up before. She growled menacingly. "I can't believe you talked me into this."

"Hold still." Sarah tugged on Jayce's shirt to get the collar adjusted. "There," she said and stood back for a final review. "Perfect. Tiara won't be able to keep her hands off of you." Sarah brushed a stray lock off Jayce's forehead, then plopped Jayce's hat on her head.

Jayce rolled her eyes dramatically. "I don't think that's a problem for her."

"Then she's a fool." Sarah leaned in and kissed Jayce's cheek. "You're irresistible."

Jayce asked, "Why couldn't I keep you, then?"

Sarah shook her head. "You know why. You're too much woman for me."

"Always the smooth talker."

This time Sarah laughed and said, "Snake charmer, more like." They both laughed. "Take care of my Arabelle," Sarah said, and glanced in the horse's direction from her place behind the buckboard that Buster would be pulling.

Jayce took a deep breath. "Okay. Guess I'm as ready as I'll ever be." She turned around and climbed onto the bench seat of the buckboard. After making sure the picnic basket was safe under the seat, Jayce picked up the reins, grinned at Sarah, who slapped Buster's hind end to get him started.

"Bring Tiara home before dark, young lady," Sarah yelled out.

"I still don't understand why I'm doing this," Jayce mumbled as she pulled the reins to the right, and steered the horse down the dirt driveway. "I'm no better than Aunt Edna, always waiting on a Summers to catch and keep us. Sheesh." Her nerves got the best of her, and Jayce wanted to turn the buckboard around. Or head it down the road and away from Falling Down Acres. Instead, she turned it left and pulled in front of the porch.

No one was there.

Hurt filled Jayce. *Well, that answers that. Guess Tiara seriously isn't interested anymore. What foolishness was Sarah thinking?* Jayce tried to count to ten, got to four before she snapped the reins, and guided the horse toward the pasture that separated their properties. She hadn't gone more than twenty feet when she heard a panicked shout behind her. "Whoa," she said and pulled back on the leads. Jayce twisted on the bench and looked behind her. Darla stood on the porch, breathing heavily and holding her stomach as if the baby would slide out if she didn't hold on. "Oh my word," Jayce muttered as she turned the buckboard around and brought it in front of the porch once again.

"Oh, thank goodness," Darla said, as she rubbed a hand over her swollen stomach. "Tiara's running a little late, and getting dressed right now. Please, give her a moment." Jayce stared at Darla with disbelief. The tall woman grinned. "Honest. She'll be —"

"She's right here," Tiara said as she exited the screen door. "Sorry I'm late, Jayce." She turned to Darla and glanced to where the woman was rubbing her belly. "Are you okay?"

Darla pulled Tiara into a hug. "I am now." Pulling away, Darla said, "Get up there, and have a great time."

Jayce looped the reins through a metal ring on the dashboard, jumped down, and bowed as she took the cowboy hat off her head. "Ma'am, it would be my honor to escort you on a buggy ride and picnic." She extended an arm in Tiara's direction and said, "Shall we?" She didn't know what was going on in Tiara's head, but Jayce was glad when Tiara tentatively took her hand and let Jayce assist her onto the bench seat.

"Have her home at a decent hour, Jayce," Darla said in mock scold.

Putting her fingers to the hat's brim, Jayce dipped her head slightly and said, "Yes, Ma'am. I'll do that." *Inwardly, wondering at some preternatural issue with Tiara since everyone was worried about her being out after dark. Did she shape shift when the sun went down?* Picking up the reins and with one quick wave to Darla, Jayce started the buckboard toward her back property.

Chapter Thirteen

NEITHER JAYCE NOR Tiara spoke for a good twenty minutes of the ride. Arabelle must have found that fact disconcerting as she snickered loudly from behind them. Jayce glanced back at her. "Hush, and concentrate on your training."

"What kind of training is she getting?" Tiara asked quietly.

Jayce stared at her a moment. Much as teasing came naturally to Jayce, she knew Tiara's sense of humor was more mercurial, and decided she should probably stick with a straightforward answer. "Um, just to get used to walking behind the buckboard, the noise, the dirt and dust, stuff like that. Arabelle already believes herself a star. She doesn't like *not* being in control of the moment."

"I know the feeling," Tiara's voice was so low, Jayce pretended she hadn't heard the remark. More loudly, Tiara said, "Thank you, for this invitation."

"Thank you for accepting. I thought for a moment you might hide from me." Tiara turned red.

Jayce said, "You did think about it, then?"

"Well, yes, but Darla wasn't going to let me get away with it. She can be quite persuasive with guilt. She must have had a Catholic upbringing."

"I see." Jayce felt a twinge of hurt. She had hoped Tiara might want to spend time with her. How had she let Sarah talk her into this? "I can take you back to Slim's."

As she started to pull back on the reins, Tiara placed a hand over Jayce's, and shook her head. "I'm sorry, please don't turn around. I want to do this, be here with you, cross my heart."

There was a tiny bit of reluctance in her tone, but Jayce decided to accept Tiara's decision. "All right, then." She took a deep breath. "Then let me finish showing you the very best parts of Silver Waters, right here on Mansfield Meadows."

Tiara raised an eyebrow. "Conceited much?"

"Nah, no conceit needed when the topic is my property," Jayce replied with a teasing smile. "It honestly speaks for itself."

Tiara shook her head and seemed to relax some and actually enjoy the scenery, pointing out landscape that had caught her eye and asking questions that Jayce excitedly answered. In Jayce's mind, she had only been forthright, not bragging, when she stated her land was the best components of Silver Waters. Her land had a variety of sites that included timberland, streams, hills and flatland. A point she enthusiastically brought up to Tiara. "The incentive to specializing in training Arabelle, and other horses before her, was from a terribly lost movie location director."

"How do you mean?" Tiara asked with what seemed genuine interest.

"He was surveying areas for potential filming sites, originally intending to use Cañon City. Taking the back roads got him all confused with directions, and subsequently very lost. I was out for a ride with one of the boarded horses when I caught him just walking around snapping pictures."

Amusement flashed across Tiara's face. "How bad did you scare him?"

"Hey." Jayce grinned crookedly in dismay. "It's my property. I am duty bound to defend it." The statement brought a giggle from Tiara. Jayce gave an offended huff, but was immensely pleased she and Tiara had reached a more relaxed standing. "Anyway," she said, adding a playful roll of her eyes, "when he regained consciousness—" She paused to watch Tiara as she held onto the seat and laughed hard. "I brought him home to Edna."

"Who promptly gave him milk and cookies," Tiara finished for her.

"Yeah, Edna's enduring cure-all."

Tiara's laughter subsided, but a smile remained on her lips. "I'd take it any day of the week," she said, honesty in her tone. She turned and a lump formed in Jayce's throat, witnessing the turbulent emotions in Tiara's gray eyes. "But were the cookies from Edna's cooking?"

"What makes you ask that?" Jayce felt the flush of embarrassment.

Tiara's smoky gaze held hers for a long moment, before she looked away. "There are sides to you I wasn't aware of." She sighed. "Or have totally forgotten. Thank you, by the way, for the cookies the other night. I almost hated to share with the crew, not that I had much say in the matter."

Jayce didn't respond, afraid she'd lose control of the jealousy she barely kept contained, remembering Craig's version of hello at the mention of her crew. Apparently, Tiara didn't expect a reply.

"So, what happened next?"

"Huh? Oh, well some folks came back to film different locations, for background on other projects and, realizing I did horse training they made some phone calls and hired me on a temporary basis to teach a particular stunt to an Appaloosa they were using. Nine years have passed since then. Basic boarding and training became more than work. Now I have a career. Guess I did okay."

"Is that how you met Ms. Juarez?"

Tiara's voice was so low that Jayce almost missed the question. She didn't want to *not* answer, or need to lie, but hadn't the right to divulge Sarah's private life without permission. Jayce settled for a simple answer. "We met before then, under different circumstances entirely."

"I see," Tiara said quietly.

"Do you?" Jayce asked of her, with a frown. She cared for the Tiara from over ten years ago, and those feelings were resurfacing with each moment they spent together, but Jayce would defend Sarah, if the need arose, as she would a beloved sibling. There must have been something in her tone, because Tiara stared at her for a moment.

"No, I guess I don't," Tiara said. "But I've no right to invade your personal life, when I won't grant the same courtesy to you."

Time seemed to stop in their silence. Jayce focused on the landscape and realized they had reached her favorite spot, and the destination for their picnic. "Here we are," she said, wrapping the reins round the metal ring near the brake handle, crossed in front of Tiara and jumped down from the buckboard. When she landed, Jayce held up a hand to assist Tiara down. "Hope the view meets with your approval."

Hesitant at first, Tiara allowed Jayce to help her from the seat. For just an instant, their bodies met and warmth consumed Jayce. She released Tiara as soon as it was safe to do so, and took a step back, hoping her breathing was under control.

Tiara's gaze took in her surroundings. "Oh, Jayce, it's gorgeous."

"Thank you," she said. Noting the mischievous twinkle in Tiara's eyes, Jayce added, "on Mother Nature's behalf, of course, as I had no hand in it." Tiara giggled causing Jayce's pulse to quicken. "I'll get the food and a blanket." Jayce needed some space. Maybe Tiara in a bad mood was the safest atmosphere. Tiara in a good mood elicited responses in her body that were becoming difficult to control, wreaking havoc on Jayce's emotions. She was acting like a hormonal teenager.

Tiara unfolded the blanket with a quick snapping motion, and placed it on the thick grass under a tree near where Jayce had stopped the buckboard. She sat and Jayce placed the picnic basket on the corner edge and joined her. Leaning against the tree trunk, Tiara pulled her knees toward her chest and draped her arms over them. "This is exquisite, Jayce," she said, breathing deeply and closing her eyes.

Jayce beamed at her comment. "Glad you like it," Jayce said, opening the basket's lid and pulling out plastic containers of food, one by one, and arranging them neatly between the two of them. "Just the pleasure of hearing you laugh, even once, is worth giving you anything, my lady fair."

Tiara opened one eye speculatively. "Lady fair?"

"In all my vast land." Jayce gave as gallant a bow as possible from her sitting position and raised her hand to indicate the open area surrounding them.

Tiara sniffled. "Did Aunt Edna pack your head with that stuff when she packed the basket? Or is this sentiment residual from your TV star?"

Jayce put a hand to her heart. "I'm wounded. To insinuate such a thing grieves me greatly."

"It doesn't answer the question. Or does it?" Both eyes opened wide and stared directly at Jayce. A hint of the ever-present sadness seemed to return, before she blinked it away.

"No, it doesn't. Not in the way you're thinking." Jayce pulled a bottle of wine from the basket, then two gold colored plastic goblets. She uncorked the wine and laid it on a small wire rack she'd brought along to let the wine breathe. "You'll have to excuse the uncouth picnic ware, it came with the basket. To clear your obvious misconception, Edna didn't fix this repast or pack it. I did. Therefore, she couldn't have filled my head with anything. As for Ms. Juarez, it wouldn't be right to take advice from the woman I'm ignoring so I get to spend time with you."

Surprise danced across Tiara's features. "You really do cook?" Jayce was astounded that Tiara focused on the news of food rather than bring up another woman. Tiara's interest in what lay beneath the plastic covers appeared to have been piqued as she pulled lids off. After Tiara had opened every container, she gasped. "You did all this? The fried chicken, the pasta salad, the pie, all of it was made by your hands?"

"All but the fruit. I only washed and sliced those, and the cheese, which I painstakingly chunked." Her face warmed in embarrassment, Jayce suddenly worried if it had been a good idea to be honest, at least on this matter. Maybe she should have let Tiara believe Edna had prepared it all. What if she knew Jayce actually enjoyed cooking?

"I let Darla cook, since she wanted to be useful while we fixed Dad's place." Tiara pulled a couple spiral pasta free from the bowl with her fingers, tilted her head back as she dropped them in her mouth. "Oh, heaven," Tiara crooned, rolling her eyes.

When Tiara lowered her head and groaned, Jayce panicked and asked, "What's wrong?"

"I lied," Tiara said in a bare whisper, shaking her head.

"It's not heaven?" With the sun setting, shadows from the tree branches crossed Tiara's face. Jayce hoped the same was happening for her, not wanting Tiara to see the hurt she felt, the expression probably racing across her face. Jayce had wanted to impress her, and hadn't realized how much until now.

"No...I mean, yes," Tiara said nervously.

Jayce picked up the wine, filling the goblets half way. "Maybe you can wash it down with this." Jayce passed her one. "Hope you don't mind a sweet red."

Tiara took the cup. When Tiara's fingers grazed hers, a tingling rushed through Jayce. She started to pull away, but Tiara clasped a hand in her own. Jayce didn't stop the smile tugging at her lips.

Tiara's thumb was gently stroking the back of Jayce's hand, as she said, "Yes, it's heaven. No, it wasn't what I lied about." Jayce wondered if Tiara was aware of the action of her thumb. Certainly she wasn't about to ask because the physical contact felt too good. Then Tiara finally let her go. "I lied before about letting Darla do the cooking because she needed to feel useful." Her voice dropped before she mumbled something else. Jayce craned her head forward to catch it, but couldn't make it out.

"Huh?" Jayce said, "I missed the last part."

With an exasperated sigh, Tiara said, "Really, Jayce. You could have been kind and ignored it." Tiara picked up a chicken leg and glowered at her. "I can't cook," she said, then chomped a massive bite out of the meat.

Jayce laughed as Tiara chewed indignantly and turned away. More relaxed, now that her culinary ability wasn't at fault, Jayce filled a plastic plate with food. "I thought it was important and I didn't want to miss it."

"Miss the opportunity, you mean."

"Here," Jayce said, offering Tiara the plate. "What opportunity?"

"For teasing me later, for one more thing this woman can't do, and for lying in the first place." Tiara dropped her gaze to the plate and almost spilled the food in the process.

"Wow, Red." She groaned. "Sorry. I mean Tiara." Jayce purposely gave her full attention to filling a plate for herself. She inhaled deeply and let it out slowly. "I apologize that every word from my lips is mistaken for, or expected to be, a slur and an insult to you. I'm trying to make amends for earlier, and I honestly thought we moved beyond that, actually enjoying each other's company. Guess I was wrong."

Tiara squinted for a moment, and then leveled a steady gaze at her. "You're right. I should be the one asking for forgiveness." She looked down at her hands, now firmly clasped on her lap. "Even Darla mentioned I've been unfair to you." She raised her head and looked into Jayce's eyes. "I admit I came back here with way too much baggage, so much more than I left with. Though I feel some is justified, some is definitely not. Please, Jayce, be patient with me." She swallowed hard. "I want us to at least be friends again."

Jayce didn't know what to say, especially when she saw the dampening of Tiara's eyelashes. She bit her bottom lip, hoping it would hide the tremor from her own emotions. "At least," Jayce said in a whisper. "I cherished our friendship those many years ago. I'd like to get back some of those really great times."

More relaxed, Tiara said, "Me too." Then, her face took on a frightened expression.

A knot built in Jayce's stomach. "What's wrong?"

With a glare, Tiara demanded, "Promise, no horse feed baths."

SARAH GAPPED THE last spark plug and bent toward the carburetor when she heard from behind her, "Hey, Dude, know where I can find Edna or Ms. Juarez?" Barely contained wrath ready to spew from her mouth at the insult, Sarah raised herself and moved away from the engine hood, and turned. She heard the surprised intake of breath from the young blond man next door.

"Dude?" Sarah glanced down at her blue coveralls. Old and new stains generously decorated the cotton material from work she'd performed on the car. The coveralls were comfortably baggy, but she never expected to be mistaken for a man because of them.

"Ms. Juarez," he said, "I...I uh...I never..."

With a slight smirk, Sarah said, "Why does that not surprise me."

"Huh?"

"Exactly." Noting he was still confused, she shook her head in annoyance, deciding to let him off the hook. But not so far off that she acknowledged her television persona. She wanted to enjoy being herself for a while longer. He was terribly cute. "Juanita and Edna are in the house."

"Huh?"

She rolled her eyes. "Really kid? You spoke a complete sentence when you thought I was a guy." Sarah spoke slowly. "They're in the house." When he remained standing, staring at her in confusion, she extended a hand. "Sarah Marsh. I'm Juanita's body double, stunt woman, and most-times mechanic."

The introduction worked as the icebreaker she intended. He took her hand and gave a couple quick, firm shakes. "Craig Walters. I'm from the next property over. Well, Tiara's property, and we're here helping. " He leaned closer to her and whispered conspiratorially, "It's my boss on the, uh, date with the lady over here." He gave a wry grin.

Sarah wanted to wipe the grin off his face with a good hearty slap. Placing hands on hips and giving her best glower, she said, "Mr. Walters, please state your business. If you're here to insult my friends with closed minded drivel, you can leave before I do something you'll regret."

"Something I'll regret? Somehow I don't think I'd much mind anything you did to me." He ran a hand through his thick mass of blond hair. "Forgive me, Sarah. I guess that came out sounding a bit prejudiced. Wasn't what I meant."

She crossed her arms over her chest. "And what would that be exactly?"

Craig shrugged uncomfortably, actually seeming regretful for all his comments. "Starting over?" Sarah grinned at that remark. "Really, I just didn't want to upset Ms. Juarez, if she happened to overhear, since she is obviously interested in Jayce, too. I've nothing against two women going out." When she raised an eyebrow in doubt, he added, "Or caring about each other."

"Well, that's nice of you, Craig, thinking of Juanita and all. It's refreshing to meet a guy who's so open-minded," she said rolling her eyes.

He blushed as if it was a compliment. "Yeah, well, I knew there had to be something going on when Tiara wouldn't go out with me."

Sarah felt her own face redden. "And you're such a catch?

With a wide toothy smile, he answered, "Well, yeah, of course."

"State your business and leave, Mr. Walters." Sarah turned back to working on her tune up. She paused a moment to breathe deep and get control of her anger, not wanting to damage the tension hoses on the distributor cap. The sound of shuffling feet alerted her Craig had moved closer.

"What'd I say?" he asked. When she didn't respond, he finally got to his point. With a sigh, he said, "Darla would like to invite all of you to dinner tomorrow night, over at the house."

Without more than a quick glance at Craig, she said, "I'll be sure to let the folks inside know. I'm sure Edna will be calling...Darla, did you say?" He nodded. "I know Edna had some plans of her own to welcome Tiara home."

Craig grinned at that. "Great. I'll let Darla know to expect a call." He walked away and Sarah watched him leave. After a couple feet, he turned back around. "It was nice meeting you, Sarah. I look forward to a chance to make up for whatever I said to upset you." He flashed a wicked grin. "After all, I'm too awesome to ignore."

Sarah laughed, in spite of her anger at his insinuations. Cute and a sense of humor. She liked that, even if he was too full of himself. Then, she shook her head and returned to her tune-up. She didn't need an arrogant cutie-pie flirting with her so soon after Johnny. Not that flirting wasn't good for her self-esteem when applied to Sarah and not Juanita. She closed the hood and wiped her hands on her coveralls, glancing over to Tiara's place. "What am I thinking? He probably likes the idea that I look like Juanita. Besides, he looks to be barely out of high school."

Chapter Fourteen

BETWEEN THE TWO of them, Jayce and Tiara had consumed every last crumb from the basket. They leaned against the tree's trunk and watched the clouds overhead as dusk approached. Still a gorgeous day, the sky was darkening quickly, the wind picking up and carrying the smell of an impending storm. A fine example of Colorado's ever changing weather. "Gonna rain." The belief confirmed with a few stray drops. "Maybe we should head back," Jayce said.

They gathered up the picnic stuff and stashed it under the seat of the buckboard. Jayce helped Tiara up onto the seat, did a quick check on Arabelle's tether, jumped into the seat and picked up the reins. It was a good thirty minutes back to the *Meadows*. Even if she urged Buster to pick up the pace, they wouldn't make it back home before the brunt of the storm hit; and, from the smell in the air, it would be a doozy. As the raindrops fell faster, Jayce made a decision to get them out of the storm before they were soaked, and the horses spooked. Less than five minutes away was a line shack, constructed by the studios for some of their filming. Jayce tugged the reins to the left, off the main path, and toward a lesser traveled course.

"Where are we going?" Tiara asked, just as the skies opened up and released a steady, hard rain that nearly obscured the path.

"A line shack. It's too far to make it home, and I don't want us or the horses out in this, especially since night's coming and I can barely see as it is."

"We're going to be out after dark?" Tiara asked in a choked whisper.

Jayce glanced over and noticed Tiara had a death grip on the seat. Just then, lightening flashed and thunder boomed. With a squeak, Tiara flinched. Automatically, Jayce put the right rein in her left hand, reached over and put her arm across Tiara's shoulder. "Hey, it's okay."

Tiara gave a tremulous smile, scooting closer to Jayce. "Sorry, I just hate thunderstorms."

With a quick squeeze to Tiara's shoulders, Jayce asked, "Do you hear me complaining?" Jayce was able to make out the shack through the rain. She clicked the reins so that Buster pulled up in front, and jumped down, extending her arms to Tiara. "Let's get you inside, and then, I'll tend to the horses."

Because the line shack was on her property, Jayce never kept the cabin locked. She pushed the door open just as a bolt of lightning illuminated the sky and the interior. Tiara's eyes widened in fear, she gave a blood-curdling scream, and whirled around to run back into the pouring rain. Realizing her intent, Jayce barely had time to clasp onto

Tiara's left wrist and pull her back into the small cabin. Panicky, Tiara slipped in the mud and landed heavily against Jayce, her arms wrapping around Jayce's waist for support.

Another blaze of lightening and Jayce was able to see a new form of trepidation in Tiara's expression from their unexpected embrace. They were both soaking wet, yet Jayce couldn't remember another time that Tiara had looked so beautiful than right at that moment. Part of her knew her next action could end badly, yet Jayce still brought her lips to Tiara's, pressing eagerly. Tiara responded, her body losing some of its tension. The soft swell of breasts pressed into Jayce. Even with the compromised material wet from rain as the only barrier, Jayce felt warmth from Tiara's skin as she pulled Tiara closer, tighter. Heat flowed through Jayce's body, and she knew she had to stop before she went too far.

As another flash of lightning, followed by a crack of thunder sounded, Jayce pulled away, but did not release Tiara. Huskily she said, "I should have warned you about the mannequin. I keep him to ward off intruders." She could feel that Tiara still trembled, so she added, "Please, just wait here, in the doorway. I'm going to let go of you and light the lantern. Okay?" With Tiara's nod, Jayce let go of Tiara's wrist.

Night fell quickly, and with the darkness from the clouds, Jayce relied more on memory than sight to lead her to where the lantern rested. Beside it was a small box of campfire matches to light the wick. Then she opened the lid on the large wooden trunk beside the mannequin, and pulled out spare blankets. Jayce turned to a trembling Tiara in the doorway. Jayce tugged her across the threshold, and toward the bunk on the left wall that was about two feet off the ground, where she turned Tiara and gently nudged her to sit, tossing the blankets alongside.

Jayce cupped Tiara's chin and raised her head until Tiara met her gaze. "You okay?" At Tiara's nod, she said, "I've got to get Arabelle and Buster under the awning, and out of this weather. Take off those wet clothes and wrap one of the blankets around you. I'll be back in a few minutes." Jayce rushed out slamming the door behind her against the onslaught of rain.

SHOOK UP AND cold from her soaking wet clothes, and minus the heat that had been radiating from Jayce, Tiara stood and undressed as quickly as possible, hoping to have the blanket around her before Jayce finished outside. Clothes off and blanket around her she sat back down on the bed and glanced around the small shack.

Behind her was a four-paned window, which she wished she'd have noticed before undressing in front of it. The bunk took up the majority of the wall, a small wood shelf at the head. On the wall opposite the door, a trunk, another window, and gazing forlornly outside from against the right wall sat the lifelike cowboy mannequin, a melancholy expression permanently marked his features. Just slightly off center in the room was a table that the lantern and a box of matches sat on, and tucked into one side a lone scuffed chair, matching the one the dummy sat in. On the wall with the door was a humble fireplace. *Does it burn as hot as Jayce's kiss and embrace?* Tiara felt her face heat up at the unbidden thought. She continued her inspection. A gallon sized metal tub with a meager offering of firewood beside the fireplace, a cross-stitched picture of *Home-Sweet-Home* surrounded by bluebells hung above in a frame of twigs. She had expected to see dust coating the shack's contents, but the furniture only had a minor coating.

The shack was a cozy place, despite the horrid storm outside. The idea of spending the night here petrified Tiara, because, in her heart, she wanted more from Jayce; and, wanted Jayce to desire more from her. After a wonderful picnic in Jayce's company, new responses flared, and memories sparked of the same ease and security Tiara had felt all those years ago when spending time with Jayce. No matter what, Tiara realized, Jayce had always made her feel safe. It was too soon to rekindle feelings, no matter how quickly they came flooding back to her. Not to mention that the thought of a relationship with anyone, especially Jayce, terrified her.

Tiara was startled from these thoughts when Jayce rushed inside, rain following in her wake until she banged the door shut against it, and dropped an armload of firewood near the metal tub. "Wow, it's really coming down out there," Jayce said, shaking her head to dispel the drops lodged in her hair, then finger combed the short length into place.

A small puddle of water formed at Jayce's feet, Tiara noticed, as her gaze traveled upward, clothes so drenched they plastered against Jayce's body. Tiara registered, even in the dim light from the lantern, that Jayce wore a black lace bra under her lavender colored shirt. Tiara's heart raced. Quickly, she looked away. "You should get undressed, too, before you catch cold." Tiara flinched inwardly at hearing the strain in her own voice, clenching her hands tighter to the blanket to fight against the perplexing impulse to reach out and touch Jayce.

"I should get a fire started first," Jayce said. "By the way, behind Hank," she pointed to the sad mannequin, "is a toilet and sink. Not fancy, but better than going outside or using a bucket." It took barely a minute for her to get a small blaze started. Then, Jayce went to the trunk and raised the lid, pulling out various items, cataloging them as she did so. "We have energy bars, twine, and bottled water. Oh, yeah, and a first aid kit in the event someone gets a boo-boo."

"Twine?" Tiara asked, curiosity helping her pulse return a bit closer to normal.

Jayce turned toward her with a smile. "If I stretch it across the cabin, we can use it as a clothes line." She, or someone, must have done this before because there were already nails placed in the walls for Jayce to run the line. "Between this and the fire, our stuff should dry. Sorry I can't offer you something more palatable for an after supper snack. Bet if I dig in far enough, I might find a can of beans." Jayce flashed a mischievous smile.

Tiara couldn't help but respond with a laugh. "I'm sure we can pass on that particular delicacy for tonight." She gave a shrug. "Besides, I'm fine. Really."

"Mm-hmm, yes, you are. Totally."

When she glanced into Jayce's eyes, she was sure that raw desire stared back. It was then Tiara realized the blanket had slid from her shoulder and left her right breast showing. Hastily, Tiara tugged the blanket closer.

Jayce finished securing the twine, and was now picking up Tiara's clothes and hanging them across the improvised clothesline. Tiara couldn't be certain, but it looked as if Jayce's hands were trembling. "You need to get undressed, Jayce. You're cold."

"I'm fine," Jayce said sharply. Once she had finished with Tiara's clothing, Jayce walked over to the bunk, snapped up the other blanket, then tossed it over the line. She walked to the opposite side of the barrier, and Tiara realized Jayce was also undressing. The blanket barrier shifted as Jayce pulled it around herself, and carefully swung her own clothes across the line. When done, Jayce dropped into the chair at the table and stared intently into the fire.

Even from the bunk, Tiara could feel the tension radiating from Jayce. It was at that moment Tiara knew Jayce was also uncomfortable with their current situation. She wanted to say something to dispel the awkwardness, but feared making the matter worse. However, Tiara had to say something because the silence, fine when alone, was torturous with someone in the room. Especially when that someone made Tiara's pulse race with her very presence, her every breath. Just keep it simple, Tiara's inner voice told her. "No cards or checkers in your magic trunk?"

"Why didn't you ever write me back?" Jayce asked in a faint tone.

Tiara blinked in shock. Where did that come from? So much for keeping things simple, she groused. "I did, after the first couple months. At the beginning it was hard to find the time." Tiara pulled the blanket tighter, though she wasn't cold anymore. "Then things settled down, and I couldn't seem to fit in at school. I wrote for news of home. I never got anything back." Tiara shrugged, but the reminder felt like a fist slammed to her stomach. "I figured no one missed me, no matter how much I missed them."

"You are *so* wrong, you know." Jayce shifted in her chair uneasily, and Tiara sneered. She turned away again, and stared into the fire. "Something you said the other day has been tickling the back of my brain."

"What might that be?"

"You said the road ran both ways."

"Yeah, so?" Tiara frowned.

Jayce took a deep breath. "Did you know Angie had a restraining order against Slim and me?" Tiara felt the blood drain from her face. A restraining order for what? Why prevent Jayce for seeing her? Why prevent her father from seeing her? She shook her head. Jayce continued. "I can't give the specifics for Slim, but I wrote to you every day for a month, and once a week for a couple more after that. I knew they made it to your house. Angie made certain that I knew. I stopped writing you on my nineteenth birthday."

All this time Tiara believed Jayce had abandoned her, but she hadn't given up, not at first, anyway. "Jayce, I swear, I never saw even one letter." Then something Jayce said snagged her attention. "Was the restraining order to make sure you stopped trying to contact me?"

Slowly, Jayce shook her head, and then turned to stare at Tiara's face. This time, Tiara shifted uncomfortably under the scrutiny. Tiara had no choice but squirm, the hurt reflected in the blue depths painful to witness, knowing that she was the cause, even if inadvertently because of her mother.

The emotional turmoil dredged up inside the shack seemed mirrored by the force of the storm outside. Tiara's focus was on Jayce, yet the thunder still cracked, flashes of lightening lit the room like a strobe. And, with each strike, her nerves strained to snapping.

She almost gave up hope that she'd get an explanation when Jayce stood and walked to the fireplace, tossing another log on the fire. "One of my letters was returned to me opened," Jayce said, keeping her back to Tiara. "I expected you were letting me know you weren't interested, maybe to leave you alone. But it wasn't from you."

"What did Angie do?" Tiara grimaced, afraid of what she'd learn in the answer. Circumstances forced her to live with Angie for too long, not to realize what kind of vindictive woman her mother had been. For years, Tiara had assumed herself the only victim of Angie's hatefulness. Had she been so wrong as to shun the only people — the one person — on her side the whole time? Tiara wanted Jayce to turn around, but part of her feared what she might see. "Jayce, look at me."

After she said the words, Tiara was almost sorry. When Jayce turned around, Tiara noticed a lone tear, glistening in the fire's light, trickle down Jayce's cheek. Witnessing emotion, usually so uncharacteristic from the cheerful, playful woman, caused Tiara to stiffen in dread. She wasn't surprised to hear the trembling of her voice when she asked, "What did Angie say in the letter?"

Jayce didn't meet her gaze. In a whisper, Jayce said, "She wrote, 'You are perverted. Tiara wants nothing to do with your filth. Keep your aberrant behavior away from my daughter.' Angie used a very bright red marker to write the message." Jayce inhaled deeply. "Since I never received a letter from you..."

"You took it as my agreement with Angie's point of view." No wonder Jayce had given up on attempts to keep the channels of communication open. Jayce nodded solemnly. Tiara swallowed against the constriction in her throat from sentiments she held at bay — barely. Rage and excitement battled for release. Tiara was mad at Angie, however useless it was now, for keeping away the one person who ever made her feel alive inside. Excitement that maybe she would have had a chance at "happily-ever-after" if she'd come back sooner. One point niggled at Tiara, and she asked, "Then why kiss me? Hell, why even give me the time of day after that?"

Before Jayce answered, a boom of thunder, imitating cannon fire, shook the shack. Tiara screeched and shivered violently enough to make her teeth clench. In less than a second, Jayce was in front of her, wrapping Tiara in her arms. "I've got you," Jayce whispered against her ear. "Nothing's gonna happen to you." Just as Tiara acknowledged the statement in her head, she heard the audible gulp in Jayce's throat. She pulled away a little and gazed up into Jayce's eyes. Even in the meager lighting, Tiara saw the blue depths darkening with desire, with need. "Well, almost nothing is gonna happen," Jayce whispered against her lips, just before claiming them hungrily.

Chapter Fifteen

JAYCE HAD WORRIED this would happen, knew she couldn't stop herself from kissing Tiara. She didn't understand her own reactions when near Tiara, she simply responded as her heart compelled her to do. They were part of the same whole, Jayce incomplete without Tiara. Jayce also realized she'd said too much about Angie. She couldn't stop herself, she wanted Tiara to know the truth, because Jayce wanted more than friendship from Tiara. She wanted what could have been. Even through her other relationships, short as they usually were, including with Sarah, Jayce kept linking memories of Tiara and using those in comparison against the other women. If soul mates truly existed, Tiara was hers, and she'd known it that summer in the barn.

Though Jayce doubted Tiara was ready for the entire truth, she needed an honest answer to her question. Breaking the kiss, Jayce pulled away, and realized from Tiara's sharp gasp that the blanket no longer covered her. Aware of Tiara's discomfort with her nudity, Jayce pointedly ignored it to concentrate on one matter at a time. Gently she clasped Tiara's face in her hands and tilted Tiara's gaze upward so she would only see Jayce's face. Once she had Tiara's attention, Jayce said, "Because I very much wanted it to be a lie. Since our first kiss, I wanted you to return at least a smidgen of the feelings I have for you."

Tiara didn't appear convinced. "Why'd you run away that day?"

Embarrassed and flushed, Jayce replied, "I didn't *run*."

"Why?"

"Oh, Red," Jayce muttered in agony. "You were a thirty-plus year old soul in a fourteen year old body. I didn't know what to do with the situation. I wanted you so badly that I physically hurt. Touching you as I wanted would have bordered on illegal, my being weeks away from eighteen." They were close enough that Jayce could feel heat radiating off Tiara's body, the warmth of her expelled breath caressed Jayce's face. Her own body responded to Tiara's proximity, tingling as if zapped by a bolt of the lightening's current. "Before I could work anything out in my head, Angie took you away. After what was written on my returned letter, I thought I'd been mistaken, fooling myself into believing I read more in your response to our kiss." Jayce released Tiara's face, and gently ran her hands up and down Tiara's blanket covered arms. "Angry, and hurt, I simply quit believing we were more than just kids who grew up as neighbors."

Tiara wrinkled her nose. "Angry because Angie classified you as deviant?" she asked, tenderly poking a finger into Jayce's bare abdomen. "Maybe she thought that meant bully."

Arousal coursed warm and sweet as melted chocolate through

Jayce's blood. She groaned, trying to concentrate on the topic. "No, Angie knew exactly what she meant. After the restraining order, I had no doubts Angie would have me arrested if given the chance."

"I'm sorry she hurt you," Tiara said.

"Yeah, well, you're the one who had to put up with her full-time." Some of the lightheartedness drained from Tiara. Jayce continued, fighting the urge to comfort her. "Actually, I guess I hurt because I knew that kiss in the barn would be the first and last kiss we'd ever share and I never told you how I really felt about you." Jayce was on dangerous ground with the admission and her nudity and her need. Pulling away and snatching the blanket from the floor, Jayce wrapped it around herself and backed up. She did what she should have done long ago. Jayce had confessed her feelings, and explained the circumstances of the past. Obviously, emotions truly were all on her side, as Tiara wasn't returning any admissions. "You should get some sleep."

"Don't you mean 'we' should get sleep?" Tiara asked.

"Well, yeah. I'll use the chair or stretch out on the floor." Jayce wished Hollywood had thought to use bunk beds in here. Maybe she'd see to that matter later.

Tiara scowled. "You'll never get any sleep that way." As if an everyday occurrence, Tiara stretched out on the bunk, blanket still tight around her, and scooted back against the wall. With a quick pat to the space beside her, Tiara said, "Come on. I promise to behave myself."

Immediately, Jayce felt flustered. Being close to a naked Tiara, she didn't think she could make the same promise. In a voice that croaked, Jayce turned her back, blew out the flame to the lantern and said, "Get under the covers, they're clean. Edna takes care of that every week. I'll sleep on top." When Tiara chuckled, Jayce felt her entire body heat with embarrassment. "Oh...that's... that's not what I meant."

"I know," Tiara said softly, a hint of laughter remaining. "Okay, your turn."

Jayce carefully climbed up, trying to keep the blanket secured around her. Then she stretched out stiffly, her body as aware as her brain that, despite the barriers, Tiara was mere centimeters from her. Shivers of pleasure ran through Jayce. Both were silent for a long time, and Jayce could feel that Tiara's tension matched her own.

It appeared neither was going to get any sleep tonight.

THE RANDOM FLASHES of lightening no longer eclipsed the soft golden illumination cast by the fire. Her fear of storms no longer an issue — much — since Tiara felt safer as long as Jayce was with her. As Tiara lay still, trying not shift and unintentionally brush against Jayce, her head endeavored to make sense of all she'd learned tonight.

Those last years under Angie's roof had taught her how self-centered and hateful her mother really was. But she'd never expected that selfishness had extended beyond Tiara's own personal dealings. In all the years after Angie's death, Tiara's beliefs of abandonment had never wavered. Never would she have considered that Angie had intercepted her incoming, and obviously outgoing, mail. Never, not even remotely, expected that Angie would file such harsh legal papers against the two people Tiara loved and needed most. She didn't know why she should be surprised, though, since the crux of Angie's reasoning was to isolate Tiara's affections. Only it had elicited the opposite. Being with Angie was like a prison sentence she had to endure until she could escape.

All the bottled up anger she'd felt toward her father and Jayce seemed pathetic and useless, in light of the new information. Now Tiara didn't know if she could move beyond all those years of torturing herself about never measuring up to their expectations. She certainly wasn't going to overcome it in a single night.

Cursing Angie for causing all the lost years that she could have shared with Jayce, knowing she had a place here, with people who loved her for simply being herself. How many other things had she been wrong about? Jayce had told her that Slim didn't gamble, but the evidence, Majestic, was in a corral proving otherwise, so how could she be wrong about that too?

One question replayed in her mind. Did the new knowledge ultimately change anything? No, she couldn't let it. Tiara had a wonderful business, a house of her own, and co-workers who were the closest things to friends than she'd ever expected to have. Knowing Jayce cared for her, had for these many years, was wonderful, however, it didn't change the fact that Tiara would resolve a few issues, while waiting for Slim, and would eventually leave. The last thing she needed was to start a relationship—not that Jayce had offered one. Jayce had just cleared the air.

Did she even want to explore an emotional association with Jayce? Of course she did. Why else was she laying here, the strain building from wanting to touch Jayce, even if the contact fleeting. Tiara realized if she touched Jayce, it would lead to sex. Was sex enough? Would that be fair to Jayce?

"HEY, YOU OKAY?" Jayce asked. So close to Tiara, though both pretended not to be bothered by their proximity, was torturous. She had to know how far Tiara would let her go.

"Yeah, I'm fine," Tiara answered.

Hearing what she perceived as tension in Tiara's voice, Jayce could tell Tiara was far from fine. "You sure?" Jayce shifted onto her side, facing her. "You seem ready to explode."

Tiara tensed at the subtle shift in distance as Jayce eased a little closer, her body absorbed Tiara's warmth, and it took every ounce of effort not to reach out, draw flush against Jayce's body. "Is it the storm? I can take your mind off of that for you."

"Jayce, don't joke."

"Who says I'm joking?"

Tiara groaned, "I admit I'm attracted to you. Nevertheless, we're like cats and dogs lately. I can't make a commitment, shouldn't—"

"I'm asking for tonight, not expecting forever." Jayce leaned toward Tiara and she came eagerly into Jayce's arms. Through the material of her blanket, Jayce could feel her body's warmth as Tiara embraced her. Jayce ran her hands over Tiara's shoulders.

"Strong," Jayce commented, as if surprised.

"Construction workers are like that," Tiara said her lips against Jayce's throat. She laughed, and Jayce felt some of the nervous tension drain out of her.

Jayce used her lips to trace the line of her jaw, then brushed Tiara's hair aside and began to kiss her ear.

Tiara gasped, and Jayce felt her shiver.

Slipping both hands under the blanket, Jayce caressed the warm length of her back, then the smooth skin over her ribs. When Jayce felt the swell of breast against her hands, she paused. Tiara made an inarticulate sound and, fitting her body closer, put both hands in Jayce's hair, gently drawing her closer, kissing her so soundly Jayce thought she'd melt from the heat.

Jayce felt a jolt of electricity travel directly from her lips to somewhere far lower. First, Jayce was aware of the exquisite softness of Tiara's lips, then, as she pressed her mouth firmly to Jayce's, the warm satin wetness of her tongue. It entered between Jayce's lips slowly, gently, as if asking permission. Then, more urgently, meeting with an insistence that left no doubt as to what she wanted. When Tiara withdrew, Jayce clutched her tighter.

Breathing hard, Jayce finally broke off the kiss, leaning back, weakened as her hand caressed, and then rested atop Tiara's hips. If they hadn't already been lying down, Jayce knew she would probably have oozed to the floor like goo.

In the half-light of lightening and the fire, Tiara's kisses were more fierce, more urgent. So much passion surprised Jayce, but then Jayce believed she understood. Tiara was holding back the fear, of the storm and of the emotions required for intimacy. A fine decision, Jayce thought, making love was one of the sweetest distractions she knew.

Jayce ran her hands over the incredible softness of Tiara's skin, and Tiara shuddered, taking Jayce's hands and putting them on her breasts. Tiara's nipples hardened under Jayce's palms, and she bent to brush them with her lips. Jayce took each hard bud in turn in her teeth, and Tiara moaned. She put her hands in Jayce's hair, not gently this time, and raised Jayce's head from her breasts. Looking at Jayce for a moment, Tiara kissed her with a demanding tongue. Jayce slipped her hands around Tiara, clasping her firm buttocks and held her tighter, as she pushed a knee between Tiara's legs, Tiara began to move against Jayce in a rhythm of her own.

"Please, Jayce," she breathed, taking her mouth away, gasping for breath.

Jayce brushed her hand from Tiara's behind to her inner thigh and found her hot, wet center. Tiara gasped, her arms tightening around Jayce as she stroked Tiara's lovely velvet wetness until she began to tremble.

"Now, Jayce," she gasped, "now."

Jayce slipped two fingers inside her, Tiara immediately closed around her fingers in a series of fluttering spasms. Tiara clung to Jayce and gasped her name, some of the sharp, sweet pleasure that claimed Tiara, claimed Jayce, too, and pierced her heart to her soul by the wonder of holding in her hand the throbbing center of Tiara.

As the spasms subsided, Jayce put both her arms around Tiara and held her, stroking her hair and kissing her. Jayce pulled the blanket over them, running her hands along the warm, lovely length of her back, and Tiara sighed.

"Thank you for that," Tiara said.

"You don't need to thank me," Jayce told her, smiling.

Tiara tapped Jayce's nose with one finger. "Hmmm," she said thoughtfully, shifting to kiss Jayce, more gently this time.

Through barely parted lips their tongues met turning Jayce's blood to molten lava. Tiara's tongue invited Jayce to speak her need without words. For Jayce's part, she was fast becoming unable to tolerate much more of this. Her desire now as urgent as Tiara's had been, and Jayce at the point where it was impossible to delay much longer. As Tiara ran her hands over Jayce's breasts, taking her nipples between her finger and thumb, a nova flared in the pit of Jayce's stomach. Jayce groaned, and Tiara needed no further invitation.

Kissing Jayce once more, quickly, Tiara slipped a hand between Jayce's thighs, and found the place where she needed to be touched. Tiara's clever fingers opened her like a flower, entering once, and then withdrawing. Beginning a gently, rhythmic stroking, Tiara managed to fan an already red ache of desire to a white-hot flame of urgency. Jayce gasped, feeling like an eager climber approaching the peak of some mountain: almost there, almost there. Then, just when Jayce thought she might faint from desire, a hot wave of liquid came boiling down along nerve endings and swept her away to a place where there was neither sound nor light; no sensation save the ecstasy that had seized Jayce.

Afterward, in the ebb tide of pleasure, when neither could breathe or speak, Jayce realized Tiara was looking down at her. She brushed Jayce's lips with hers, smiled beautifully and smoothed back Jayce's sweaty hair.

"Sweet," she said. Then, settling down beside her, Tiara put her head on Jayce's shoulder.

Jayce put one arm around her, and was about to say something — nothing important — but when she looked down, Tiara was already asleep.

Chapter Sixteen

TIARA WAS NESTLED in the crook of Jayce's arm as she stared at the approaching dawn outside the window, Tiara's hand gently rubbing across her chest and abdomen. Jayce heaved a contented sigh. If she could stay like this forever, it wouldn't be long enough. When Tiara shifted, removing her hand, Jayce wanted to draw her back.

"Hey, do you think Edna and Darla believe we've killed one another?" Tiara asked softly. Then she sat up and giggled. "Maybe, right this minute, they're organizing a search party, ready to bust through that door."

"We probably should be getting back," Jayce said, raising herself on the arm she'd used to pillow her head seconds ago. With her free hand, Jayce reached forward and ran her finger down Tiara's bared spine. Jayce shivered with excitement from the contact. Tiara was so soft, so girlie, even with the firm muscles she'd acquired from manual labor.

"Stop, that tickles," Tiara said playfully, before her features set in a serious expression. "Thank you." Tiara lay down, her own arm bent to pillow her head as she faced Jayce.

"For what?" Jayce asked, running the same finger from Tiara's abdomen to her breasts, circling the contours and flicking her nipples teasingly. "After what you've shared with me, I should be thanking you." Jayce placed a kiss on each breast, reveling in Tiara's soft moans. "Do you need rescuing?" Jayce leaned forward and placed her lips on Tiara's, kissing her until she responded with warmth of her own. Jayce pulled away slowly, desire to make love to her once again building to fevered heights. Tiara's response, filled with matched desire, also seemed a ploy to distract Jayce. "Do you?"

Shaking her head, Tiara said, "Not really, but we need to talk Jayce."

"That sounds ominous." Jayce could feel the muscles in her stomach clench in panicked anticipation.

"Look, I really enjoyed last night," Tiara started, clutching the blanket to cover her exposed flesh, as if suddenly conscious of her nakedness. "It's just that..."

Was Tiara regretting their shared night already? Did she fear Jayce would take what they shared to mean it was more than sex? She had, of course. Not that she didn't want so much more, Jayce understood she should take what she could get from Tiara—even if for only a little while. People did this kind of fling-thing every day and she could too. So why was her brain having difficulty grasping a love 'em and leave 'em mentality? She could do this, Jayce reasoned, could pretend intimacy with Tiara wasn't life altering for her. "Afraid I won't understand I'm just a booty buddy?"

Jayce hadn't expected stating the obvious to upset Tiara, too late to take the words back now that the damage was done. Tiara crawled over her, jumped off the bed, and started pulling her clothes of the line and dressing. Jayce reached for her, but Tiara jerked out of her grasp.

"Thanks, Jayce."

"Red, I'm sorry," she apologized, knowing Tiara wasn't accepting it. In fact, Tiara had grabbed her boots and shoved them under her arm as she stormed away, buttoning her shirt. Jayce jumped to her feet, uncaring she hadn't even considered dressing, only wanting to stop Tiara from leaving the line shack. "Damn it, wait a minute." Jayce grasped Tiara by the elbow, just as she opened the door. "I can't keep up. Your mood swings are like dealing with Poe's pendulum, honey."

"Then why try," Tiara grumbled.

"Because I care about you," she explained, "I thought that was obvious. I realize you don't return my feelings. However, you set the ground rules and I'm good with working with that, if it's all I can get."

"Right, booty buddies." Tiara jerked her elbow free of Jayce's grasp, and sneered while raking her gaze up and down Jayce's naked body. She sighed heavily and walked back inside to the cabin's empty chair, and finished getting dressed. "Get your clothes on, please."

Jayce closed the door, and did as told. Wow, Tiara shouldn't have been so sensitive, when she was the one who classified their non-relationship. "Didn't mean to hurt your feelings, and I was teasing, Tiara." She picked up her own boots and hopped up on the bunk to put them on. "I'm trying to be all modern and new millennium here." This wasn't all about Tiara's feelings anymore, and Jayce would make certain of the revelation. "In case you never figured it out, or even cared to, I'm the white picket fence and happily ever after kind of gal." Jayce felt her temper rise. She restrained it as best she could, yet heard it tingeing the words. "I'll take all the blame, Tiara," she said walking to the door and jerking it open, before twisting to glare at Tiara. "More than that, I concede the war to you. I'm tired of fighting. You win." Jayce turned away. "I'll get the buckboard ready to take you to Slim's place." Tears burned behind her eyes and Jayce slammed the door as she left the cabin.

As she approached Annabelle and Buster, Jayce muttered, "Gotta get someone here to make bunk beds."

DARLA FELT COMPLETELY drained by the time she reached the Mansfield porch. The walk had seemed a great idea when she'd started out, going early enough to beat the heat of the day. Now, she just wanted to make it up the final step and to the screen door. She hadn't planned on how treacherous the rain from the night before had made the landscape. "Oh, sweet lord," came a female voice behind her. When she turned, Darla came face to face with Ms. Juarez, her yet not exactly her. Obviously, the stunt woman Craig mentioned. The woman swung an arm around Darla's massive waist, and tucked a shoulder under her arm. "Let me help you into the house."

"Thank you," Darla said, allowing the assistance without complaint. "Guess I overextended my ability to take a bit of a walk."

As the screen door closed with a comforting thwack, a voice called out from further in the house, "Jayce, is that you?"

Darla, assaulted by a strong floral scent that made her light-headed and already breathing heavier than normal, weaved unsteadily on her feet. The other woman tightened her grip reassuringly.

"No, Aunt Edna, it's me, Sarah," she said, steering Darla in the direction of the voice. Confidentially, she whispered, "Sorry about the smell. Juanita's gift from some guy, Sparretti, I think."

Nodding, Darla replied, "Ah, the little purple gangster."

"That would be him." Sarah laughed, and it sounded familiar to Darla. "Someone's supposed to pick them up today to take to the hospital and the nursing home at the edge of town. All too many of the residents don't get visits from family, some relatives having moved to the bigger cities, or the folks don't have relatives or anything left. Sad isn't it, not to have someone in your old age. Here we are." Darla realized they were in the kitchen. A short, skinny woman stared at a kettle on the stove. "Edna, you have company."

Sarah pulled out a chair and gently guided Darla onto it. "Thank you, again," Darla said.

"No problem, I'll be right back," Sarah said.

"Tea will be ready in a minute." When Darla looked toward the stove, Edna gave her an encouraging grin. "Ah, here's Sarah returned."

Sarah had a small foot ottoman in her arms. She dropped it in front of Darla's chair and proceeded to raise Darla's legs atop it with an, "Up they go."

"Sarah, you don't—"

"Yes, she does," Edna announced, placing a mug of tea near her hand. "You should have let us come to you, Darla. Or you could have let Sarah get you in that fancy Mustang of hers."

"Now that would have been quite the treat, I must admit," Darla said. She placed her hands on her swollen belly. "Couldn't say I'd be able to get in and out of the thing, though, not when I'm big as a barn."

"Oh, pooh," Edna said, with a dismissive waive of her hand. "Pregnant is beautiful, and you're every inch that and more." With a hot tea of her own, Edna sat at the table as Sarah went to the refrigerator to get iced water, before sitting across from Edna. "Now, down to particulars," Edna said. "Craig tells us you want to have us all for dinner. We would be happy to accept."

Darla supplied a time.

"Also, we would like to throw a barbeque, country style, to show some hospitality to new friends. So, I suggest we work together."

"Hopefully," Sarah said, taking a drink of water, "we can keep Jayce and Tiara from killing each other, while we help them see they are made for each other."

Darla frowned. "I don't know all that happened a decade ago, but I know Tiara cares deeply for Jayce. I also know she's doing everything in her power to push Jayce away."

"Jayce is also at fault," Edna stated, "not being sensitive to poor Tiara's feelings. Things haven't been easy for her, you know." From Edna's facial expression and the glistening in her eyes, Darla could tell the older woman had strong maternal feelings for Tiara.

Sarah shook her head. "Edna, we all care for Tiara, but she's the one being too sensitive. She wasn't the only one hurt by Angie's choices. We all have been, in one way or another." After a drink of her tea, Sarah said, "So I've sort of come up with a plan that could work, or could blow up in my face."

"I'm certain we all wish to avoid that particular end," Darla said quietly. "Maybe if we talk out the details, we can devise a plan with the fewest challenges and repercussions. Our goal is to help, not hurt, either of them."

"That has my vote." Edna leaned forward conspiratorially, prompting Darla to mimic her actions, as they listened to Sarah's plan, interjected with ideas to fine-tune certain aspects. After a couple cups of tea, they believed they had covered every possible scenario, delighted with themselves and their scheme to bring Jayce and Tiara together. "So, we can present them with this tonight at dinner," Edna said.

"Although, it could be a moot point." Darla leaned back in her chair and rubbed her swollen belly. "They did, after all, spend the night together somewhere."

"Despite the warnings," Sarah teased, "to have Tiara home at a decent hour."

"Be nice," Edna said. "I'm certain Jayce would have done as much if the storm hadn't come in."

"You do think they're okay, right?" Darla asked. "You don't think they're out there hurt, do you?"

Just then, the front screen door slammed, followed by boots stomping up the stairs, and Jayce yelling, "She'll be the death of me."

Darla noted Edna and Sarah shaking their heads. With more humor than she felt, Darla said, "At least that confirms they're both alive."

Chapter Seventeen

AFTER JAYCE DROPPED her off, Tiara had hoped to see a friendly face at home. As it was she had to go outside to find Mark and Craig, hard at work and sweating. "Where's Darla?" she asked Mark.

Mark indicated the *Meadows* with a tilt of his head. "Visiting the neighbors. Wish she'd let me drive her over, though."

"She walked?" Tiara asked. Mark nodded.

"You okay, Boss?" Craig asked. "I can go get her if you need her."

"No, I'm fine. I'll catch up with her later."

Craig guffawed. "Can't wait to gossip about your date?"

"Like I'd tell you." Tiara didn't want to gossip as much as get in her point of view before the increased tension with her and Jayce became apparent. "I'm gonna change and get back to work myself."

She went inside, changed into work clothes. It wasn't long before she had made her way back to the old barn.

Work kept Tiara busy and happy. Her achievements were productive and visual. One could always step back and say, "I built that, or I created that." However, today her work was unfocused, her brain continually drifted to the morning and the frustration she'd unleashed on Jayce.

In all fairness, Tiara knew Jayce had given her exactly what she had asked for, and with the expected Mansfield witticism. Tiara couldn't find the same comfort in Jayce's humor as she usually found. Worse, she felt stricken when Jayce seemed to accept a one-night-stand calmly and willingly. So now that she received exactly what'd she asked for, Tiara wondered why she felt so utterly empty.

Tiara saw an old metal pail, turned it over and sat down with elbows on knees and head resting in her hands.

The intimacy she'd shared with Jayce last night was exactly what Tiara wanted and had waited for since the kiss in the barn over ten years ago. Not only that, the experience had turned out far better than the fantasies she'd imagined all these years.

So why had she blown up in anger at Jayce? Because now she knew what could be hers if she'd give in to her heart and Jayce, the voice in her head exclaimed. "Oh, shut up."

"Excuse me?"

Startled, Tiara jumped and spun toward the voice. "Darla." She looked tired, but still had a smile on her face. "Are you okay?" Tiara glanced around for something Darla could sit on, obviously she was in no condition to take the pail. Standing on end inside one of the open stalls was a bench that had seen better days. Crossing her fingers that it still retained some stability, Tiara grabbed it and after a quick examination to determine its soundness, she brought it to where Darla stood. "Here, sit down before you fall down."

"Thank you," Darla said, sighing as she lowered herself to the bench. "Guess I'm gonna have to start taking things easier. I've pushed myself a bit too much today, and I still have a dinner to make."

Tiara shook her head, pulled the bucket closer and sat in front of Darla. "No, don't you worry about that. The guys and I can make sandwiches. I do know how to make tuna salad, and we've plenty of canned tuna, as you know."

This time it was Darla's turn to shake her head. "Not tonight, sweetie. I've invited guests for dinner. The folks next door are coming over."

"We'll just cancel it then. They'll understand." Tiara suspected that Edna might blame Jayce, but she didn't care—not really, anyway. Right now, she didn't want any harm to come to Darla and the baby.

"You'd just love that, wouldn't you?" Darla asked, a mischievous grin on her face.

Tiara had the courtesy to blush.

"I'll take an extra long nap and be just fine." Darla placed her hands on her knees, blew out a long breath, and asked, "What in heaven's name happened last night?"

"Wh—wha—what do you mean?"

"You disobeyed curfew, and Jayce seemed a tad upset when she came home."

Tiara quietly asked, "Did she say anything too bad about me?" She wasn't certain she wanted an answer.

"Does she have reason to?" Dara glared at her as she asked.

"Depends on the point of view, I guess. I'm more at fault for this latest, um...misunderstanding," Tiara said.

Reaching forward, Darla tapped Tiara's knee. "Don't worry, Tiara. I'm not leaving here until this is squared away."

Feeling lightheaded from the panic, Tiara squeaked, "What?"

Holding her extended baby-belly, Darla laughed until tears gathered in the corner of her eyes. "Not leave Silver Waters, I meant. I'm going in for a little rest right now." Tiara felt some of the panic leave her rigid posture. Darla strained to stand, a chuckle escaping as she got to her feet. "Don't think this is over, young lady, not until I get all the details. I'm not exaggerating, either. I want every last juicy morsel of what happened last night between you and tall, dark and sexy."

"Be careful what you ask for," Tiara mumbled as Darla made her way to the open barn door entrance.

Turning as quickly as a seriously pregnant woman could, Darla grinned and said, "Oh, this is going to be worth waiting for." She placed her hand tenderly on her belly. "Hope this isn't so stimulating that Baby Chester decides to come out early."

At Tiara's shocked expression, Darla left her alone.

MUCH AS TIARA wanted to pass on the evening's events, she knew in good conscience she couldn't hurt Darla that way. Darla had spent a lot of time (after a good two-hour nap) in the kitchen, on her poor swollen feet, to make this a night to remember; and Tiara didn't doubt that would be the outcome. She hoped it wasn't negatively influenced by some transgression between her and Jayce.

Scrubbing the washcloth over her face, Tiara groaned. What had she done to deserve all this? She'd been happy on her own. Now, she was replacing acquaintances with friends, nights alone in front of the television for chats over coffee with Darla, and even going on a date. As torturous as this all was, Tiara knew she wouldn't have traded a moment of it all—even the threats by a weird little man, and dealing with a horse—for anything. She wouldn't give any of it back. A few days ago, Tiara would have considered these changes punishment for a wrong; however, staring at her reflection in the mirror, she was reminded what a blessing it was to have people around who cared about you. The tension between her and Jayce notwithstanding, Tiara realized she had changed. She didn't talk to empty rooms, but had conversations with people. She didn't eat solely because her body needed nourishment, but actually looked forward to meals. She didn't turn off the alarm because she had a job to do, but because she couldn't wait to see what the new day would bring. Even her clashes with Jayce emphasized being alive and not simply existing.

Tiara would better appreciate these changes if Slim had shown up to witness even a little of her transformation. Was that his purpose in arranging this trip? Tiara heard a loud knock from downstairs (country folk didn't need doorbells), then animated voices. With a pointed look in the mirror, she told her reflection, "Be on your best behavior. It's show time." Turning off the bathroom light, Tiara made her way downstairs.

When Tiara reached the bottom step and looked into her living room, she gasped and her stomach fluttered at the sight. It was an image she never expected to be a part of in her home. Edna, Darla and Sarah sat on the couch, Mark in the chair with his hand bridging the space to rest on his wife's, and Craig casually sitting on the couch arm next to Sarah. All were in a friendly conversation as if they had done this a million times.

Then it hit her. Jayce was absent. Where was she? As if the very thought produced her, Tiara felt a brush of air as Jayce whispered from behind her, "Warms the heart, doesn't it?" Tiara desperately needed to put some distance between them as her body immediately responded to Jayce's presence. Her skin prickled with electricity, her heart beat faster, and most embarrassingly, Tiara's nipples pebbled at the warmth from

Jayce's breath in her ear. Tiara fervently hoped her body's reactions weren't evident to the others, especially to Jayce. She didn't know if Jayce's comment held sarcasm, so she spun around to look at Jayce. Tiara believed she caught a flash of desire in the blue depths before Jayce had the chance to squash it. Now all she saw was sincerity as Jayce softly said, "You can be proud of the friends you've made, Tiara. They're good people."

Tiara looked over her shoulder into the living room. Jayce was right. She had friends to be proud of in her life, though she hadn't recognized them as such before coming back to Falling Down Acres. "Yes, they're great," she acknowledged, turning her attention back to Jayce. "Jayce, I—"

"You two get in here," Edna commanded. Jayce complied first, Tiara following. "No offense, but you two alone tends to induce verbal explosions. I plan on having a great evening."

Jayce hung her head, more subdued than Tiara had ever seen her. "Aunt Edna, it isn't like we intend it to happen that way."

Sarah snickered. "Yeah, come on Edna, we all know Jayce is a lover, not a fighter—unless it's over a girl. Maybe this is some bizarre mating ritual with these two." Tiara felt her cheeks flame, and noted the immediate flush to Jayce's face. Sarah winked at them. "I'm thinking maybe we should feed them." She leaned forward and directed her attention to Darla. "If we keep their mouths full, they can't argue, can they?"

Darla laughed. "You may have something there."

"What can I do to help?" Edna asked.

"It's all ready. I thought we'd have dinner buffet style, if you don't mind."

Edna patted Darla's leg affectionately. "Don't mind at all." She stood, moved to stand in front of Tiara, gently tapping her on the cheek. "We tease in good fun, because we care about you."

Tiara nodded. She understood, not that it changed her discomfort.

After filing into the kitchen, piling plates with the vast array of food and taking places at the table that had all the leafs extending it, Tiara realized she and Jayce had been maneuvered once again. Shuffled to the back of the line, the others had taken seats that left two directly facing each other across the table.

"Like we don't know this was orchestrated," Jayce said.

Tiara glanced at her. She didn't know what was wrong. Jayce wasn't herself tonight. There were no smiles, no teasing. Did she regret having to spend time with her, because of how their time at the line shack had ended?

Tiara realized Jayce had moved away and she stood alone at the counter. She made her way to the last available chair. Before her return home, this would have been awkward because Tiara hated social gatherings. Now she felt uncomfortable because something was wrong with Jayce, and most likely had been her doing. If the lack of conversation from her and Jayce disturbed anyone, Tiara couldn't tell. She, herself, paid a fraction of attention.

Edna seemed to carry most of the entertainment by relaying stories of Jayce, Sarah and Tiara during their youth, even a couple stories of Slim that Tiara had never heard. The food was wonderful, as usual, and everyone had seconds, the two men managing to consume any remainders. The stories of Sarah seemed to have piqued Craig's interest.

"So you're not just a friend because of Miss Juarez?" Craig looked surprised as he watched Sarah.

"Nope, I'm a product of Silver Waters," Sarah said, a touch of melancholy in her tone.

"That's great," Craig said excitedly. Tiara cringed inside knowing he hadn't heard the emotional timbre in her words. "Now I know someone who can show me the town. When can you give me the tour?" He flashed Sarah his pearly whites.

Sarah rolled her eyes. "I'll try to fit you into my schedule."

"I look forward to it," Craig said. Then, as if an epiphany hit, he asked, "So, if you were raised here, how come you stay with them instead of your own house?"

The pain that flashed on Sarah's face was so raw that no one spoke for a moment. Since Craig was here because of her, Tiara intervened. "Because nobody passes up Aunt Edna's cooking."

Edna smiled at her, adding, "Darla wasn't a known commodity, either. I may have had some formidable competition."

Jayce placed a hand on Sarah's shoulder, which seemed to catch Craig's attention. "Crap. I put my foot in it, didn't I?"

"Looks like it," Mark said and glared at Craig.

"No, it's all right," Sarah said. She took a deep breath, and then turned directly to Craig. "Both my parents have passed away. I haven't been back to the house since."

"I'm sorry, Sarah," Craig said. "I never meant to upset you, bringing up painful memories."

"Sooner or later, I'll to have to go back and face the house."

"Well, if you need company, I'd like to help." Tiara didn't doubt the sincerity of his words, since it matched the expression on his face.

"I may just hold you to that, Craig." Sarah winked at him.

"Great," Edna said, clapping her hands together. "Now on to new business."

Jayce smirked and sank in her chair. "I thought this was a friendly get together?"

"It is," Edna said. She glanced to Tiara. "How are the renovations coming along?"

At any other time, Tiara would've taken the question at face value, but her intuition blared a warning. "Uh, fine. Do you have some concerns, Aunt Edna? Are we too noisy?"

Edna snorted. "No, dear, I quite enjoy the activity. I'm curious because I'd like to suggest a game, of sorts, that Sarah has proposed."

All eyes turned to Sarah, who responded with a barely noticeable shrug. "Don't blame her alone. She had an idea, and Darla and I agree with it."

Mark cleared his throat noisily and directed his attention to Edna. "Um, excuse me, ma'am. Even though my wife seems to have aligned herself in some scheme, Tiara is boss to Craig and me. I think it best he and I leave you ladies to whatever you are about to spill."

Craig pushed back his chair with an eerie squeak across the linoleum. "Yeah, I don't want any part of women stuff." He and Mark had made it to the entryway of the hall before Craig spun around and said, "But don't forget us when dessert is ready."

With the men gone, Tiara looked around her, finally recognizing the seating order. Sarah was across the table beside Jayce, while Tiara sat between Edna and Darla. A headache began to build. "What's going on?" Tiara asked, dismayed by the tremor in her voice.

"Nothing to be fearful of, dear," Edna said.

Sarah nodded. "We think you and Jayce need to better understand each other and what each does."

Barely above a whisper, Jayce said, "Oh, we understand each other quite well, thanks."

"That's emotion talking, Jayce," Sarah stated softly. "Remember I told you something about the grass being greener?"

With a smirk in her direction, Jayce reminded, "No, Ms. Juarez brought it up, Sarah."

"We're trying to help. Anyway, we think the guys don't know Sarah and Juanita are the same." Darla and Tiara nodded. "Try to take this seriously, Jayce," Edna admonished.

Jayce scowled at her aunt. "And I'm letting you know that Red and I have already handled this. She stays out of my way and I'll stay out of hers. I'm only here because you wouldn't let me stay home."

Tiara felt horrible at that moment. The other three couldn't have missed the hurt in Jayce's voice, because it was too raw. "Jayce—"

"What?"

Sighing heavily with hurt, Tiara said, "Let them speak. We don't have to agree to do anything."

"Fine." Jayce sat up in her chair and placed her elbows on the table. "What game is supposed to make us buddies?"

"We thought the best way would be to understand what the other does for a living. In other words, switch jobs. Tiara learns to work with horses, and Jayce learns carpentry work."

She raised an eyebrow. Tiara had wounded Jayce more than she would have believed possible. What she didn't understand was why? Jayce could have any woman she beamed that Mansfield smile upon. Had Jayce truly envisioned Tiara in her domestic fantasies? Didn't she grasp that Tiara could never stay in Silver Waters? Once again Tiara had managed to disappoint a person she truly cared about. She knew she had been harsh at the line shack, but the way it ended had hurt Tiara, too.

She got so angry when Jayce called her booty buddy, even though it was how she was about to end things herself. Tiara didn't know how she could rebuild the harm she had done. Jayce should never be negative; she was the ever-happy one.

Now was the time to take a leap and fix this mess, so Tiara accepted the challenge. Focusing her gaze on Jayce, Tiara said, "I'll only agree if Jayce adds a cooking lesson."

Chapter Eighteen

JAYCE HADN'T EXPECTED Tiara to take them up on the challenge, or to add an assignment to their imposed time together. Hadn't she already explained they'd come to an understanding? Why couldn't Tiara leave well enough alone? What had she missed?

"Wonderful," Edna exclaimed. "I have a request."

Groaning, Jayce asked, "Another one?"

With remarkable agility, Edna reached across the table and slapped Jayce on the side of the head.

"Hey, we're not at home, you know," Jayce said.

"You should be thankful a fork wasn't handy."

"Fine. What's your request?" Jayce asked, and then blew a raspberry at her.

Edna snorted as she returned to her seat. "I'd love to have a fancy table for the hall entrance." She glanced at Tiara. "You know, for keys and purses when you walk in."

"Whatever. What else?" Jayce asked, rolling her eyes. She noticed Darla stared at her with a strange expression. Shifting slightly in her chair, Jayce managed to blot her from her vision.

Sarah added, "Teach Tiara a little about horses, make her more comfortable around Majestic."

Tiara rasped. "Is that possible? Maybe we could use a really old and tame horse."

Edna patted Tiara's leg. "Majestic is a good horse, Tiara, we wouldn't steer you wrong." With a wink, Edna added, "Only Jayce is the chauvinistic beast."

Tiara blushed.

Jayce sighed and asked, "And finally?"

Darla bit her bottom lip, before she said, "Teach Tiara to cook a — meal. It can be a small one, for Edna and Sarah."

Jayce studied Darla and Tiara. "Why not for everyone?"

Tiara snickered. "They don't want me sending Darla to the hospital, because I've poisoned Baby Chester." Jayce had to strain to hear Tiara add, "Told you I can't cook. I wasn't being modest, just saving the lives of people who would have to eat my culinary disasters."

"No one is that bad, Tiara," Jayce said.

Simultaneously, Darla replied, "Yes, she is," as Tiara said, "Yes, I am."

That had them laughing, but Jayce couldn't manage more than a wry smile. "Great, it's all settled. Can I go now?" Pushing her chair from the table, Jayce stood.

"Jayce," Edna warned.

Sarah also stood. "Jayce can go home, make sure the animals are okay. We can clean up while Darla watches us. Gotta make sure we do it accurately, right Darla?"

"Thank you," Jayce snarled. She started toward the door, but her guilt at taking out her anger on everyone kept her from leaving without showing her gratitude. "Um, Darla, the meal—and most of the evening—was wonderful. Thank you. Also, please accept my apologies for my bad attitude. You shouldn't have had to be part of that."

"You're welcome," Darla said, as she slowly stood at eye level with her. Before Jayce could respond, Darla yanked her into a hug and whispered, "Trust us. This has a chance to work, Jayce."

Unable to speak due to the emotion choking her, Jayce nodded. "Good night, Darla. Rest well." Unable to face in Tiara's direction, she rushed through the screen door and onto the back porch.

She didn't get far. "Please, Jayce, wait." Tiara stayed on the porch. She held on to the column, as if it were the only thing keeping her from falling, the porch light brightly illuminating her.

Despite her misgivings, Jayce turned around and placed a booted foot on the bottom step, and crossed her arms over her chest. "What now?" She almost apologized for her tone when a grimace flashed across Tiara's face, but managed to bite it back. "Well?"

"It's just that..." Tiara plopped down on the top step, and buried her face in her hands. Jayce moved to her side to offer comfort, but then Tiara's hands dropped. "Can we start over?"

"Pretend last night never happened?" Jayce asked, her voice incredulous. Yeah, like that's gonna work.

Tiara's face flushed quickly, as she shook her head. "Pretending won't change that it did happen." She glanced away. "I don't want to, nor will I, forget making love to you, Jayce. I want to forget the argument this morning."

Jayce hoped this to be a mutual apology and sat next to Tiara. "That's a relief." She motioned wiping her forehead with her arm. "Thought I'd lost my charm. What would I do if I couldn't suitably woo the ladies?"

"Nah," Tiara denied, knocking her shoulder into Jayce's, "you've definitely still got it, handsome." Jayce turned to her in surprise. Tiara gave a nervous laugh. "Could we add that to the list of stuff we're pretending didn't happen?"

No way would Jayce forget the compliment. Her stomach fluttered with the knowledge that she appealed to Tiara. Some of the frustrated anger from dinner left her. "Where do you wish to start over from?" She extended her hand to Tiara. "Hello, my name is Jayce Mansfield."

Tiara startled her for the second time, when she clasped Jayce's extended hand and held it tightly in both her own. "From this moment on, Jayce, I've returned and left the baggage in the trunk. We can't forget the hurt we've heaped on each other, but maybe we can forgive. Let's agree we acknowledge what happened, file it away, and we move forward, okay? When I return home, I'd like us to be friends who communicate."

A twinge of pain fluttered in Jayce's heart. It hurt her to know Tiara would leave, yet she was excited by the prospect that Tiara wanted to move forward in their friendship. "Okay, I can give you that."

"Good, because if you can teach me to cook half as good as you do, I'll be awesome."

A mischievous grin crossed Jayce's face, as she shook her head slowly. "I'm marvelous, not a miracle worker." Tiara lightly slapped her on the back of the head with one hand, yet hadn't released Jayce's hand from the other, pleasing Jayce no end. "Hey, I can't perform for the folks inside if I've a concussion. What was that for?"

Tiara chuckled. "That comment would have hurt if it wasn't so true. And, somehow I doubt anyone has complained about your performance."

Tiara bit her bottom lip and Jayce decided it best to ignore any comeback she wanted to make. "You don't think I'm a miracle worker?" Jayce placed her hand over her heart. "You've wounded me to the quick."

"You know I don't cook, barely know my way around the kitchen." Tiara appeared pained to have to make the statement. "You would have to be a miracle worker if I can manage something edible without burning down the kitchen."

"No problem," Jayce said with a nod. Then, she looked directly into Tiara's beautiful grey eyes, while waggling her eyebrows, and asked, "And your thoughts to my being marvelous?"

"YOU CAN'T DELAY the inevitable much longer, Slim." Edna moved behind where he stood and gave his arm a gentle squeeze, and then wrapped her arms around his waist, laying her head against his back. "You have to tell her the truth. Let Tiara know how you feel, have always felt. Girls need to know their daddies love them. That's especially true in Tiara's case."

Slim rubbed his long fingers across his jaw line. "Edna, honey, you make it all sound so easy. It ain't simple anymore."

"Pooh. I'm fed up with excuses. When is everyone going to try to correct their actions, or inactions, rather than whine about it being hard? Anything worthwhile has to be fought for, and no one ever says it's easy, so you can't expect easy, either. That's what makes us appreciate the winning most." She dropped her arms and moved away from him. He spun around to grab at her, but she moved out of reach and leveled a glare at him.

"Can't we just postpone my dealing with Tiara until after our honeymoon?"

Edna slammed her fisted hands onto her hips. "If you think I'll marry you now, when you haven't mended fences with your own daughter, then you're crazier than I know you to be." With a snort, Slim moved closer to Edna and put his arms around her waist, facing her. She didn't relent. "I do not jest, Edward Michael Summers."

"Goodness, my full name, honey?" Slim muttered, moving a couple steps back. "You really are sticking to your guns here, aren't you?" He slowly walked to the armchair and plopped down. "When do you suggest I have this itty-bitty conversation with my little girl, darlin'?"

Snorting, Edna said, "It should've taken place already. You Summers are a stubborn bunch." Edna sat on the couch, closed her eyes, and sighed. Then she stared at him again. "We have a barbeque planned in a couple days. Maybe it would be best if you talked then, with a bunch of folks around."

Slim paled and he ran a trembling hand through his thinning strawberry-blond hair. "You want me talk to Tiara with a heap of people around?"

Shaking her head, Edna said, "No, privately, but this way she'll have a lot of folks around, limiting where she can run if she gets upset."

"You think I'd hurt her?" he asked.

Edna patted his hand gently. "Not intentionally." Tears began to cloud her vision thinking about how often she or Jayce had witnessed the pain Tiara carried around with her, though she usually hid it. "When Tiara gets to feeling cornered, she tends to gallop fast and far toward safety, the perfect example of the flight part of fight or flight."

"All right, honey, I'll find a way to take her aside at the barbeque and have a daddy and daughter chat. Anything else?"

She recalled the phone call she'd made to him the day the limousine appeared at his place. He'd reluctantly admitted he expected that, and he'd talk to the man. They hadn't heard from Elmo since. "Thank you, by the way, for telling him that Juanita Juarez went back to Hollywood. I couldn't handle whatever he may have had planned after the damned flower debacle." At his nod, she said, "Tell me about Elmo Sparretti."

Slim guffawed and slapped his knee. "What a hoot of an idea, right?"

Edna gritted her teeth. "Talk."

Leaning back in his chair, Slim extended his booted feet, crossed them at the ankle, and smiled. "I bought Majestic from a man willing to work the poor horse to death. Figured it was time to let the dang critter get some rest. Only living creature to care for Majestic is an annoying goose."

"Yes, we've met." Edna tapped her fingers impatiently on her thigh. "About Elmo?"

"Heh-heh. That was a flash of genius, if I say so myself."

"Which you are," she growled, "at a morbidly slow pace, I might add."

"Okay, honey, keep your pantyhose on. Sheesh." Slim sat up in his chair and appeared to get serious. "Well, I knew I had to get my little girl back home where she belongs."

"But she owns a business. Her life is elsewhere, now."

Slim's expression darkened. "She could move down here, couldn't she, if she truly wanted? Once she realizes how much —"

Edna got up from the couch and sat in Slim's lap. She pulled his head to her breast, squeezed gently, and then pushed it back. "We're working on it, sweetie. Now, please, tell me about Elmo's part in all of this."

Pulling her into an embrace, Slim chuckled. "All right. He's an actor who does odd engagements. Elmo was just supposed to show up, startle Tiara so Jayce would get kinda protective, and they'd both realize they're made for each other. He's not really coming back for the horse."

She remembered something Jayce told her about the incident. "And that huge guy, he went with Elmo?

"Aw, darlin' he's no one to worry about. He's Elmo's baby brother. Peter won't do anything Elmo doesn't tell him to do."

Tapping the top of his head, Edna said, "There were quite a few aspects of the plan you didn't account for. You didn't expect Tiara to bring folks to fix up your place. The changes are long overdue, by the way. You didn't expect that Sarah would be here with a new horse. And, you didn't expect Tiara to be so insecure she'd fight Jayce the entire time."

"No. No I didn't plan on any of that," Slim said, frowning. "Don't worry, honey. Between the two of us, we'll revamp the plan and get our Tiara and Jayce a happily-ever-after." Giving a sly grin, Slim pulled her in for a kiss. "Then we can finish arranging ours."

Chapter Nineteen

TIARA WASN'T IN a rush to reach the corral where Jayce would teach her to train Majestic. Up ahead, the corral fence came into view, Tiara could see Jayce inside the barrier with Majestic. Two people sat close together on the top fence rail with their backs to her.

She recognized Craig as one, and had to assume the second to be Sarah. A smile came to her lips immediately. Craig, young and often childlike, was a good person, funny and loyal. Tiara wondered if Craig had figured out that Sarah and Juanita were the same person. After seeing the difference in responses of people when they thought they were speaking to Juanita compared to how they responded when speaking to Sarah, Tiara understood why the woman didn't immediately announce the deception to anyone, let alone Craig.

Tiara, though not experienced with relationships, did recognize that Sarah had strong feelings for Craig. Sarah would need to garner a level of trust between them to make sure he wasn't another Johnny, using her for what it could bring him.

Tiara stopped behind them. "Are you treating Sarah with respect, Craig? If not, Mr. Sparretti will turn the huge bald guy on you just to earn brownie points with Ms. Juarez."

Craig looked at Sarah before he turned toward Tiara. "Not that the big guy isn't incentive enough, but I would never intentionally hurt her."

She didn't want to be party to any games Craig had in mind. Since her talk with Sarah in the barn, Tiara remembered more details about Sarah. Mostly things learned from conversations between Jayce and her family, when the Mansfields spoke freely around her. Tiara waved Craig over. He jumped down from the fence and they walked a short distance away.

"What's up, Boss?" his voice slightly above a whisper.

"Craig, I know you're an adult, and I have no place in your business—"

"Do I hear a 'but' in there?"

Back in school, Sarah had always put herself wholly into any relationship and Tiara doubted that had changed, with friend or lover. "Sarah is a friend, and I wouldn't want to see her hurt."

"You're afraid I'm playing around while we're here, 'cause she looks like Juanita?"

"It's a possibility I can't ignore."

Craig grinned. "I see. Well, Boss, my intentions are honorable—at least where her heart is concerned." He shook his head and leaned in closer to her. "And, if you want honesty, here's some for you. I'd be more afraid of pissing off Jayce and you than I would be Elmo's henchman."

Tiara snorted. "As well it should be. As you were, young man." Craig returned to his place beside Sarah, and Tiara turned her attention to the corral.

Inside the corral, Jayce put Majestic through the paces, racing him in circles, forcing sudden stops, trotting him in zigzag patterns. Tiara felt the familiar leap in her pulse at catching Jayce comfortably herself, uncaring about anyone or anything other than the work she tended. She was more magnificent than mere words could ever capture. Joy was evident in Jayce's unguarded smile and the stately way she held her posture using her body to transmit commands to Majestic. Watching Jayce as she worked, Tiara recognized that the emotions churning within her were more than simple appreciation, or infatuation, for the handsome dark haired woman. Tiara loved her — always had despite her vocal denials to the contrary.

What the hell was she supposed to do with that? She had a good life, even though it wasn't in Silver Waters. She was not sticking around. A couple of weeks, then she'd be gone. Right? She sighed heavily.

A ghastly honk started Tiara.

She couldn't put this session off any longer, especially after that ridiculous goose announced her arrival. Pasting a smile to her lips, her insides churning like a storm about to erupt, Tiara said, "I didn't realize there'd be an audience."

At the sound of her voice, Jayce stopped Majestic and faced her. Tiara hadn't realized she'd spoken so loudly, though she expected Jayce had been anticipating her arrival. Jayce pushed her cowboy hat back and raised a hand in greeting. "Hey."

Hearing what she thought was a nervous tremble in Jayce's voice, Tiara understood they were both anxious about this undertaking of job reversal they'd agreed to. As the first of three, this task would be the most telling. "Hey, you." Tiara climbed up the fence rails and jumped into the ring, after a pointed glare to the goose. Jayce had dismounted and stopped a foot back.

"I can send them away," Jayce said quietly. "They can take Majestic's babysitter."

Tiara was tempted to do just that, but she feared being alone with Jayce more. Only now, she feared what she'd do, not what Jayce might do. Not to mention, there was no telling how Majestic or the goose would react if separated. "No, they're fine."

Jayce seemed to relax a little, her body lost some of its tension. Tiara fought the urge to laugh at the skittish Jayce before her, responding like a teenager on her first date. "So, what do I do first?" Tiara asked, squinting a glare in Majestic's direction from under her ball cap visor and silently begging him to be on his best behavior. Her look at Majestic encouraged another honk from the goose, this one seemed more of a gentle warning than open displeasure. Tiara turned back to Jayce. "I can guarantee there is no way I'll be able to do what you were doing when I arrived."

"Oh, honey, I wouldn't expect that of you, or anyone," Jayce said.

Tiara wondered if Jayce was aware of the spoken endearment, if it meant anything to her. Leave it alone, she chided herself. "So what *are* we going to do, cowgirl?"

Jayce beamed her pearly-whites at Tiara, and Tiara had to stifle the urge to rush into Jayce's arms, bask in the warmth and comfort promised with that smile. The woman was uniquely compelling, Tiara realized. "Just some basic ground manners, first. A horse needs to respect you, as you should the horse. This is a companionship, a partnership between you and Majestic."

"Well, we're done with training already, then," Tiara said with a smirk. "Majestic doesn't like me."

Nodding, Jayce said, "I understand your position, but that's not entirely true. He toys with you because he senses you're afraid of him."

"No kidding, Jayce, he's about two thousand pounds," Tiara said, slamming fists on her hips in a show of stubbornness. From the corner of her eye, Tiara noticed the goose begin to pace. Stay where you are, she silently pleaded.

"Then you'll see him coming before he squishes you," Craig hollered from the fence, before busting into laughter. Sarah promptly elbowed him roughly in the side. "Ouch."

Sarah smirked, raising an eyebrow daring him to respond.

"Okay, I get it. Shut up, Craig," Craig said, eyeing Sarah.

Sarah reached over and squeezed his cheek as if he were a four-year-old. "You're so cute when the light bulb goes on."

Jayce chuckled and shook her head. "I wouldn't let anything happen to you, if I could prevent it." With a serious tone, Jayce asked, "Don't you trust me, Red?"

Despite the teasing tone moments ago, Tiara didn't miss the hurt in Jayce's eyes in expectation of a negative answer. Before she could stop herself, Tiara clasped one of Jayce's hands in hers. "I do trust you, Jayce." She just didn't trust herself. "Let's do this." With a quick squeeze, Tiara released Jayce's hand. "Teach me those ground manners," Tiara said, then cleared her throat loudly, "and preferably with me staying in a standing position."

"You pick up tasks quickly," Jayce said, "so this will be a lot easier than you're expecting." Jayce walked to the fence with the reins in her hand and Majestic casually followed. She took the rope Sarah held out, removed the bridle and attached the rope to his harness. Then Jayce walked Majestic back to where Tiara stood. "First you need to recognize the horse's mood." Tiara started to comment, but Jayce held up a finger to her lips. "Shush. We're going to imagine you both adore each other."

Jayce rubbed Majestic's nose. "How do I know he's relaxed?"

Tiara shrugged.

"His head is low, eyes are hooded, and ears are back. If his head was high, ears forward or twitching, then it would be best if we both left him alone."

"He needs to look post-orgasmic." Craig chuckled, before another, "Ouch."

Tiara and Jayce glared in his direction. The goose loudly added his two cents, with a quick peck at Craig's ankle.

"Okay, look for the lowered head to know he's in a good mood."

Jayce nodded. "You need to be the alpha-horse here. The minute a horse realizes he can be aggressive with you, push you around, you have a major problem."

Tiara frowned. "But he *can* push me around, he's huge." Not that she wanted to bring up her embarrassment from her second day in front of Sarah and Craig, but Tiara reminded her, "Majestic proved his strength by dragging me across my yard, Jayce."

"Horses are playful, Red. Plus, you're being too literal. He has the strength to overpower you, yes. That's why you can't be afraid, why you have to be the alpha." Jayce pulled a pair of leather gloves from her back pocket and handed them to Tiara before glancing down at the lead rope. "Now, you never want to wrap a lead rope around your hand, as that's the fastest way to lose a finger or worse. You don't want the rope to drag the ground, as it could be harmful to both you and the horse. Make sure you don't hold too tight, as Majestic will need free head, which means the ability to move it freely and not feel confined. Both of you need be relaxed and comfortable in each other's company. Go ahead and put the gloves on." As Tiara did as told, Jayce continued. "Should Majestic get spooked, the gloves will help. Bare hands would mean rope burn, and that's not fun. Not to mention you'll need your hands in great shape for your real work."

Tiara smiled playfully at Jayce. "And the second part of my instruction in the kitchen?"

"Yeah, there's that too." Jayce handed the rope over, and moved to stand behind her. Tiara felt the warmth of Jayce's body against her back. As if unaware of the distracting sensations she created, Jayce wrapped her arms around Tiara and tugged at the rope in Tiara's hand. "Okay, loosen the grip just a tad. Great." Jayce adjusted the rope so it had a bit more slack and Majestic had his free head. "How's that feel?"

Closing her eyes and taking a deep breath, Tiara wondered if Jayce could feel the quickening of her pulse from her position against Tiara's body. She managed to whisper, "Feels okay," without too much tremor in her voice. She refrained from leaning back into Jayce and increasing their contact. "What next?"

Jayce shifted her left hand and rested it against Tiara's waist, her other hand moved to Majestic's shoulder. "When you need him to move backward, giving you some space, just nudge him here." Jayce tapped the shoulder area below his neck that she'd pointed out a moment ago, and Majestic took a step back. "See how easy that is?" Not trusting her voice, after a flutter of goose bumps ran across her skin from Jayce's warm breath in her ear, Tiara nodded.

"You try it," Jayce said and stepped away. Her absence was immediately evident to Tiara. Hopelessly lost, Tiara realized she'd never be able to maintain a platonic relationship with the handsome Mansfield woman.

Tiara did as instructed. Docile, Majestic took a step back, and Tiara gave a pleased giggle before doing it twice more. The look of pleasure on Jayce's face made this instruction worthwhile. "What next?"

From a step away, Jayce said, "Practice walking forward and then backward." Tiara did this for about five minutes, and then Jayce had Tiara walk Majestic around the circular corral. No matter how quickly or slowly Tiara's pace, Jayce kept up with them. Tiara felt relieved to have her close, not because she expected Majestic to do anything harmful, but because she took comfort in knowing Jayce was prepared to protect her.

She was so relaxed and enjoying herself that she was surprised when Jayce called a halt. Perspiration had plastered her cap to her head, and her clothes adhered to her body, yet she felt more happy and alive than she had for nearly a decade. An unexpected euphoria came over Tiara and she clasped Jayce in a tight hug of appreciation. "Oh, Jayce, thank you."

Gently returning the hug, Jayce asked, "What for, honey?"

Being held in Jayce's embrace, referred to as honey, and the surge of comfort that coursed through Tiara were too much to handle. Before she knew it was happening, Tiara felt the tears pour down her cheeks. With a nervous sob, Tiara replied, "For just being you, you big lug." She stepped away from Jayce's arms and playfully punched her on the shoulder.

Startled concern spread across Jayce's face. "Are you all right? I'm the chauvinist and the beast, remember?"

Those questions started her sobbing in earnest. Tiara glanced toward the fence, uncomfortable with the thought of an audience witnessing her breakdown. Only the goose remained, and he appeared to be asleep. "They left about twenty minutes ago," Jayce said.

"How long have we been out here?" Tiara asked, lengthening the space between she and Jayce, roughly rubbing the tears from her face.

"Almost two hours." Jayce said. "Red, what'd I do to make you cry? We don't have to do this, you know. Let me take the blame. I'll just—"

"No, Jayce, please don't say you'll stay out of my way." Tiara said pleadingly as she turned to face her again. "That would be worse."

Jayce nodded. After a minute, Jayce grinned. "Actually, I was gonna tell you I'll just quit calling you Red."

That was the moment for Tiara, the epiphany of her life. The instant she realized how in love with Jayce she had truly fallen. What was she to do now?

FROM BEHIND A stand of trees marking the entrance to the forested area of the tall woman's land, Peter Sparretti lowered the binoculars. As they left the corral with Majestic in tow, he wondered what had made the short woman, Slim's daughter, cry. She seemed to have had a good time exercising his brother's horse, but then she just lost it. "Maybe she has problems like me," he whispered. It didn't matter, he reminded himself. Elmo had looked after him his whole life, never abandoning him as their parents had, and Peter was determined to do the same.

Elmo had told them Majestic was his property. Elmo had even given them time to hand the horse over, being more than polite, too. It didn't look like they were going to do as asked.

Peter realized he would have to make sure they didn't cheat his big brother. He'd seen a little place in the woods that he could use. Maybe he could take the goose, too. He never had a pet before. Yeah, but he'd have to do a lot more thinking, try to make sure he didn't do anything too stupid. Usually Elmo did all the thinking. Elmo wasn't simple like Peter. Elmo was smart. Elmo took care of him. It was Peter's turn to take care of Elmo. That's what brothers were for, to take care of each other.

"I'll get Majestic back, so you can be proud of me, Elmo." Despite his size, Peter quietly slipped back into the forest.

Chapter Twenty

A COOL BREEZE blew through the kitchen screen door. Jayce, leaned against the sink counter, a mug of coffee clutched in her hand and enjoyed the feel of the early morning breeze against her skin as she waited for Tiara to arrive. It was nearly three weeks since Tiara had arrived. Their time together had become more relaxed, each encounter proving less stressful than the last. Both had agreed to break the time up with their real work. Darla's dinner night the week before had them agreeing to give their best to the tasks set before them. Their time working with Majestic had gone quite well. In fact, last night it was unanimously agreed upon by Darla, Sarah and Edna that since neither had so much as threatened one another, they could try to go without chaperones this morning. Jayce hoped the cooking lesson would be as amiable.

Gazing at the counter, Jayce did another mental inventory ensuring all the items they'd need, minus the refrigerated stuff, was already out and ready. She had decided to start small, picking a single item at a time, rather than attempting an entire meal preparation. She didn't want to put that much stress on Tiara. So, they would start simple, with homemade biscuits, a staple of rural America. Once she'd evaluated Tiara's comfort level and ability, Jayce would plan the next phase.

A soft knock came at the door. "Come in."

Tiara entered in her standard worn jeans and t-shirt, with an expression similar to the one Jayce wore when called to the principal's office. Jayce chuckled, "How 'bout a cup of coffee?" At Tiara's nod, she poured coffee in to a mug and handed it over. She shifted a bit so Tiara could have access to the sugar. "This isn't an hour of torture, you know. You just may find you like to cook."

Tiara smirked. "Yeah, as much as having teeth pulled at the dentist office when they're out of Novocain."

Jayce guffawed. "Aw, it's not gonna be that bad, honey." She swallowed, hoping Tiara hadn't noticed the endearment. The same one she couldn't stop yesterday while they worked with Majestic.

"Huh. Is that why we needed such an early start? I mean, really, Jayce, we beat the sun in rising." Tiara pursed her lips to blow on the hot liquid before she sipped and Jayce had to stifle the urge to kiss the puckered lips. Too late, Jayce realized she'd been staring, when Tiara took a step back and asked, "What?"

Shaking her head, Jayce said, "Nothing, just thinking of something, um, I want to do later." Yeah, she wanted to kiss Tiara in a bad way. Jayce's heart beat erratically in her agitation. What had possessed Tiara to agree to this? She put down her mug and went to the stove and set the temperature to preheat the oven. "It's gonna be another scorcher today. Don't want to heat the house too fast, if we can help it."

Tiara nodded, not showing any indication she noticed Jayce's discomposure. Then Jayce pulled out the tray that she'd placed all the perishable items on, so she would have them handy, and put it on the counter beside the others. "Okay, I think we're ready," she said, picking up the piece of paper with the instructions that she'd written down earlier, before turning back to Tiara. "Just one more thing. I knew for a certainty that you were out of your element yesterday with Majestic, so I may over explain each step. I don't want you to think I'm treating you like an idiot, so please," she said while handing the recipe to Tiara, who began to read it, "tell me how you want to go about this. Should I wait until you ask questions? Do you want me to assist, leave the room, what?"

"What's the matter, cowgirl? Afraid I'll attack you with the kitchen utensils?" Tiara asked with a mischievous grin.

Jayce waggled her eyebrows. "Under other circumstances that suggestion could prove fun." She was glad Tiara only blushed, and didn't use the comment as a reason to run.

"I'll remember that for another time."

It was Jayce's turn to flush, as an image of a naked Tiara holding a pastry brush in hand jumped to mind. Does she realize she's torturing me? *"Touché."*

Tiara chuckled and winked. Jayce concluded Red knew exactly what she had done. Luckily, she let Jayce off the hook, much to Jayce's relief.

"I'd like if you stayed near and watched. If you see me about to make a mistake, let me know. And if I have a question or am unsure about something I'll ask. Deal?"

"Done." Jayce shoved her trembling hands into her pockets, hoping her voice was steady.

Tiara pulled the large mixing bowl closer to her, and set the paper beside it. She read and combined the ingredients as directed. Jayce watched Tiara's lips moving as she read and noticed she bit her bottom lip when she concentrated. Tiara poured the dry ingredients as if they would combust otherwise. Whisking went well, Jayce marveled at the precise movements of Tiara's hands. Lost in the economy of motion Tiara used, Jayce focused on her hands and remembered how they felt against her bare skin. They'd been strengthened with calluses yet gentle and soft when grazing her flesh. Jayce could feel them hot against her skin, her body wanting their touch again. Not until a hand grabbed her shoulder, and she stared into Tiara's grey eyes did Jayce realize where her thoughts had taken her. "What?"

"Are you all right?"

"Yeah, fine, why?" she asked.

With a frown, Tiara released her. "I asked if turn out the dough meant remove from bowl. Your answer was to moan. You didn't appear to be focused on my question, so I won't take it personally. We can do this later if you aren't feeling well."

There was no way Jayce could explain she'd been lost in a flashback of their night at the line shack, or how her body tingled from those recollections. She pulled herself together, and fast. Focus. "Uh-huh. The dough can be messy to work with when rolling out, so I usually lay waxed paper down first, and flour it heavily. That's it. Now let it set for a couple of minutes."

"Is it tired?" Tiara asked, picking up her coffee mug.

Jayce stared at her, confused, until she realized that Tiara hid a grin behind the mug. Her own response took a moment. "I can see daydreaming is a dangerous pastime around you."

"Anything you want to talk about?" Tiara asked, her tone serious.

"No," Jayce squeaked. With herculean effort, Jayce pulled herself together giving attention to the task before them. "Knead the roll for about a minute."

"You'll need to explain," Tiara said, raising an eyebrow.

Jayce worked her fingers in the air as she said, "You manipulate the dough by pressing, folding, and stretching it." When she caught the darkening of Tiara's eyes, Jayce shoved her hands in her pockets, realizing how her visual example must have looked. She couldn't finish this farce. Earlier, Jayce had believed her selection to be a good one, relatively simple for a first cooking project, but it was difficult to concentrate on anything but her attraction to Tiara. Every nerve and muscle screamed for her to flee.

Jayce didn't want Tiara to be this close and to pretend their night together had never happened. Tiara doesn't want to acknowledge her lovemaking, so she can leave without a guilty conscious. That's what she needed to help her through this. Jayce needed to remember Tiara wasn't staying in Silver Waters. Accepting this challenge was just a means for her to pass the time until Slim returned. If Tiara ever returned, it probably wouldn't be for another ten years.

Taking a deep breath to bolster her courage, Jayce pointed to the rolling pin and the flour canister. "Lightly flour that and roll the dough to about half-an-inch thick." Tiara silently did as told and placed the rolling pin on the counter. Jayce pointed to the biscuit cutter. "Use the cutter to section off the biscuits. No, no," Jayce said, staying Tiara's hand with her own. "You want to cut them as close together as possible without over lapping. You want to get the most of each round, before you attempt to reroll the dough. You want to get the maximum production with minimum effort."

Tiara began to cut the pattern closer. "I get it," Tiara said. "Make 'em quick and fling 'em in the oven so there's time slop the hogs, mend the fences, get the children off to their one room schoolhouse."

Despite herself, Jayce laughed. "Yeah, something like that."

"Done." Tiara absently wiped the back of her hand across her forehead, leaving a flour trail, before she wiped her hands on her thighs. "Okay, what next?" Tiara asked.

Impulse nearly had Jayce wiping the mess from Tiara's face, but she recognized that touching her would be the worst move Jayce could make. "We put them on an ungreased cookie sheet, spaced evenly apart, and bake at 425 degrees for about twelve to fifteen minutes." Tiara did as told, picked up the metal sheet and opened the oven door. "Thar you go, woman, fling them thar biscuits into the oven. We got fences to mend."

Slowly, Tiara closed the oven door, and set the timer on the stove for twelve minutes.

Jayce swallowed hard, realizing Tiara's mood had subtly shifted.

"Yes, Jayce," Tiara whispered tenderly. "We have fences to mend. The sooner, the better, too."

Jayce picked up her forgotten mug, took a sip and grimaced at how cold the coffee had become. She tried to buy herself time by dumping the contents into the sink and preparing a fresh cup. "Isn't that what these challenges are about? I learn to view work from your perspective and vice-versa."

Nodding, Tiara sighed. "Yes, ultimately, but I'm the one who agreed for the both of us. This was my idea. You were prepared to distance yourself from me, weren't you?"

"Yes." Jayce couldn't see any point in lying.

"You're still upset with me for my anger over our words at the line shack?"

Jayce shook her head. "I'm not upset any longer with poor word choices, no."

Confusion registered on Tiara's features. "Please, Jayce, I can feel you closing yourself away. I'd hoped we were making progress, even having fun. Aren't we?"

Jayce nodded, aware of the distress in Tiara's tone.

"Then why erect the walls?"

Despite her best efforts, Jayce felt tears pushing for release. She didn't want to answer, but couldn't lie. "Because I can't, nor do I want to, forget our night together, Red." She turned her back on Tiara, put her mug on the counter and grasped the edge to steady herself. "And every time I'm near you, I want you in my arms again. Want *you* to want picket fences, too." She spun around, glanced at the timer, saying, "Biscuits are almost done." As quick as she could, Jayce strode to the back door, pushing open the screen. "I'm not strong enough to know you'll leave without ever looking back. I know I'm not enough to make you want to stay."

Before Tiara could respond, more afraid she wouldn't, Jayce stomped out the door, silently berating herself—honesty made her every kind of fool.

Jayce couldn't believe she'd spilled her guts like some damned teenager, and even blubbering over it now. She needed to immerse herself in work. Work was the best medicine for her to feel better. Now, it could only offer a diversion. She went into the barn, grabbed her saddle and carried it to Arabelle's stall. "Morning, gal. Up for a long walk?" Arabelle whinnied.

"Hey, where're you going?" Sarah walked over and rubbed Arabelle's nose.

"Training."

Sarah raised an eyebrow. "Done making biscuits already?"

Gritting her teeth, Jayce tightened the cinch, pulled the bridle from the peg by the door and placed it on Arabelle. "Yeah, we're done." Using the reins to lead the horse outside, Sarah steps behind her, Jayce was about to swing into the saddle when Sarah's hand on her arm stopped her.

"Please, Jayce, talk to me," Sarah said.

Jayce considered telling her, for about a second, but heard Craig's cheerful voice, "Hey, ladies. Awesome morning, isn't it?"

She didn't look at Sarah as she jerked her arm free and climbed into the saddle. "There's nothing to talk about. Gotta go," she said. Jayce kicked Arabelle into a gallop, putting as much distance as she could between her and the heartbreak cooking in her kitchen.

Chapter Twenty-one

SARAH WATCHED AS Jayce disappeared on Arabelle, wondering what had happened to put that much hurt in Jayce's expression. She knew the reason was Tiara related, and promptly wondered if Slim's matchmaking intentions were worth it. So far, all Sarah could see was fun loving and perpetually happy Jayce more often upset and crying.

"Was it something I said?" Craig asked as he stopped beside her. When she shook her head, Craig kissed her on the forehead. "Ready to go?"

She wouldn't be able to enjoy the day until she did something about the current fiasco, before the situation got completely out of hand. She shoved her hands in her jean's pockets. "I've gotta take care of something. I can come get you when I'm done," she told Craig.

"If it's all the same to you, I'd like to follow along," Craig said. "You're clearly worried, and I'd like to offer my support, if you'll allow me."

Sarah considered whether that was a smart idea. She had a notion where Slim had been hiding himself, but couldn't guarantee what type of a greeting they'd get, especially since she suspected Slim had something to do with Elmo and it wasn't related to Majestic. Since Jayce and Tiara were supposed to be happily playing in dough, Sarah figured Edna would be with Slim. At least she prayed that was the case, because she'd need Edna's calming presence and clear head. Hers was already telling her to throttle Slim the second she laid eyes on him. Craig could hold her back if it came to that. "All right, let's go find Slim."

"Tiara's dad?" he asked, easily keeping pace with her angry stride. "He's finally home, huh? Tiara never mentioned it."

"That's because none of us is supposed to know."

"Oh, okay."

With a snort, Sarah snapped, "No, it's not okay. I presume Slim and Edna have hatched this plan to bring Tiara home, for good, and she and Jayce can live happily-ever-after."

"The way those two are at each other's throat?" he asked incredulously. "Besides, Tiara has a business in the city."

"Parents, even parents of adult children, almost always want their children home. And, I don't think Edna's going to tie the knot with Slim until he's patched things up with Tiara."

Craig had put a hand on her arm, halting her. "You know the whole story about Tiara and Jayce? Care to share?"

Sarah considered his request. It really wasn't her place to bare the history. Much as Craig could be a welcomed ally, and as her friend, a family friend, he was still Tiara's employee first. But he would find out all the dynamics once she confronted Slim, and Sarah believed she should make him aware of that fact. "The history isn't mine to reveal," she said, holding up her palm when he opened his mouth to respond. "However, if you pay close attention when I talk to Slim, you should come up to speed quickly."

"I'll be an eager student then." A grin spread across his features, and Sarah was almost taken aback by how nearly angelic he appeared as the amusement sparkled in his eyes. For an instant, Sarah berated herself for falling for him, as certainly as she breathed. He was younger, and she just recently released from a relationship. Maybe she should slow this down, even halt it, before either of them were hurt.

"Oh, no you don't," Craig said, pointing a finger in her direction. "The focus is Tiara and Jayce. Don't start evaluating our relationship," he ordered.

Sarah guffawed. "What makes you think we have a relationship?"

Crossing his arms over his chest, Craig said, "If you want to call this 'friendship', go ahead. I know you care for me. I'd love everything to be about us, but I can wait a bit. We *will* talk before you return to being Ms. Juarez." The corner of his mouth twitched on his announcement.

"How long have you known?" she asked.

"Since Darla's dinner. I can see a star not wanting to hob-nob with the little folk, but it was just too curious that you two are never together at the same time. Juanita is supposed to be smitten with Jayce, after all." He shrugged. "Besides, you're too similar, even for a stand-in double."

Swallowing her surprise, Sarah said, "Another topic to add to the list of items for our future conversation." This added a gargantuan item for serious examination by her later. "Okay, one problem at a time." She walked toward the bunkhouse.

The structure hadn't been used much since about the 60s, when ranch hands lived on the property. In the last decade, the building housed the men when a snowstorm made it impossible for someone to leave the property, or when the Hollywood representatives stayed over for filming. The bunkhouse had all the amenities and simple comforts for short stays; which is why neither she nor Jayce would have considered it as Slim's hiding place.

They stepped up on the creaking wood slats of the porch, and the main door opened, Edna motioning them in. The room looked much like Jayce's living room with the couch and matching chair in front of a thick wood coffee table. On the coffee table was a silver tray with matching tumblers evenly spaced beside a pitcher of lemonade. A large flat screen television adorned the largest wall. Slim sat in an old wooden rocker, leaning forward with his elbows resting on his knees, concern etched lines in his forehead. Edna said, "I figured we'd be found out, but I thought Jayce would be the first here." Edna indicated the couch, as she moved to the chair. "Sit down and tell me what has brought you out here." Directing her gaze at Sarah, Edna added, "From the expression on your face, it isn't good."

Shaking her head, Sarah said, "No, Aunt Edna, something's made this whole situation worse."

"Is Tiara all right?" she asked.

Sarah snapped, "I wouldn't know. But your niece is a mess, if you're interested."

Injured surprise flashed across Edna's features. "Of course I'm interested. How could you possibly think I wouldn't be? Jayce is resilient, and always pulls through just fine."

"Well, you both," Sarah shot an accusatory glare at Slim, "may have pushed too far this time. Strong, buoyant Jayce is a chaotic mess." She added, curling her lip in disgust. "Tiara is playing her like a xylophone in a kindergarten class, rough and uncaring of the tune. Poor little princess, my ass."

Edna gasped. "You've made your point, Sarah."

"I don't think I have. Everyone is so worried about all that Tiara has gone through. I doubt either of you has considered what a toll this would take on Jayce, the one person who supported both of you the entire time." Sarah noticed Slim squirm in the rocker. "Yeah, more a daughter to you than your biological, yet absent, one." Sarah's body trembled as bad as her voice had during her tirade. Craig placed a hand on her back and gently rubbed in a rhythmic circular motion.

"You don't know what you're talking about," Edna said.

"Sarah, honey, this whole setup was with Tiara and Jayce in mind. We didn't intend either to be wronged. We only wanted them happy."

Sarah shook her head. "Then you've failed miserably."

"Stop it, Sarah, please." Sarah, along with the others, turned to see Jayce standing in the bunkhouse doorway. To Sarah, Jayce looked worse than she had moments ago.

"Jayce—"

"It's all right, Sarah," Jayce said. She walked closer, poured a glass of lemonade, took a long drink and sat herself on the corner of the coffee table closest to Sarah. "Tiara hasn't done anything wrong, really. This is my doing." She took another drink. Then, as if she and Jayce were the only two in the room, Jayce lightly tapped her hand on Sarah's knee and said with a grimace, "Tiara was frightened by the storm the night at the line shack. I wanted to take that fear away and..."

Then, the crux of the matter from Jayce's point of view came clear for Sarah. Fresh tears clouded her vision as she drew Jayce into her arms. "Oh, honey, I'm so sorry."

SLIM DIDN'T WANT to acknowledge the anguish swimming in Edna's cornflower blue eyes, it was too raw. How could he not have noticed as Jayce's eyes had held the same ravaged emotion, consuming any hint of her lightheartedness, her normal joviality? Edna apparently understood what the private communication between Jayce and Sarah meant. Much as his curiosity was piqued, he knew better than to ask. However, Slim knew one question did need asking. "How can I fix this, Jayce?"

"Time, Slim," Jayce told him, pulling away from Sarah's embrace. "I just need time," she said. "I hear it heals all wounds. Now, if you'll all excuse me, I've work to do." Jayce laid a hand on Sarah's shoulder, seemed to purposely ignore Edna, strode to the door, where she turned and focused on him again. "Slim, good to see you, as always. But I think it's about time you came out of hiding and let your daughter know you're home." She let the door slam loudly behind her as she exited.

Slim doubted he was the only one to flinch. Slapping his hands to his knees, Slim stood. "Well, I believe it's time to get reacquainted with my little princess," he announced with more bravado than he felt. He looked squarely at Edna, "May I walk you home, honey?"

Edna nodded. "Just know this, Eddy, I won't assist you in this. If Tiara is still at *Meadows*, I'll be going directly to my room. You brought her here for a purpose, and she should know what it is, even if a part of that objective has backfired."

"Yes, backfired badly," Sarah said, anger strong in her tone. "As in blunder, boo-boo, big ass mistake."

"Sarah," Craig said softly, taking her hand in his own. Sarah looked at their joined hands. "I kinda suspect Tiara's daddy is aware of the situation. I think we should leave him to it, preferably without more synonyms." Slim thought he caught a smile on her lips, as she nodded agreement.

As Craig and Sarah rose from the couch, Slim moved next to Edna. He extended his hand to Craig. "Sure wish we'd met under better circumstances, young man."

"Craig. Name's Craig Walters, and I work for you daughter." Slim nodded, surprised when Craig added, "Sure hope you get this mended 'cause I don't care to have my boss, who's also my friend, hurt. Jayce may be a new friend, but I'm not too happy about what you've done to her, either. You need to make this right, sir."

"That is my intention, Craig."

"All right, then. I have some sightseeing to do with this incredible woman," Craig escorted Sarah to the front door. "Think you need to get along with it."

Slim turned to Edna. "Ready to go home?"

"Ready to face Tiara?" Edna asked with a sympathetic smile.

"No, but I think it's long overdue."

"You'll feel better when you've got it over and behind us."

"I don't know, honey," Slim said, shaking his head. "Why do I get this gut feeling I'm about to put a Band-Aid where I should be applying a tourniquet?"

Chapter Twenty-two

TIARA HAD CLEANED up and placed all the biscuits into miscellaneous plastic-ware she'd located in the cupboard. She sat sullenly at the table staring into her mug of neglected coffee. When she heard someone enter through the kitchen's screen door, Tiara turned around to see Edna walking in. Tiara jumped up and rushed over to give Edna a hug. "Thank goodness you're home, Aunt Edna. I've upset Jayce and don't know what I did."

Edna patted her back and pulled from the embrace. "I know, honey. Come to my room when you're done, and we'll talk about it."

"I've already finished. Oh yeah, I used some of your containers to put the stuff up in."

Shaking her head, Edna nudged Tiara back a step to shift them away from the door. That's when Tiara noticed the person behind her, shifting uncomfortably from foot to foot. "Papa Slim?"

"Hey, there, princess," he replied hesitantly, as if uncertain of her welcome.

With a reassuring squeeze to her shoulder, Edna said, "I'll be upstairs."

Tiara focused on her father as Edna left the kitchen, her steady tread sounding on the stairs. Other than more grey hair, he looked exactly as she remembered him from a decade ago. So much time had passed, and Tiara's brain reminded her of his abandonment. Her instinct was to close the distance and lock him in her arms. She didn't know what to do. The little girl in her won. Closing the distance, Tiara flung her arms around her father. "Damn it, Dad, where have you been? I've messed up so much without you."

"I'm here now. We'll fix this." His tears dampened the side of her cheek. "I'm sorry, princess, that I left this go on so long."

She pulled away, giving a watery chuckle, as she scowled at him. "Don't let it happen again." Tiara returned to the kitchen chair, pointing to a chair beside hers. "We need to talk. You know I'm very mad at you, right?"

He nodded gloomily. "You have every right to be angry."

"According to Jayce, not entirely as much as I thought I did. Look, Dad, I need to understand some stuff to fix what I've messed up with Jayce."

"Is that what you really want, Princess, to fix things with Jayce?"

"I'd at least like to keep our friendship, yes." She frowned. "Where were you?"

"Edna's bunkhouse," he said and his face flushed.

Tiara was hurt. "You've been here the whole time?"

"Got here the morning Majestic did." Slim straightened in his chair. "Look, Princess—"

"Yeah, I'm hurt you didn't come see me, first thing. But, I need answers not excuses, right now. You said you won Majestic." Tiara paused. "No, that's not important, either." She didn't want to bring up Angie, but there really wasn't a way to avoid the topic forever. "Angie said you didn't want anything to do with me, and that's why you never came around or asked me to spend the summers or holidays."

"That is purely a lie. I've always wanted you with me at the *Acres*," Slim said, his voice rattled with sadness.

"Jayce mentioned Angie had a legal document preventing either of you from coming near me. I'm sorry about that, by the way. I never knew. And I certainly didn't know she was destroying all our letters to each other, either."

Slim inhaled deeply. "Truth told, Princess, your mother had a lot of problems. Unfortunately, by the time I figured it out, it was too late. Our divorce never finalized, so some of her rights were always as my wife. One being I couldn't exactly fight over custody issues. You also need to realize it was a different time. Nowadays, dads are getting a better deal with rights, even if they aren't always the better parent."

"Then how did she get the protection order?" Tiara asked.

"Convinced the court we were separated and working through counseling." He frowned. "Tiara, I may not have physically been around, and I'm sorrier about that than you can know, but I paid your mother's bills, and I had people who understood the situation, help me get word about you and what your needs may have been." He nodded sadly. "Maybe not the emotional needs, Princess, but, well, there were limitations to my involvement. I was terrified of upsetting your mother too much, as I suspected she turned that bitterness on you."

He hit that nail on the head, certainly. Angie had done that very thing. She was surprised, however, that he had been as involved as he had been. Tiara knew part of her wasn't forgiving him completely, but she felt better. There would still need to be venting and healing time. Nothing could change the past, just her perception of it, and she realized she needed to do that. "What do you do for money, if not gamble?"

"I'm an investor. I started with venture capital when I was with Angie, now I mostly stick with investment counseling and mutual fund portfolios." He shrugged. "So, in a manner of speaking, I do gamble, first with my own money, now with other peoples." Slim scooted closer and leaned his elbows on the table. "As for winning Majestic, I own him outright. When I said I won him, I was also being vague. Majestic's previous owner wanted to keep him at the ranch to stud. I wanted to bring him here to rest, maybe give Jayce a chance to work with him. That was gambling because it was determined with a coin toss."

She smiled at her father. Jayce seemed to know about her father's profession, and did spend time with him, as he thought of her first when it came to the horse. How much involvement did she have in Slim's plan to get her to Silver Waters? "Dad, did Jayce know about your contrivance to get me here?"

Shock replaced his smile. "No, honey, she certainly did not. Edna only learned of it after I'd set the plan into motion. Neither one can be held accountable. This was all my doing."

"But I don't understand why?"

"I wanted to see if you'd come." He cleared his throat. "Also, I know Jayce has had it bad for you for a long while. When that cop started visiting, I didn't want Jayce to give up the chance you'd come back. So, I helped the situation along."

That was a surprising turn of events. Once she realized who Sarah was, Tiara didn't take chasing Juanita seriously; but, Jayce hadn't mentioned a female cop. Immediately, her heart tightened with jealousy. But she would be leaving Silver Waters, returning to her business and a life elsewhere. She should give Jayce her chance at happiness.

Slim didn't appear to see her distress. He continued with his explanation. "It wasn't just for Jayce, though. I'm being selfish, here. Princess, I proposed to Edna and she won't have me until I make things right by you. I don't expect you to come back, but I want you to be part of our future life together." He shook his head. "I'm not sure what transpired between you and Jayce, but it wouldn't have happened if I'd left things alone."

Left Jayce to her cop and a happily-ever-after? Tiara shivered. "Well, Papa Slim, I'm kinda thinking the rift between Jayce and me is my doing, not yours. I also suspect your fiancée will have a better understanding of what happened with Jayce."

"Are you upset about my upcoming wedding?"

Tiara and he stood simultaneously, and she gave him a heartfelt hug. "It's long overdue, Dad, and I couldn't be happier. I hope you realize what an incredible woman you're getting." He broke out in the loopiest, dopiest grin she'd ever seen on anyone. "Guess you do realize. Right now, I need that wonderful woman's advice." She turned away and then she remembered Elmo. "So I don't really have to worry about the little gangster and his henchman?"

Slim burst into laughter. "No, Elmo's an actor friend who owed me a favor. The henchman is his brother. Both are harmless."

Just remembering the pair sent a strange niggling disquiet through her. "I hope you're right." Tiara didn't know why, but intuition told her she hadn't seen the last of Elmo and his huge brother. The feeling left her feeling strangely apprehensive.

SARAH'S STOMACH TWISTED in knots as she sat in the driver's

seat, not ready to leave the car. It had been a long time since she'd been back to the family farmhouse, and usually Jayce came along with her. Now it felt simultaneously disturbing and right to have Craig with her. Oddly, to her at least, the idea that she could easily fall for the younger man, disturbed her. Craig seemed older on some levels. She did recognize he easily lapsed into immature behavior a bit too readily. However, overall, he came across as truly caring, a good listener, and an honestly kindhearted man. She smiled, and he was a great kisser. If anyone mentioned her recent breakup, since meeting and kissing Craig, she'd have to reply, "Johnny who?"

Right now, she had another thing to be grateful for since her time together with Craig. He was the only one, other than Jayce, to catch the nuances in her reactions and changes in her emotions.

As if to confirm her thoughts, Craig reached across and took her right hand into his left hand. "We can do this another time."

Much as she wanted to do that very thing, Sarah knew she'd eventually need to face the house, pleased with his genuine concern. "No, I need to get over this."

"There's plenty of time. I realize this is painful for you."

Sarah looked over at him. The idea of going into her childhood home, the memories of parents who gave all they had for her, proved terribly daunting. However, those memories were such wonderful ones, and she wanted to keep them. Only Jayce knew, so far, that Sarah had been considering giving up her Hollywood life, leaving Juanita Juarez behind forever and settling down in Silver Waters. Jayce was extremely supportive of her desires and dreams. Sarah had thought Johnny would learn to want those things, too, and was glad she'd found out the truth before she moved forward with that particular plan. If she followed through with her retirement, Sarah would need to make modifications to the house, which hadn't been upgraded in twenty years or more. "I'm glad you're here for this."

Craig returned her stare seriously. "For recommendations on renovations?"

She flashed a wry grin. "That, too. Mostly because you seem to really care about and understand how difficult this is for me."

He squeezed her hand. "And you know I'm here for Sarah, not Juanita?"

"Yeah, I believe I do."

"Good, because I mean it." Craig shifted in the passenger seat so he faced her. "I'll understand if you can't go in the house yet. You wanna call me a couple months from now, I'll be here for you then, too, for you as long as you want or need me to be."

The honesty in his eyes was almost her undoing. Before she could give in to a bout of tears, she pulled the keys from the ignition, pushed open her door and exited the car. Craig did likewise. Sarah located the house key on the ring as she made her way up the stairs to the porch, and stood in front of the door. They both stepped in when she'd pushed the front door open wide.

Since Edna and Jayce had a cleaning service regularly come to the house, Sarah hadn't been surprised by the lingering smell of cleaning fluids. The pictures of various stages of Sarah's life hung up on almost every available wall space, from the entryway and curving up both sides of the walls along the staircase.

The furniture in the living room remained the same she'd reclined in while watching television, doing her homework because she didn't like being alone in her room. The room where her mother constantly slapped the bottom of her feet when she'd placed them on the coffee table, knowing it was against the house rules. Sarah and her parents had all the usual angst and arguments, but they'd always gotten over them quickly. Her childhood home more often rang with laughter and loving teasing. Sarah was loved. She thought of how blessed she had been, knowing others like Tiara, may not have had the same experiences.

As she took Craig through the house reciting memories when the moment inspired them, Sarah wondered, what were Craig's thoughts about her home? When she and Jayce were growing up, even when they dated, Sarah hadn't been a nester like Jayce. She wanted a career, the fortune and the fame. Now that she'd had it, Sarah couldn't help wanting the same things Jayce longed for. And she needed to find someone who wanted what she did? Could Craig be that man? Was he simply viewing the house as a project? He was still young. Did Craig think or care about raising a family?

"This would be an awesome home for raising kids," Craig said.

"Not usually something a guy your age would admit."

"I'm not like most guys, Sarah, I hope someday you'll get that. Actually, I had a fantastic childhood, and I can't wait to share that with someone special."

Sarah said. "I'm surprised you aren't settled down then."

"Are you kidding? That's a commitment that requires a unique person with a like mind." He shook his head. "I want a relationship like my parents had, compatible and fulfilling in all ways. I refuse to settle for just anyone." Craig waggled his eyebrows. "Still waiting for the right woman to have the light bulb go on over her head." He stared at her. "I refuse to take marriage lightly — no matter who she is."

Craig could be the keeper, but so soon after Johnny, was she ready to find out? She wondered if the last comment had been specifically aimed at her, or if she were reading more into the situation because of her own thoughts along that same path. A path Sarah needed to get off before she landed herself into trouble she wasn't prepared to handle.

"Okay, handsome handyman, tell me your thoughts on renovating my home."

Chapter Twenty-three

TIARA LEFT THE kitchen and went to find Edna. At the top of the stairs, she heard movement, knowing Edna's room was at the end of the hall and to the right she headed in that direction. On the left side of the hallway an open door drew her attention. It was the master bedroom, from the size of it, and the décor broadcasted Jayce's personality like a bullhorn. Impulsively, Tiara entered the room drawn to objects on the dresser. The top held a hairbrush, a glass bowl with change, and the wooden horse Tiara had carved that fateful day in the old barn. With a trembling hand, Tiara picked up the carving immediately noting the shiny spots of dirt worn smooth from years of being rubbed. Tiara noticed the brown spot staining the wood and she recognized it as the blood from when she'd cut herself. That spot was also shiny from years of rubbing.

"I never understood the significance of the horse, until the day I tried to remove it from the dresser." Tiara turned toward Edna, who stood in the doorway staring at the wooden carving she held. "I didn't know where she had picked it up, no idea of the significance, only that she had it all dirty. How healthy could that be?" Edna smiled crookedly in memory. "Jayce walked into her room just as I was picking it up, rushed over and yanked it from my hand, demanding that I never touch it again. 'Touch or take anything from my room, Aunt Edna, but this, this is the only part of Red I may ever have.' " Edna blinked, focusing on Tiara now. "And I never touched it again. To my memory, no one has."

"It's not great workmanship, and I wasn't very good at it."

"It's beautiful, a part of you that Jayce was able to hold and cherish. It meant the world to her." Edna moved all the way into the room and stood beside Tiara. "When Jayce gets sad, which luckily isn't very often, she holds the carving and gets terribly quiet, focusing internally. After a while, she's worked through whatever has upset her and is able to move on. Her own personal therapy totem."

Tiara indicated the bloodstain. "She caught me carving this in dad's barn. I was alarmed, not expecting to get caught whittling. I thought my carving would instigate some wisecrack from her, and I ended up nicking myself." The memory brought tears to her eyes as she stared down at the carving. "That was the first time Jayce kissed me. But then she ran away."

Edna nodded. "She told me about that. She said at that moment she knew."

Tiara gave a wry grin. "Knew what?"

"It's not my place to say," Edna said, shaking her head. "Let's focus on this morning. Can you tell me what happened? Why you think you did something wrong?"

"I wish I knew. One minute we're joking and laughing, teasing about mending fences, and Jayce got weird on me. I thought we'd come to a truce, but Jayce indicated wanting more." Tiara got up and paced, reluctant to get too personal with Jayce's aunt. After all, Edna had a duty to defend her niece. Tiara didn't want to put her in the position to need to do so, but she herself needed to understand whether things were more desperate than she imagined them to be. "I can't stay in Silver Waters, Aunt Edna. I have a life, and it's not here. Not anymore. I wish you could all see and accept it."

"I'm confident that realization has finally come to both Jayce and your father." Edna stood and stopped Tiara from her pacing, placing her hands on Tiara's shoulders. She met Edna's resolute gaze. "I hope you don't blame Slim for how poorly things have turned out. He truly meant well, wanting to do right by you. Even for Jayce, though he didn't understand all the dynamics involved."

Tiara frowned, not understanding what Edna alluded to concerning Jayce. "I realize Dad had the best of intentions for everyone, yes."

"Good." Edna released Tiara's shoulders, and looked away. "Has your father mentioned anything about us?"

"He has, and I'm very happy for you both."

"Also good because I hope you'll come back and be present when we finally wed. I no longer have reason to delay him."

Was it her imagination that Edna didn't sound as enthused about her attendance anymore. Was it because Tiara refused to stay?

"Jayce and Slim can handle Majestic now, and we're so pleased with the changes you've made with the *Acres*." Edna still didn't meet her gaze, and had moved to stand in the doorway to Jayce's room. "The barbeque is tomorrow and the town is looking forward to seeing you and your friends attend." Now, Edna raised her head to stare into Tiara's face, tears building in the Mansfield blue depths.

"I know Darla and the guys are looking forward to it." Too late, she should have added herself as eager, to avoid hurt feelings.

"The following day is Sunday. You and your friends could beat weekend traffic if you leave early. That way you don't have to wait to get back home." As if of their own volition, Edna's tears fell. She had taken a deep breath, said, "Good-bye Tiara," as she rushed away. Seconds later, Tiara heard the closing of a door.

She stood stunned and confused in the middle of Jayce's room, barely aware she still clutched the carving, trying to fathom what had just happened. Had Edna just asked her to leave Silver Waters? Or had she acknowledged that no one would stop Tiara from leaving? What the hell did she expect, after making it perfectly clear she didn't want to be here anymore?

Tiara didn't know if she should be hurt or angry. Ten years ago she was dragged away by Angie. She didn't want to leave then. Today, she felt as if she was being dismissed. Tiara was given the very thing she wanted, a reason to leave again. She hadn't wanted to come in the first place, hadn't wanted to dredge up old memories and feelings. Finally, they were allowing Tiara to decide what was best for her own well-being. And what was best was to go back to finishing work on the chiropractor's house, back to her own home and her classic movies, back to take-out and eating in the living room, sleep when and where she felt like it.

Finally, Tiara was her own person again.

So why did it feel like Edna had just ripped her heart from her chest?

SHE WAS SO intent on rubbing down Arabelle, Jayce startled when she heard the car horn. When she turned around, Alison Stewart exited her Sheriff's vehicle and waved. The tall, athletic blonde was stunning as ever, especially in uniform and flashing that sexy grin. The first time Jayce had seen that grin on Ali's lips she thought it contrived. After a year in her position as sheriff, and as a friend, Jayce realized Alison was completely unaware of the affect she had on people. The unassuming qualities bound their friendship in a true sense, giving Alison a place in Jayce's life for as long as Alison wanted, much as Sarah had done.

Jayce put down the brush, and walked toward Alison, her spirits lifting at the sight of a friendly face. "The uniform's on so you're not here to ride. Hope it's not official business bringing you to *Meadows*."

"Not exactly. Why? Have you done something bad I'm not aware of?" Alison laughed. "I'm not opposed to locking you up, if it could result in you finally going out with me."

Deep in her heart, Jayce wished she cared for Alison in a romantic way. Her life would certainly be easier. Alison had no problem with small town life in Silver Waters. Blushing, Jayce said, "Oh, Ali—"

"Please, don't finish and break my heart." Alison leaned against the hood of her cruiser, propping a booted foot on the fender, as she crossed her arms over her ample chest. "You look like hell, Jayce. Is everything okay?"

"I've had a rough week."

"Want me to rough someone up for you?" Jayce thought she heard a bit more than a hint of seriousness in the question.

"No, but I'll keep it in mind next time Edna gives me a hard time." Jayce wished she could see and feel for Alison as she did Tiara.

"Uh-oh," Alison shook her head as if disappointed. "Can we make sure that doesn't happen until after the barbeque tomorrow?"

"I'm wounded, and you're thinking with your appetite, again," Jayce said. Her heart clenched as she remembered thinking the same about Tiara. Damn it, why wouldn't Tiara leave her head? Suddenly,

Jayce felt nauseous.

"Hey, take it easy," she heard Alison say near her ear. Before Jayce realized she was mobile, Alison had wrapped an arm around her waist and walked her toward the front porch. Alison urged Jayce to sit on the swing and sat beside her. "Should I get you a wet cloth, a bucket, something?"

Jayce found her concern endearing. She gently tapped Alison's cheek with her fingertips, then took one of Alison's hands in hers. "Relax, Sheriff, I'm just a little queasy. I'm fine now. Thank you."

The corners of Alison's eyes crinkled as she laughed. "Thank goodness, because this is the last of my clean uniforms. I've been saving laundry for tomorrow morning, before the barbeque."

"Your clothes are safe, for the moment at least." Jayce realized how that came out, and felt her face heat in embarrassment.

Alison smiled broadly, and then shook her head. "Okay, I've so got to let you off the hook, or I'm going to do something very un-sheriff-like." Pulling her hand free of Jayce's own, she said, "I've heard from some folks about seeing a stranger while they were on the road behind your property."

Jayce frowned. "I assume they didn't recognize this person?"

She shook her head. "Both times, I've been told, the person was in shadow and moving fast. I'll let my guys know, and we'll keep an eye out during patrols. Tomorrow's my day off. Maybe, after laundry," she said, grinning, "you can saddle up a horse for me and I can check it out for you."

"I'm sure it's nothing, Ali. Please don't use your day off chasing shadows."

"It's my job, Jayce." Alison patted Jayce's thigh. "I don't want to see anything happen to you," her voice sincere, "or Edna," she added.

Just then, the screen door opened. Jayce expected her aunt, but saw Tiara instead. Fresh pain washed through her. Alison must have read her reaction because she rose from the swing and stood beside Jayce.

Tiara glanced at Jayce first and then Alison, not settling on either as she said, "Sorry to interrupt. I was heading home." Jayce thought she noted stress on Tiara's face.

Alison stepped toward Tiara, and extended her hand. "I'm Sheriff Stewart."

"Tiara Summers," she said, shaking Alison's hand, "I'm Slim's daughter."

"Nice to meet you, Ms. Summers. I know a little about your father." At Tiara's raised eyebrow, Alison added, "Mostly by reputation. I've only had the pleasure on one occasion." Resting her hands on her utility belt, Alison assessed Tiara from head to foot. "This a visit or a permanent move for you?"

Tiara startled Jayce with her response. "No need to worry about me, Sheriff Stewart. My crew and I will be leaving Sunday. We're just sticking around for the barbeque."

The news was just one more unexpected squeeze to Jayce's heart. Even though she'd expected Tiara's leaving, hearing it from Tiara's own lips brought on a new rush of hurt. Did Tiara hate Silver Waters, or just Jayce, so much that she couldn't wait to get away? It didn't matter. With a little time, Jayce knew this too would pass.

"Well, guess I'll see you again." Alison turned her back on Tiara and walked toward Jayce. She smiled. "Jack and the boys are excited about playing tomorrow. I was hoping you'd give me the honor of at least one dance with you, please? Preferably before I have to bust drunken heads and get all dirty."

Jayce impulsively smiled back, standing to face Alison. "The honor and pleasure, Ali, will be all mine."

"Thank you, ma'am." Alison pulled Jayce in for a hug, which appeared to be an excuse to whisper, "Want me to escort her home?"

Returning the hug, Jayce said, "Thank you, but no." She took a step back and caressed Alison's cheek. "You're the best cop I know. Go do cop things and I'll see you tomorrow." Jayce gave Alison a gentle nudge. "I probably don't have to remind you to bring your appetite?"

"Are you kidding? Hunger's with me twenty-four-seven." Alison nodded to Tiara, who hadn't moved, and said, "Nice to meet you, Ms. Summers." Alison got in her cruiser, turned around, and headed down the driveway, with another wave out the open window.

"She's beautiful, your lady cop friend," Tiara said quietly.

Jayce didn't really want to talk about Alison with Tiara. Tiara, who would be leaving in two days, going back to her more important life, far away from the people who cared for her. "Yes, she is." Mustering every ounce of strength she could, Jayce spun to face Tiara. "Anything else I can do for you?" At Tiara's hurt surprise, Jayce said, "No? Good. I've things to do." Before Tiara could respond, or Jayce give in to the impulse to apologize, she jumped over the porch rail and headed for the barn. Jayce repeatedly whispered, "Be smooth, don't turn around." She managed to do both—until reaching the barn, and closing the door to an empty stall.

Chapter Twenty-four

THE LARGE NUMBER of people to show up at the barbeque astounded Tiara. Apparently, any reason for a get together planned around a huge meal was a good one. She gave up trying to remember everyone Edna and her dad introduced, or who had introduced themselves, to her. Besides, Tiara didn't want to concentrate on people she'd probably never see again. While her head hadn't any difficulty with this conclusion, her heart chastised her for being a fool.

Some of the folks brought in huge grills and smokers on their pickup trucks, for the event. An entire row of barbeque grills was going, each with a different item. The choices were chicken, ribs, steaks, etc., one vegetarian and a tofu meat-lookalike. The tantalizing smell of roasting meat filled the air. Large tables were set edge to edge in front of Jayce's front porch, disposable plastic tablecloths of red and white on top. Huge beach umbrellas were strategically located to shade all areas of the tables and their contents, where metal pans of ice were set for people to place the various pasta salads and other cold food items.

Children of various ages ran around the yard, laughing and playing, teasing siblings and often being reprimanded by a parent for their behavior. Families had brought their own picnic furniture to use, while other wooden tables of various sizes and shapes had been pulled out of pickups and arranged over about half an acre of the front property. Everything had come together in such an orderly fashion that it confounded Tiara.

On Jayce's front porch, the band had set up and played a variety of music, though mostly country tunes. A few people danced in the area where Jayce usually parked her truck. Tiara searched for Jayce and the Sheriff in the same area. She didn't see them and hoped to have a reason to abandon this party before she did.

"Hey, Princess." Her father approached from the left. "Having a good time?"

Tiara knew she couldn't tell him of her desire to hide at home. "Yeah, fine." She pointed to the huge tub of ice and bottled water. "I wanted to get some cold water for Darla. Don't want her overheating herself or the baby."

"That's sweet, honey." He glanced around him. "Quite the turnout."

"Edna and Darla did a good thing, here."

He lightly nudged her in the side. "I like your friends. Too bad you've gotta go home so soon. Edna tells me you'll come back for the wedding so I'm glad to hear that."

Since their talk yesterday, neither Edna nor Tiara revisited the topic of her leaving. To Slim it seemed like a foregone conclusion, too, since he hadn't attempted to change her mind either. A part of her was wounded that everyone had given in so easily. "Just let me know when and I'll be there, Dad."

He kissed her forehead and absently mumbled, "That's great, Tiara, that's great. I'm gonna look for Edna, see if she can spare a moment to dance with me."

"Okay," she said, wondering at his quick dismissal. Tiara expected this reaction from Jayce, even if she didn't entirely understand it, but not from her dad. Shaking her head, hoping to dislodge her confusion and make the most of the barbeque, Tiara grabbed three of the bottled waters from the ice tub, and made her way to the tree where she'd left Mark and Darla sitting in the folding chairs Slim had brought for them. They had a good view of everything. She handed a bottle to each, and twisted the cap off her own. "They're about ready to serve food."

"Thank you, Tiara," Darla said. Mark nodded his thanks.

"No problem. How are you holding up?"

Darla shrugged. "Not bad. I've met quite a few folks, all very sweet. This has been entertaining." Darla reached over and clasped Mark's hand. "After we eat some of that incredible smelling food, I'll probably need to go to the house for a nap, and then do our packing."

A cowbell rang from near the porch and a man with an old-fashioned handlebar mustache hollered, "Come and get it."

Mark kissed the top of Darla's head. "I'll be right back, honey." He glanced at Tiara. "Get you something, Boss Lady?"

She shook her head. "No, Mark. I'll get something in a little bit." Truthfully, she had no appetite.

As soon as Mark walked off, Darla motioned to his now empty chair. "Sit with me for a minute." Tiara did. "I had some of those biscuits you made this morning."

"Yeah." Tiara had forgotten all about them.

"They were wonderful. You had a great teacher." Darla shrugged. "Not that I'm surprised after those incredible cookies." She groaned, held her belly a moment, and blew out a slow breath. "I think the baby's looking forward to chow. So, you want to talk about what happened?"

Tiara wiggled uneasily in her seat. "I wish I knew for sure. Working with Majestic went great, then we're seemingly doing fine in the kitchen. Suddenly, she's telling me—she's talking fences, and not being strong enough. I don't understand where it all came from. We're adults after all, but Jayce has been acting peculiar since the line shack, all hot and cold."

"It's probably a good thing we're leaving tomorrow."

"Uh-huh, I guess."

"You don't seem happy about it anymore. I understood you couldn't wait to get away from here."

"I can't," Tiara said with more conviction than she felt. "I want to get back to my normal life."

"Are you happy with your normal life, Tiara?"

"Just dandy," she said. Tiara had meant to sound upbeat, but heard bitterness instead.

Darla flashed a wry smile. "There are a lot of women like me out there, Tiara, you're bound to encounter them."

Tiara said, "If you mean straight, I have encountered a few."

Sighing wearily, Darla shifted in her chair. "I believe you know what I mean. More women looking to have hearth and home, the fences built to nurture and protect, not trap you inside. From what I've seen of your handsome Jayce, she's just that kind of woman. Maybe she had hoped you were, too."

"Then she *let* herself get misguided." Tiara's temper flared. When had Jayce won Darla over? Gritting her teeth, and lowering her voice, she added, "Since when does a night together mean a person is ready to play house? People have one-night stands all the time. Damn, we're adults. What the hell does she want from me?"

"More than a one-night stand, maybe?"

Tiara stared, dumbfounded, trying to grasp what Darla said. This was ridiculous, hadn't Jayce been the one to use the reference of booty-buddies, accepting of the situation for what it was between them? Then, clear as the cowbell ringing earlier, Tiara realized Jayce had only acquiesced when Tiara started to blow her off. Had Jayce been harboring hopes that she'd stay, leaving behind the life she'd worked so hard to build?

Jayce would always have a special place in Tiara's heart, but she couldn't stay simply because she cared for Jayce, cherished their night together. There were too many factors, too little hope they could make a relationship work.

When Tiara saw Mark was returning, she got up and stared down at Darla. Quietly, she said, "I'm sorry, Darla, but I can't stay here. Jayce will realize it and move on." Tiara watched Mark pass a plate to his wife and take his seat again.

"Are you gonna get some grub, Boss?"

Tiara looked at Darla, "Get some rest," she glanced at Mark, "after the grub."

Weaving between some kids playing tag, Tiara made her way toward the porch, and stopped dead in her tracks. Elmo's massive brother stood next to the barn watching the party, as if looking for someone in particular. Their eyes met and held. She moved in his direction, preparing herself to confront him. He must have realized her intent, because he hastily moved out of sight. By the time she reached the place where he'd been standing, she found no sign of him and suspected he'd escaped to the forested area behind the barn.

Why'd he run? she wondered. Didn't he know her father had explained everything to her? With a shrug, Tiara turned back to the activities just in time to see Sheriff Stewart escort Jayce toward the dance area.

JAYCE ALLOWED ALISON to escort her to the other dancers. "A promise is a promise, Jayce." Alison winked playfully. "And my chores are done." She suspected Alison had finagled a slow dance from Jack and crew as one queued up as soon as they reached the designated dance area.

One arm gently rested at her waist as Alison clasped Jayce's right hand with her own left. Her movements were precise and fluid, proving Alison was a fantastic dancer. Jayce felt comforted by Alison, but she also felt like a fraud. "Ali, I really welcome and enjoy our time together."

Alison smiled down at her, "But you've got a thing for the cute little redhead. Slim's kid."

"Yes, not that anything will come of it." Jayce acknowledged.

"And you know I'd like our friendship taken to the next level. Are you protecting the local law from a broken heart, Jayce?"

Jayce chuckled at Alison's directness, always threaded with warmth and humor. "How's it possible that you've stayed single this long?" She thought she caught a flash of pain cross Alison's face. Once Tiara left, she'd have to spend more time with Alison. Jayce didn't like the idea of her friends concealing heartache when friends were supposed to support each other at these times.

Scowling, Alison said, "If you spout some nonsense about different circumstances, I'll arrest you, Ms. Mansfield."

"Okay," Jayce said, chuckling. More serious, she added, "I couldn't bear it, Ali, if I hurt you because I wasn't honest from the get-go. I've got to get my head on straight."

The music had changed to a fast dance, and Alison led Jayce from the writhing mass. "I understand, Jayce, really. I do." Alison leaned down and kissed her cheek. She smiled, and batted her eyelashes. "You could ease my breaking heart, Jayce."

"What do you have in mind?" Jayce asked with a roll of her eyes.

"Could you get me an autographed picture of Juanita?"

A burst of laughter escaped at the request. "Have I been replaced so quickly? Oh, woe is me."

"Actually, I have a niece, Jennie, visiting next month. She's recently come out, and my sister thought I'd best understand how to cope with her."

"And Sarah's picture will help how?"

"Instead of being cop aunt, I'm the cool aunt who personally knows a famous TV star."

Jayce nodded. "Then it's yours. Did you want to get something to eat?"

"Do you think Edna would mind putting a plate together for me to pick up later? I'm going to drive that old back road and take a look around."

"Sure, I'll take care of it myself, Ali. It'll be in the fridge waiting for you."

"Thanks. I'll come back when things quiet down and check on you." Alison chucked her under the chin. "Hang in there, Jayce. Just because things seem messed up right now, doesn't mean it will always be this way." With that, Alison walked away.

She didn't know how much time had passed while she stood there watching Alison drive off. "Damn." Jayce wondered why she had to go and fall in love with Tiara, when someone as wonderful as Alison was alone.

THE DAY CONTINUED to be wonderful fun. Sarah wished the parties in Hollywood were as enjoyable, rather than the emotionally draining exhibits of people flaunting too much wealth, bad manners passing as eccentricities, and conversations so boring she wondered how she'd never fallen asleep standing up. The most remarkable point being no one expected Juanita to show up. Of course, anyone in the community who knew or remembered Sarah never expected her television persona to make an appearance in the first place. Surprising her most, Craig seemed perfectly happy to spend time with her, plain old Sarah.

Sarah grudgingly admitted she was probably looking on the bright side where Craig was concerned. But she was frightened, expecting his kindness to be a ploy to ingratiate himself to the people who would notice, and share with her later. Was Craig making nice with the hope of using her later?

"Wow, what a scowl you've got going on there." Sarah turned to Jayce. "You okay, sweetie?" Jayce asked, handing her one of the two plates she held.

"Yeah, I'm—" Sarah didn't get to finish.

Craig was suddenly beside her, too. "Damn it," Craig whispered the curse loudly. "I'd hoped to beat all your other admirers."

Noticing he also held two plates, she teased, "Are you hungry, or is the food just that good?"

"Well, when I noticed Jayce making an extra plate, I expected it might be for Tiara. I thought I'd take my chances, as I haven't seen you eat yet, and bring some food to you."

Sarah smiled teasingly. "Are you watching me or stalking me?" she asked. From his expression, she doubted Craig had caught her joking tone. "I'm kidding."

"Okay," Jayce said. "Three's a crowd. Guess I'll take my plate back, and find someone who appreciates my efforts."

"Tiara hasn't eaten," Craig said seriously. "She went into her dad's old barn about ten minutes ago, alone and unfed."

"How many women are you stalking?" Sarah asked. Sputtering something incomprehensible, Craig turned beet-red. "Teasing you, again, Craig." She looked at Jayce. "I think he's right. You should take her the plate."

Jayce rolled her eyes. "Haven't you heard? They're leaving tomorrow?"

"Not all of us," Craig said, when she stared questioningly at him.

Sarah shook her head. "Here's your chance to say good-bye. Tiara could probably use a friend right now."

"Then maybe I should tell Darla," Jayce said, accepting the return of the plate of food. "She seems to have all the right words to soothe Tiara."

"Well, if you're too chicken, we understand," Sarah said. It pained her to bait, Jayce, knowing how deeply she hurt, but a confrontation might be just what Jayce needed to be able to move on.

"Fine," Jayce snapped. "I don't know why no one takes my side." With a glare, Jayce stomped off in the direction of the barn.

"Much as I like having you to myself," Craig said, "Do you think Jayce is safe? Tiara has quite a temper. And Jayce is currently walking wounded."

Sarah realized his concern was genuine. "So does Jayce, Craig. Her temper's just better concealed than most, hidden behind an authentic zest and blessedness for life." The observation seemed to bring him some relief. "Should we eat before the hot food gets cold and the cold food gets warm?"

Sarah now had Craig's undivided attention. "I saw a tree free of squatters, if you'd like go sit for a while."

Craig beamed a smile. "I'd be honored. I even have soda in my pockets."

Once comfortably seated, a few bites taken, Sarah asked, "So what do you honestly think of our neck of the woods, so to speak?" She didn't know why it would be important, but she hoped his impressions were positive. She wanted to ask about why he wasn't departing tomorrow, but couldn't find the strength to bring up a topic that might prove painful to her.

After retrieving the soda bottles from the side pockets of his shorts and handing her one, Craig stared off into the distance. Sarah had just about given up receiving a reply, when Craig finally spoke. "Had you asked me about a week ago, I'd have told you I couldn't wait to get back to the city. Those first couple of nights without street sounds just about had me losing my mind."

"So you miss the noise?"

"Not just that, it felt so isolated out here."

"And now?" Sarah asked, not certain she wanted his response, and not sure why it was important to her that he like Silver Waters.

"I could seriously get used to it," he said. "Your house was an impressive motivator. And, after today, meeting some of the people and being treated and feeling welcomed like I'm part of big family, I don't know why more people don't moving to the country."

"Well, actually, we country folk don't want them. Too many people, and you've only got another city growing too fast for its own good." She sighed, her gaze taking in Jayce's property. "Most people can't appreciate the simpler things in life, the simple beauty that surrounds them. Here we work with nature to preserve the beauty." Sarah turned back to Craig. "That's not to say that even small towns don't have folks wanting to muck it all up. We do. But most folks here are farmers or ranchers, they work the land and the land works with them to keep them alive, an even give and take."

Craig frowned. "Then why do you work in the biggest city of them all?"

"Not everybody can work the land," she explained, smiling. "I thought I needed to get away from small town mentality, but quickly learned how much I missed it. Now, I need to make enough of a nest egg to retire young enough to enjoy it. I'll need to do like Tiara is doing to the *Acres*, fix my parents' place up, modernize a few things, as you noted."

"Your parents left you a remarkable place." Sarah felt the tears build in her eyes, and Craig noticed them. "Hey, I didn't mean to upset you. We can change the subject."

Sarah still missed her parents very much. They'd been in their forties when she came along had been a surprise for them; and, probably to most the town. She had wanted for nothing, as long as she was willing to work for it. Her parents had instilled a proper work ethic into her. One thing she had most of all was the love and affection so many other children don't ever get—like Tiara probably had to do without. Sarah had listened when Jayce and Edna spoke of Tiara over the years. Now that she'd actually spent time with the woman, Sarah better understood Tiara's actions, or lack thereof. "My father passed away soon after I graduated high school and my mother a couple years ago. I've been thinking lately that it's about time to settle down and enjoy it all while I still can. This last visit has reminded me just how much I've missed all this, the people and camaraderie."

Now that Sarah had said it aloud, the prospect of retiring from her career seemed more than just an idle wish. She only had another two years on her contract for the *Deadly Aimes* series. Hollywood only offered more of the same—people taking what they wanted from her and not giving anything but grief back. More guys like Johnny were out there in the world, wanting to use her for their personal social climbing, not caring how their actions hurt her emotionally.

"Well, not that you're old enough to retire," Craig said with raised eyebrows, "but life has a way of sneaking up on us with the unexpected. Who wants to live with regrets?" He leaned back against the tree trunk and crossed his arms over his chest. "And, I gotta tell ya, I'm not getting any younger."

Sarah asked, "You think you'd be one of my regrets?"

Craig gave her a cocky smile. "If you insist on including me, who am I to stop you? I knew you couldn't resist my adorable charms."

"You have quite the opinion of yourself."

"I intrigue you, admit it." Sarah rolled her eyes. He laughed. "You need to renovate your place, I know a wonderful contracting company with this remarkable employee. You need to hire my services before I'm too old to swing a hammer in a way that will impress you."

Sarah couldn't help herself. She stiffened at what his remark implied. "Why would you want to impress me, exactly?"

Craig seemed surprised by her question. "You're hot, lady, why wouldn't I?"

"Is it so I fall for your charms, and you can brag to your friends you know Juanita Juarez or her stunt double?"

The blank stare Craig gave made her nervous, not knowing what he could be thinking. "Not that you'd believe me, but I haven't thought once about Ms. Juarez since seeing you in those coveralls." With surprising speed, Craig pulled her onto his lap, and Sarah didn't resist. His hands cupped the sides of her face, forcing her to look directly into his eyes. "Know this, Sarah Marsh, I will prove it's you and only you that I want, not some vapid television star. I'm offering my labor services when I'm free to make adjustments and renovations to your home."

Craig then attacked Sarah's lips in a kiss so incredible, her toes actually curled.

Chapter Twenty-five

JAYCE FELT THE nervous tightening in her stomach, fearing another confrontation, as she carried the plates of food to the barn, where Craig had told her she'd find Tiara. Every cell in her body wanted her to give up this useless venture; however, she consoled herself somewhat by remembering Tiara would be leaving tomorrow. She vacillated on whether Tiara going was good or bad. Good would come in Jayce's little piece of Silver Waters going back to normal, no more hammering and sawing as renovations were made. Good, with no distractions from a chance meeting of Tiara, with her slightly freckled face and grey eyes, the cute compact body as she stood on a ladder teasing with her adorable behind. Good because Jayce wouldn't feel compelled to entertain Tiara with Danish and coffee, sharing kisses at the sink. Bad would be...well, bad would be almost the same. There would be no glimpses of Tiara, no teasing over breakfast, no supper get-togethers with friends, and no proof of life at *Acres* without the steady rhythm of construction. How could one tiny woman leave such a marked impression and not even know it?

She took a deep breath, hoping to steady her nerves and pasted a false smile on her lips. Jayce walked through the open barn door, and lost her breath all over again.

 Tiara's back—derrière, actually—was pointed toward Jayce as she furiously sanded the leg of a table that stood in the middle of the open room. From the doorway, Jayce figured Tiara was covered in sawdust, if the front matched the back. Tiara wasn't holding power tools, but Jayce still didn't want to startle her unnecessarily. "Tiara."

She jumped anyway, and Jayce wondered what topic held her concentration so strongly. "Jayce?" she asked as though perplexed.

Eyes wide feigning fear, Jayce quickly looked over one shoulder and then the next before nodding to Tiara. "Did I sprout horns? Is that why you're unsure it's me?"

Blushing, Tiara shook her head. "No. I didn't expect to see you is all."

Jayce blew out a loud breath. "Whew, had me worried." She held up both plates in her hands. "I brought you something to eat, suspected you hadn't eaten yet. The food's probably congealed into goop or ready for scientific donation, just a warning. It took a while to get in here."

Tiara raised an eyebrow in question. "Really, why's that?"

"I was outside this door, wrestling with myself on whether I should come in. Since we were an even match, I had to agree to call it a draw before a decision could be made."

With a quick lift of one corner of her mouth, Tiara asked, "Who wanted to come in, you or you?" She had tossed the sandpaper on top of the table, and pulled off the safety goggles, leaving an area around her eyes as the only part of her free of the wood dust. Even her hair was coated with it. Jayce tried not to notice Tiara's beauty, tried to stay put while at the same time wanting to rush to Tiara and brush the dust from her strawberry locks.

Instead, Jayce lightly kicked at the dirt floor, dropping her gaze. "Shucks, ma'am. Since it was a draw, can't we both get points?"

Tiara laughed openly, and nodded. "Yes, points awarded to both. Besides, if we keep this up I'm going to get lost in who is who, or which is which, whatever." Tiara walked to Jayce and took one of the plates. "This all looks good. Thank you, Jayce. It was nice of you to think of me."

"Aw, it weren't nuthin'," Jayce said. She had to bite her lip, then. The easy teasing tone of the conversation had her nearly asking for a kiss as payment. Luckily she stopped herself in time. Jayce wondered if she'd ever figure out—let alone get over—how Tiara brought out the merriment and tomfoolery gene in her. The one thing she liked most about herself was being able to laugh, and Jayce wanted to share all those moments with Tiara. She realized, though, that Tiara wouldn't, or couldn't, feel the same about her. Jayce also needed to remember that tomorrow Tiara would be gone. She needed to reconcile her emotions to that fact.

"Uh-oh," Tiara said, taking a step back. "That introspection couldn't have been good."

Jayce realized her thoughts must've been reflected on her face. She shrugged. "It doesn't matter Red, it's something I have to work out for myself. I won't let it ruin our lunch, and you shouldn't either. I don't want you leaving tomorrow without our achieving some kind of peace." She nodded toward the table Tiara had been working on. "Show me what you're working on?"

"Okay, but let's eat first." Tiara picked up a chicken leg and took a bite, rolling her eyes. "Gosh, I'm hungrier than I thought." Nodding to one of the open stalls on the side, Tiara made her way over and sat down on the floor.

Jayce followed her, removing plastic forks and napkins from her back jeans pocket, which she handed over, before sitting and facing Tiara. "The one thing a body can count on, in Silver Waters, is folks know how to barbeque." For a while, they both ate in silence, Jayce not wanting to jinx the moment.

"So, is this the table Aunt Edna wanted us to make for our challenge?"

Tiara nodded. "I didn't want to—to—"

"Leave. You can say the word. We both know it's inevitable."

"I'm sorry, Jayce."

"Nah, we both know that's not entirely true. If you were regretful, you wouldn't go." Jayce smiled wryly. "This is something you need to do, what's right for you. Just because it doesn't suit my wants, doesn't make it wrong." Jayce noted the tears building in Tiara's eyes, but not yet falling.

With the food completely consumed and needing a change of subject, Jayce leaned back and her hand was promptly swallowed by the barn floor. A stinging pain bit into her palm. She jerked her hand free seeing wood splinters imbedded in her flesh.

Dropping her plate, Tiara got to her knees and yanked Jayce's injured hand onto her lap. "Bet this smarts," Tiara said, pulling a Swiss army knife from her pocket and freeing the mini-tweezers. With deliberate care, Tiara removed the splinters lodged in the skin. "I'm sorry if this hurts," Tiara said without making eye contact. Most of the wood pieces were large enough to be removed easily and quickly; the rest took only a couple minutes. "Okay, stay right there," Tiara ordered. She jumped up and went to a gym bag tossed near the door, rifled around and came back with a small first aid kit. Tiara removed an aerosol container and sprayed Jayce's torn flesh.

"Yeow," Jayce squealed. "I didn't take you for a sadist, but I'm being swayed in my opinion."

Laughing, Tiara said, "Quit being a big baby, and butch up." She applied an ointment and released her hand. "There, now it shouldn't get infected, and will start feeling better soon."

"Thanks, Doc," Jayce said, turning to see what she'd fallen into. Pushing away the straw with her undamaged hand, and careful not to incur any more splinters, Jayce found a small hidey-hole with something wrapped in rawhide. She pulled it free and held it between them. Tiara paled. "You know what this is?"

"Yeah, I think so." Tiara sucked in a breath. "I think you should just leave it where you found it."

Jayce stared at the myriad emotions flicking across Tiara's face. She considered replacing the bundle, almost. Despite the discomfort, Jayce figured Tiara needed to face whatever it represented. "Maybe it's best we don't leave it. Does this contain something to bring you heartache or closure?"

"A lot of both," Tiara shifted away from her.

Tenderly, Jayce grasped an end of the rawhide, tugging upward and allowing the bundle to roll open. One by one the wooden carvings, similar to the one Tiara had given to her a decade ago, fell free into her palm. Jayce examined them individually, before placing them in a row in beside her. "Wow, these are remarkable. But I would never have believed otherwise after the incredible detailed work on my horse."

Jayce got to her feet and walked to the table. Studying the detail Tiara had carved into the trim she'd added to the table, Jayce ran her fingertips over the small swirls and grooves. "Tiara, your work is remarkable. Have you considered concentrating on handmade furniture?" Jayce immediately realized that might have sounded critical to Tiara. "Red, your construction work is great and I'm not bashing you or your capability, honest. But, really, the intricate design, the structure of your work, is fantastic. I know people who would pay a small fortune for furniture like you create."

A blush flared across Tiara's cheeks and she shook her head. "You're a little prejudiced because you've stared at your carving for so long."

Jayce sighed. "I stick by my assessment. You're entitled to your own opinion of your capabilities on this matter, but I see more potential in you than you do."

Tiara shrugged. "I appreciate it, but I think the popularity of Summers Construction speaks otherwise, so I think I'll stick with what I'm doing."

"Hence, going back to that life tomorrow. Point taken." Jayce made one more pass of her hand over the table's top. "Guess I should get back to Aunt Edna and the barbeque."

"Jayce—"

"No, Tiara." Jayce bent down and touched the carvings lovingly, as a lone tear fell. "I just need to say, before I go, that I understand your need to leave." She inspected Tiara's face for signs that she would run before Jayce spoke her piece. "*Meadows* will never be the same without you, and neither will I. I also know our night together didn't mean the same to you as it did me. Please, be safe in whatever you do, whatever life throws at you." Jayce dropped her gaze, unable to handle any emotional expression Tiara's face might expose. "I realize I look at you and only see the happy home we could build and share together, and that you don't share that vision for the future. I love you, Tiara, I always have and I always will. But I also accept that it's time to let you go. Time for me to move on. I need to cut the ties to those memories and feelings."

Standing, pulling Tiara up with her, she said, "However, there is something I have to do one last time." Jayce leaned in and kissed Tiara's neck in a slow sweep of her lips, delighted when she felt Tiara shiver, and then she claimed the parted lips before her. Gently placing a hand to the nape of Tiara's neck, Jayce forced the kiss longer, deeper. Their mouths melded, tongues swirled and caressed. Tiara tasted delicious, sweet like honey. When she groaned into Jayce's mouth, she fueled the fire growing hotter at Jayce's core, the sensation nearly reaching incendiary proportions.

Tiara pulled back, breaking the seal of their lips. "Jayce," she whispered hoarsely.

"Shush." Jayce placed a finger gently to Tiara's lips. "Good-bye, love." Before she could respond to the impulse to finish what she started, Jayce strode quickly from the barn, and into the fresh open air, sucking in great gulps to get herself under control.

"Damn, Tiara, why do I love you so much?"
No answer came.

Chapter Twenty-six

TIARA HAD FINISHED packing, leaving out the clothes she'd wear the next day, and placed all the other stuff she'd acquired in the truck. She'd gone through her bedroom, making sure she hadn't forgotten anything. At the dresser, Tiara placed her hand on the rawhide bundle Jayce had left in the barn. Tiara couldn't bring herself to dump the carvings back into the hidey-hole, not after Jayce had been so impressed. A smile appeared as she realized the strange enchantment of the wooden carvings. Both times that she and Jayce had been in the old barn with the carvings present, Jayce had given her a mind blowing kiss, only to leave her standing stunned and alone.

Also, both times Jayce had seen the craftsmanship and been impressed, her enthusiasm and praise caressing Tiara's heart—even if she didn't entirely believe the compliments. So why *couldn't* she take Jayce's appreciation and approval at face value?

She hadn't lied to Jayce. Tiara was very good at what she did. Her business thrived. Would her life have been different if she had chosen the path Jayce had mentioned? If she had been allowed to stay in Silver Waters, probably so, but Tiara hadn't been allowed that option and so life was different. Why couldn't her father and Jayce understand that she'd made her life elsewhere? She couldn't pretend it didn't exist, couldn't pick up everything and move it to Silver Waters. She'd have to give up what she'd worked so hard to obtain, and for what? Something that might fail? No. No matter how much she'd miss Jayce, Edna and her father, she couldn't stay. Her job and her life weren't in Silver Waters.

A knock sounded behind her. Tiara turned to see an exhausted-looking Darla leaning against the door jamb. "May I come in?" Darla asked.

"Of course." Tiara waved toward the bed. "Sit down before you collapse. Are you okay? Can I get you anything?" she asked, genuinely concerned by the strain in Darla's features. She sat beside Darla. "Do you need to nap? I don't want to be rude, but you don't look so good."

Darla patted her thigh. "I'm all right, really. I wanted to talk before we head back."

Tiara read between the lines. "Before things go back to the way they were, you mean?"

"No," Darla said, too quickly. Tiara raised an eyebrow. "Okay, maybe I intended that a little. But not because I'm critical, Tiara, more because it will be easier for you to fall back on what was comfortable."

"No offense taken. Any other time, that would probably be the case. However, you've been good to me when I didn't make it easy on you, and I've really enjoyed this past couple of weeks." Tiara feigned a scowl. "Even if I didn't enjoy hearing all you had to impart."

"I'll give you that," Darla said. "And I'm going to add to it. I've a few things I think you need to consider, because disregarding them isn't in your best interest. You've come too far." Darla shifted, whether trying to find a more comfortable position, or to prepare herself for an uncomfortable conversation, Tiara wasn't sure.

"You're a great person, and I have to admit, Jayce is fantastic. I know you two had a falling out, but I can see that she loves you. So, I want you to consider staying in touch with her. I know she wants you to stay in Silver Waters, and that you're unable to do that. But, Jayce is someone who'll be there for you if you let her. Why would you turn away from a friend who would do anything for you? Plus, now you're on speaking terms with Slim and Edna. I want to give you sage advice. You have to settle for good intentions."

"I understand. I do. I just don't know if that's possible." Tiara got up and walked to the window, keeping her back to Darla in case she couldn't control her emotions, not wanting her face to reflect her conflict. "You see, Jayce is the settle-down-play-house-type and she'll be wonderful at that, but I can't give her want she wants. She needs someone who can. Maybe the sheriff is that person."

"You can't or you're afraid to?" Darla asked quietly.

"Both. Just because I know people with happy marital relationships doesn't mean I'm capable of having one myself. The two of us together are like oil and water. Earlier, Jayce told me she was letting me go, moving on, making any argument moot." This time she faced Darla. "And what no one seems to understand is that I have a business to run, and it's not here."

"They understand. Maybe they were hoping you'd compromise somehow." Sighing heavily, Darla started to get up, groaning as she did so. "Gosh, I'm more tired than I thought. I should leave you to your packing."

"Actually, I'm finished. Why don't you take your nap here?" Tiara pointed to the bathroom. "And the conveniences are closer."

Darla giggled tiredly. "That's how you win an argument. Thank you, Tiara, I appreciate it." She returned to the bed, but looked once more at Tiara. "Are you okay?"

Tiara walked to where Darla sat, and hugged her. "Yes, thank you. Get some sleep. I'll be in the barn finishing the entry table for Edna. I'll keep my cell close in case you need me."

"Will the cell be on?"

Tiara pulled the phone from her pocket. "Yes. Want to check?" Darla shook her head. "Okay, then. Sleep tight."

Darla said, "See, there's a note of domesticity in you after all."

Chuckling, Tiara said, "Wow, you don't give up easily, do you?"

"Where's the fun in that?"

"I'm going now. Lie down and rest." Tiara closed the door and went to the barn, with her thoughts swirling in her head.

WHEN PETER REALIZED the people in the house were packing to leave, he panicked. The lady next door kept moving Majestic, riding and training, putting the horse in a different place each night. He guessed he'd have more time to find him if Slim's daughter left, but what if she took Majestic with her? Then how was he to help Elmo? He knew he had to do something, but he didn't know what he could do.

The party was over, and people were leaving. Maybe he should have talked to her when she saw him, but he got scared and ran into the woods, to the place he found hidden there. He liked the little house, but the mannequin kept staring at him. He didn't like that at all, he didn't do anything wrong. He was trying to do something right.

Maybe he could go to the house and talk to Slim's daughter, make her understand that if Elmo said the horse was his she shouldn't treat him like a liar. Elmo was a good man, a good brother. Peter shook his head. No, that wouldn't work. She would think her father was good, too. "Damn, Elmo, I'm trying. Why can't I think so good?" He rubbed his hands over his face. "What would you do?"

Peter realized someone had come into the barn. From his hiding place in the loft, Peter saw the daughter opening a can, stirring the contents, and then grabbing a brush. She painted the table. Now he couldn't leave until she was finished. How long would that be? Peter knew he had to be really quiet because he didn't want anyone to know he was there. Carefully, he scooted away from the edge, sat up, and pounded the knuckles of his fist against his head.

Think.

He needed to get away.

Think. Think.

Peter needed to get her away.

Yeah. Talk to her; make her see Elmo was right. Majestic was Elmo's. But if she got scared and screamed, the other people would come out and not let him explain.

Think. Think. Think.

He needed to talk to her without anybody around. Maybe take her to the little house, away from interruptions. That's what he would do. If he was real quiet, he could climb down, get behind her, and carry her off. Once they were alone, Peter could make her see. He could help his brother by doing something right.

He climbed down from the loft, carefully. A black gym bag sat about four feet from the ladder. Peter edged over, rummaged through the items, and found a roll of grey duct tape. Perfect. Then he snuck up behind her.

Peter wrapped one arm around her, successfully pinning her arms at her sides, the can and brush splashing with a *thunk*. She tried to scream, but he stopped it by fastening a strip of the tape across her mouth. That got her really mad. She struggled, even managed to kick him hard a few times.

"You stop that, now," he said into her ear. Peter grasped both her arms, shook her roughly until she moaned and weakened enough to tape her hands behind her back.

She struggled harder, her face turning bright red and nostrils flaring with her exertion, yet Peter held tight. The contents of the can bathed them both with sticky splatters, but Peter ignored the strange feeling, tossed her over his shoulder, and carried her out the barn and into the woods. After about half a mile, she had stopped struggling, so Peter stopped for a little rest, careful to place her against a tree.

Tears fell down her face, and he felt cruel. He hadn't meant to upset her. "I won't hurt you," Peter told her. She stared at him. "We'll talk. Once you understand, I'll let you go."

Growling sounded from her throat, as she struggled to stand.

"Where are you trying to go?" Peter watched the determination on her features. Then he understood what he hadn't thought of before now. "You don't want to talk about Majestic, do you? Maybe I should have your friend bring him to me." He nodded, a change to his plan forming. "You're stubborn, so a trade is all you'll accept. I'll have to go try something else."

Satisfied with himself, Peter picked her up again and continued the trek to the cabin in the woods.

Chapter Twenty-seven

THE LAST OF the party stragglers were rounded up, sent home, and the yard cleaned up. Night fell quickly, and Jayce wanted to take a shower and fall into bed. As she topped the porch, she noticed paper taped to the screen door, and read:

```
I have Slim's daughter. Bring Majestic to the
cabin in the woods. We'll trade. Come alone or I hurt
her.
```

Jayce felt sick to her stomach, the tears building in her panic. She started to rip the note down, but left it for Edna to find. Jayce only hoped her aunt would be able to get hold of Slim so he could prevent anything from happening to Tiara. Jayce knew in her gut Slim was involved in the Majestic affair. Part of her understood, and appreciated, the desire to entice Tiara to come home. However, if harm came to her because of this sham, Jayce knew Red would never return no matter the occasion.

Her greatest desire had always been that Tiara would miss Silver Waters, and want to remain permanently. Now, she knew that wasn't the case. Jayce still held out hope they had managed to reach a level of friendship such that Tiara would come back, if only for a little while. If she came to harm, Tiara would never return. Although, that may ultimately have been for the best, since Jayce had no idea how she could move on with Tiara in the picture. Damn, how did she get into this predicament? One issue at a time, she chided herself. First, Jayce need to get Tiara released.

At a full run, Jayce crossed her property heading to the back acreage where she had left Charlie to work with Majestic in the training ring. If she had left the horse in his own corral, would Tiara be safe at home, packing to leave? Was it her fault that Elmo and Tank had Tiara? She hoped this wasn't as it appeared. Jayce wanted to find Tiara having coffee with Slim and the goons, so they could all have a good laugh—after she strangled Slim for scaring her so badly. Unfortunately, her fear about to suffocate her, Jayce worried she'd miss an important clue and bring further harm to Tiara. "Focus, Jayce, focus."

After moments of strenuous running, Jayce had arrived at the corral, and waved for Charlie's attention. He responded to her urgency and jogged Majestic toward her, yanking the corral gate open as she got there. Frowning, he asked, "What's wrong?"

If Jayce had more time, she would've explained. Instead, she said, "I need to take Majestic. You should go back to the house, wait for Edna in case she needs you."

"What about the goose?" Charlie asked.

"Take him back with you." She grabbed the reins when he dismounted.

Charlie shook his head. "No way, that thing—he's dangerous."

She stepped up into the saddle. "Fine, leave him here, we'll deal with him later," Jayce said, nudging Majestic into the woods. Jayce hoped the reference in the note to the cabin was in fact the line shack. She hadn't toured the property acreage in so long, and so soon after Alison mentioning a stranger in the woods, Jayce hoped some squatter hadn't built a structure she'd never locate in time.

Jayce wanted to set Majestic to full gallop, but couldn't take the chance of a misstep, which could injure her only means of getting to Tiara in time. Majestic must have perceived her anxiety, responding by snuffing and striding faster than she'd urged him safely to proceed. She rubbed his neck in gratitude.

As she made her way through the woods, staying away from the paths worn by her truck and buckboard, Jayce tried to formulate a plan to get Tiara away from the Sparretti brothers. Her gut told her handing over Majestic wasn't going to be an option for finalizing the trade.

What confused her was the real reason behind this charade. Slim had purchased Majestic from the horse's owner. Elmo and crew were hired by Slim to encourage Tiara to ask for Jayce's help, and Slim would come in to save the day. So, why did they want the horse still? If Slim hadn't paid them enough, she would gladly pay any price they demanded.

What about poor Tiara? What was she thinking, feeling, going through? Had they hurt her? Jayce's stomach roiled at the thought of someone harming Tiara. Was she afraid? Stop it, her head screamed, and focus. Tiara's fine.

Jayce had to get close enough to the line shack so she could see what was happening inside. She didn't want to spark any negative responses from the Sparretti goons. She'd have to tie Majestic up and get closer on foot, so they wouldn't know how close their prize stood.

Off to the far right, a light shone through the trees. To the left Jayce saw the main road and realized she was close to the line shack. Backtracking about a hundred feet, Jayce dismounted, wrapped the reins around the limb of a fallen tree, and stepped in close to Majestic. "Okay, boy, I'm going over to take a look. You wait here and stay quiet. I'll be back in just a minute."

She couldn't guarantee he'd be able to stay silent, but Jayce figured he wasn't going anywhere without her. "Here goes nothing, big guy," she whispered. With as much stealth as she could muster, Jayce made her way toward the line shack.

TIARA GRIMACED AT the throbbing pain in her wrists. The damaged flesh resulted from her continued wiggling and yanking to free her hands from the duct tape binding her wrists behind her back. Her captor—Tank, as Jayce originally referred to him—stoically guarded the entrance from the chair he'd placed beside the door. The only positive action was he'd removed the tape from her mouth. The skin stung, then settled into an uncomfortable itch she wasn't able to scratch.

She couldn't believe this was happening. Hadn't Slim told her the whole gangster thing was part of a ploy created to get her to Silver Waters? Tiara couldn't believe Slim had planned or anticipated this part. He'd also assured her he had purchased Majestic honestly. So why had the little gangster sent his henchman to kidnap her? First, to allegedly talk, then as part of an exchange. She'd been horrified to hear Tank tell her he'd left a note at Edna's house.

What distressed her more than her raw flesh, was the knowledge that at any moment Jayce would come to the line shack to rescue her. That fact Tiara didn't doubt for a moment. Jayce had declared her love, even knowing Tiara had no intention of staying. And she knew Jayce well enough to realize she never let her friends down.

"Do you have a name?" she asked, tired of only their breathing in the room. "In case you don't remember, I'm Tiara."

"Everyone has a name."

"Okay, yours would be?" Tiara asked.

"Huh?" He stood as if suddenly remembering something. "My name is Peter, Peter Sparretti. Please to meet you." He bowed, extended a hand, and then looked at his hand strangely. "Guess we can't shake yet."

"Are you kidding me?" Tiara wondered how someone could keep a straight face while being so patently sarcastic.

"No, I'm really Peter."

Great, she thought, he must be trying to tick her off before stealing her father's horse. "Got it. Peter. Want to tell me why you think you deserve Majestic more than Slim does?"

His brow furrowed. "I don't know about deserving, but I'm supposed to help Elmo, that's what brothers do. He's never let me work with him before. I can't let him down."

Tiara was puzzled. Something about this wasn't right, something about Peter wasn't connecting, either, at least not with Slim told her. "Peter, what does your brother do?"

With a shrug, he said, "I dunno. He usually leaves me home, having Mrs. Dreyer check up on me. In case I need something." Peter grinned. "We don't tell Elmo she lets me drink beer sometimes, and eat delivery pizza."

Okay, maybe she'd figure out the puzzle after all. "This is the first time you've been allowed to tag along?" Peter nodded. "Did he tell you what to do and say the day you drove to my house?" Another nod. "What did he say, Peter?"

Peter looked excited about his part. "Elmo told me the words to say, and to act like the people in the *Sopranos*. He said Slim stole a horse he'd bought, and he had people to help him get Majestic back."

"You were acting?"

He sat straighter in his chair, thrilled to explain. "Yeah, and when *Deadly Aimes* rode up, I knew Elmo was right, someone to help. She always helps people on TV. Only you still didn't give us Majestic."

So Peter recognized Sarah from television. From what Tiara figured, Peter couldn't quite separate fact from fiction, not that all people could, but she realized Peter may be slow. Mentally challenged, she corrected herself. Well, that would change the dynamics of rationalizing. How do you reason with a tank of a man who had the intellect of a small child? Honesty?

"Peter, Elmo was acting. He was helping my dad." She watched closely for a reaction. His face appeared neutral, but it could be his way of analyzing.

After what seemed like forever, Peter shook his head. "No. That would mean Elmo lied to me. My brother's never lied to me." Peter scowled and jumped from the chair. "You are the one lying. Are you trying to make me mad at Elmo?"

Involuntarily, Tiara cringed at the anger in his voice. Please don't let him hit me, she begged silently. Then motion at the window caught her attention. Jayce? Crap. She had to calm Peter down before Jayce got all gung-ho on her behalf, and got herself killed. Was there any way to get rid of Peter, recommend a walk to cool off? "Relax, Peter. I'm just trying to understand. I don't know Elmo well enough, so I can't accuse him of being a liar, can I?"

He appeared to give her words thought, calming enough to return to the chair. Only now, he kept shaking one leg. Tiara took a stab at the reason, remembering what Jayce had told her about the line shack. "Peter, do you have to go to the bathroom?"

Peter looked at her guiltily, and nodded. "But I shouldn't leave you in here alone. I don't want anything to happen to you while I'm gone."

Relief flooded through her. Tiara tilted her head toward the mannequin. "There's a toilet in the wall behind him. Just push on it a little. It's not like I'm going anywhere." Peter appeared to be judging her honesty. "If you think you can hold it..."

Like a little boy, he frowned at implying him chicken. "Okay. Wait here."

Yeah, where would she go all trussed up?

No sooner had Peter disappeared into the bathroom, then Jayce silently pushed the cabin door open. Leaving it ajar she rushed to Tiara's side. Tiara smiled with relief, happy to see Jayce despite the circumstances. Jayce's gaze fell to Tiara's mouth and she drew in a sharp breath, her fingertips carefully accessing the damage. Her expression darkened. "I'll have you free in a minute, Red," Jayce vowed, tugging at the duct tape.

"You should leave. He'll be done soon." Tiara's gaze darted toward the wall. "He's not going to hurt me, Jayce. Bring Elmo and Slim here."

Horrified, Jayce stared at her. "No way in hell I'm leaving you here, like this."

"You don't understand—" Just then, the dreadful goose appeared in the doorway and honked loudly.

"No," Peter bellowed as he launched his bulk through the opening.

Clearly startled, then immediately defensive, Jayce stood between Tiara and Peter. "You asshole, you'll pay for hurting her," Jayce vowed before slamming a right fist into his jaw.

Peter barely flinched, but Tiara watched painfully when his body, reacting instinctively, threw a right hook of his own. Horrified, Tiara watched helplessly as the huge fist smashed into the side of Jayce's face, propelling her over the table, the lantern tottering but not falling, and Jayce's head slamming into the bunk. Jayce slid lifelessly to the floor. Tiara saw the blood flowing.

"Jayce," she screamed, oblivious to all else around her.

SLIM'S PACING QUICKENED with each tick of the second hand on the clock. For the hundredth time, he glared at the passing time. Occasionally he'd stare helplessly toward Edna. Finally, the knock on the bunkhouse door spurred him into action. Pulling the door open, grabbing Elmo by the lapels, Slim demanded, "What has your brother done to my daughter, Sparretti?"

Elmo's face contorted. "Honest, I had no idea Peter would ever act on his own." Slim released him with a less than gentle shove, only slightly aware of Elmo's gasp for air. "He's never tried anything like this. I can't imagine what's going on in his head."

"That's what you're supposed to be able to tell us, so I can get Tiara." Slim growled. "You're the one who included him in this debacle. You should've been able to oversee your own damn part." He stalked to the coffee table and picked up the slip of paper and thrust it under Elmo's nose. "And, what the hell, Mo? 'Or I'll hurt her'? Peter wrote cabin in the woods like this is some friggin' horror movie."

"Come on, Slim. You know Peter would never make those mental bridges."

Barking derisive laughter, Slim shook his head. "No, Mo, last week I may have believed that, but today he's threatening Tiara, over a horse that was never really yours."

"Stop it, both of you," Edna yelled. "We'll play the blame game later. Right now we have to get to them, because if I know my niece, and I most certainly do, Jayce *will* get hurt trying to save Tiara, whether she's in real danger or not."

"Okay, honey," Slim said, cowed. Inhaling a deep breath to calm himself, he walked over to Edna and hugged her. "Do you know where in the woods this cabin could be? I certainly can't remember any."

"Um, if it has four walls and is bigger than a shoe box," Elmo said, "Peter will call it a house. In this case, cabin, so that's what you're working with. Don't confine yourselves to standard meanings."

Shaking her head, Edna cried. Slim felt horrible, knowing Edna loved both women with her whole heart. He rubbed his hand up and down her back. Then she jerked out of his grasp. "The line shack, it's the only type of building that far from the house."

"Great, honey, let's go," Slim said, grabbing his keys, then Edna's hand. Outside, he tugged Edna toward his jeep, noting how dark it had become. Elmo, Slim noted, just a step behind them, pulled himself into the back seat. With a glance in Edna's direction as he started the jeep, he said, "You better call Alison and let her know what's going on. Just in case," he added, praying it was an excessive precaution.

"I should call Darla, too," Edna whispered. "She's already worried sick."

"Do we have to get so many people involved?" Elmo asked fussily.

"Shut up, Mo," Slim and Edna demanded simultaneously. Sharing a reassuring glance with each other, they clasped hands and squeezed tenderly.

"Let's go save our girls."

Chapter Twenty-eight

"PLEASE, BABY, TALK to me," Tiara begged, unable to control the alarm in her voice. No, no, no, Jayce, I can't lose you like this. She leaned atop Jayce, a wet cloth pressed to the cut on Jayce's forehead. Tiara had ordered her release the second Jayce had hit the floor, and Peter responded with more speed than expected for a man his size. The terror on Peter's face let her know he hadn't meant to hit Jayce back, and he felt shame for what he'd done. Right now, he sat in the chair by the door clutching the goose to his massive chest with all his might. Reluctant at first, the goose didn't appear to mind anymore.

"Can't," Jayce replied with a croak, eyes still closed.

Tiara felt panic. "Is it too painful to speak? Can you open your eyes for me, please?"

"Is Tank still here?" Jayce asked with a snarl.

Tiara nodded until she realized Jayce couldn't see her. "Yes, why?"

"Come closer," Jayce whispered. Tiara pressed herself almost flush against her, shifting so her ear was close to Jayce's lips. She felt the sharp intake of breath before Jayce whispered, "Because you feel too good, I don't want to open my eyes and realize I'm dreaming. And I don't want Tank to know how turned on I am."

Relief flooded Tiara. Under different circumstance, she might have been angry with Jayce for scaring her, but when Jayce's hand gently touched her waist, Tiara realized Jayce was reassuring through teasing. Well, two could play at that game. Tiara swiveled her head slightly so her lips were close to Jayce's ear. "Not that I like seeing you bleed, but I'm turned on too, Galahad." Tiara nipped the earlobe, rewarded with a groan; this one announced a different kind of discomfort from Jayce. This would also provide an opportunity to alert Jayce to Peter's mental circumstance. "Jayce, honey, Peter is a little slow. Some things he isn't going to notice because he doesn't know what to look for." Tenderly, she placed a kiss just below Jayce's lobe, then to her temple. Raising herself off Jayce, and cupping a hand to her cheek, she said, "You're wound is starting to bruise so you can't lie about the pain, but I do have the bleeding under control. I need you to open your eyes and sit up so I can assess the damage."

Tiara recognized the flash of pain crossing Jayce's face as her eyes fluttered open, they squinted against the glare of the soft lantern light. She tried to guide Jayce to a leaning position against the bunk. Jayce gritted her teeth and Tiara understood that she was in a great deal of pain, but didn't want to acknowledge or draw attention to it. When Jayce's face suddenly paled, Tiara jumped to her feet, rushed to the fireplace and upended the metal tub to remove the firewood. She returned to Jayce's side just in time to place a hand to Jayce's brow. Tiara crooned, "It's okay, I've got you," as Jayce vomited.

"She gonna be okay?" Peter quietly inquired from the chair. His face was looking a little green, too.

"Peter, maybe you should wait outside, in the fresh air." It dawned on Tiara that Majestic had to be nearby if the goose was here. "Jayce, where is Majestic?"

"A little walk that way from the shack." Jayce indicated the direction as behind her. Tiara stood up and glanced out the window, but it was too dark to see. She turned toward Peter and directed him to where he'd find Majestic. "Bring him over here, and put him in the stall at the side. Can you do that for me?" He nodded. "Good, Peter. I'm going to fix Jayce's head, and then we can go back to the ranch, okay?" One more nod and Peter was off to do as he'd been told. Tiara rummaged through the trunk for the first-aid kit.

While Tiara bandaged the gash, certain it would need stitches, Jayce asked, "You think he'll run?"

"No, he feels ashamed for what he's done to you." She sat back to assess her work. It looked like the bandage would hold until they could get her to real medical help.

"Yeah, I'm a little ashamed of what he did to me, too," Jayce said. "Guess I have to give up my hero card." Tiara realized from Jayce's expression, she was truly embarrassed about what had transpired. Did Jayce really believe she could go against a man the size of Peter and not get the worst of it?

Giggling, Tiara told her, "Just the butch card, sweetheart." The shocked that crossed Jayce's face was adorable, for the second it took for her to realize Tiara was messing with her. Tiara placed a quick kiss to Jayce's lips. Tiara's body responded immediately, and she would have pressed further if Peter hadn't walked in.

"He's in the stall, Tiara. I put the goose with him."

"Thank you, Peter." Tiara gathered up the bandage wrapper, stuffing everything else back into the little plastic first-aid container. Then she hefted the tub and took it into the bathroom, dumping the contents down the toilet and flushing. There was no way she could rinse it in the tiny sink, so she took it outside and placed it upside down at the side of the shack. Wearily, Tiara leaned against the wall.

Her stomach was in knots from the little kiss. Tiara knew her anxiety had started the instant she determined Jayce would come for her. Seeing the tall muscular woman flung unconscious across the room like a rag doll had nearly seized her heart. Then, the blood... Tiara shuddered, barely able to contain the tears of distress. Damn, one stupid misunderstanding from a plan her father had set into motion and her whole life was off kilter. Jayce could have been killed. She felt the tears fall. What would she have done then? How could she have lived with herself knowing Jayce would never give one of those mischievous smiles? Or looked at her tenderly with those beautiful blue eyes?

"Tiara!" Peter hollered from the shack in what sounded like pure panic.

"Coming." She wiped at the tears as she rushed to the door. Peter nervously danced from foot to foot focused toward the bunk. Jayce had gotten to her feet, and was currently swaying as if she'd pass out again. Even as Tiara entered the room, Jayce attempted to walk. "Grab her," she ordered Peter, as she rushed to Jayce's side. Peter latched on and supported Jayce against his right side. Glaring into Jayce's pale face, Tiara demanded, "What the hell are you thinking?"

Jayce's voice was strained as she answered, "You took too long. I got worried something happened." Her breathing sounded labored. "Can we go home? I'm tired and don't feel so good."

Peter offered, "I'll get someone, and bring them back."

"No, Peter," Tiara said, "they might not listen immediately. We have to get Jayce help soon." She gazed into Jayce's pain filled eyes. "You need to stay here, honey, I'll go get help," Tiara said.

Jayce shook her head, and then groaned. "I don't like you going out alone. But I have to agree about Peter not going. Damn, I can't think straight."

Despite her fear, Tiara tried to reassure Jayce, which would ultimately comfort Peter. "You never did think *straight* as long as I remember."

With a snort, Jayce said, "Cute, Red. What else do you suggest? Just know that I'm not sitting here no matter what the plan is."

Tiara bit at her lip trying to formulate a plan surprised when Peter made a suggestion. "Majestic will take Tiara home. I could carry Jayce until you find us."

"That's a good idea, Peter," Tiara acknowledged before realizing the full implication of the proposed resolution. "Um, I don't know how to ride." She didn't add that the very idea scared her witless. "Why don't we let Jayce ride and we'll walk back."

"I don't know if I can hold on to the reins, Tiara," Jayce said. Her voice sounded weaker, and Tiara figured that if Jayce stood on her own accord, her legs would buckle beneath her. The full impact of the situation hit Tiara. Jayce was in bad shape and needed help urgently, and it was up to Tiara to make that happen.

Trying to remember anything she could about concussions, Tiara recalled minor things like dizziness, nausea, and that the person wasn't supposed to fall asleep. Walking, or being carried, would help keep Jayce awake. Tiara also suspected that the thought of Peter carrying her would help keep Jayce alert. Did people die from concussions? Hell, yes. A fresh flood of dread coursed through her.

"Okay, everyone outside." As Peter cradled Jayce, helping her walk, Tiara grabbed the lantern, hoping it had enough fuel to keep it lit for a while longer. Jayce and Peter stood by the stall, the reins clutched in Jayce's trembling hand. "Which direction is *Meadows*?" she asked.

"Majestic will know," Jayce told her. "But go slow. It's dark and I couldn't live with either of you getting hurt. Peter and I will follow the road," she pointed toward the rough trail leading up the hill. "Anyone you find at the house will know it. We'll all meet up in a little while, okay?"

"Okay." Tiara felt anything but okay. She thought Jayce looked weaker. Tiara squeezed Jayce's hand gently as she took the reins. She hoped she'd conveyed her concern. "Be back with the Calvary before you make it the road."

"I'll hold you to that, Red," Jayce said. "Help the lady up, Tank." Peter seemed conflicted, knowing Jayce required his support.

"I've got this," Tiara announced, tension twisting her gut. Ignoring fear, she shoved the lantern in Peter's hand. Tiara placed her foot in the stirrup, grabbed the saddle horn and pulled herself into the saddle. Majestic gave her no trouble, true to his name he stood regally and still until she was settled. She adjusted the reins comfortably. The goose stood to the side of Majestic waiting for the procession to begin. With one last glance at Jayce, Tiara tapped Majestic with her heels. "Be back in a sec," she said, leaving a wounded Jayce with her attacker, even if he was relatively harmless. "Please don't let leaving her be a mistake," she begged of the darkness.

"UP WE GO, Tank," Jayce said, though walking was the last thing she wanted to do now. Her head pounded as if stampeding horses had used it as a crossing. Her vision blurred so she could barely make out Tiara being carried away by Majestic, the ridiculous goose trailing alongside. Peter pressed against her—or was it the other way around—and he was solid as a concrete structure.

Without missing a beat, or a step, Peter asked, "Why do you call me Tank?"

Jayce snorted. "Because, my friend, you're as sturdy and powerful as a tank. Gotta tell you, I didn't mean it to be nice when I first used it, but I'm glad now."

"Am I?" he asked.

She didn't know what he was asking, and decided to tell him so. "My head is throbbing, so I don't know what you're asking?"

Peter seemed uncomfortable having to explain. "Am I your friend? I'm the reason you're hurt, so are you not being nice again?"

Wow. How do you answer that with the guy who could remove you permanently from this world with a single punch? What the hell? She hadn't the strength to put up a fight even if she wanted to. She was angry with him for kidnapping Tiara, pissed that he'd hit her so hard, but like so many people doing what they thought was right, Peter believed he was helping his brother. No, if she were to blame anyone, it would—and will, next she saw him—be Slim. With the information Tiara provided, Jayce couldn't truly blame Peter for any of this debacle. And, he seemed genuinely upset by all that had transpired. "Yeah, Peter, you're a friend."

That seemed to please Peter, who grinned. "Thank you. I don't mind if a friend calls me Tank. I think I like it."

"Good," she told him. "'Cause I like nicknames for people I care about, that's why I call Tiara Red. When we were younger, her hair really was red." She smiled at the memory. "Boy, did I tease and pull a lot of pranks on her."

"She still likes you after you did it," he said.

Almost there, Jayce noticed. Maybe once they hit the main trail the walk would get easier. But it didn't. As they reached the hilltop, Jayce felt queasy again. "Let go," she ordered Peter, shoving him away. Reluctantly, he complied and she stumbled a few steps away, leaned into a tree slipping to her knees as she vomited for the second time that night. Using the tree to lever herself to her feet, Jayce stood, though wobbly.

A handkerchief appeared to float in the air to her left. "To wipe your mouth," Peter told her. She wished for something to rinse her mouth, too. As this thought ran around her head, Peter placed an arm around her waist and the other under her knees, drawing her into his chest. "We'll go faster if I carry you." He bent and picked up the lantern he'd put down while she was retching.

"No way are you treating me like some toddler," Jayce groused. "Put me down."

Suddenly, rustling sounds came from further down the trail. Jayce looked in that direction but she couldn't focus. From the darkness, she heard a voice say, "Yeah, mister, put her down." Jayce thought she recognized the voice, but couldn't be certain. A moment passed before two men with rifles came into the sphere of weak light from the lantern. She couldn't concentrate to recall their names, but they seemed to know her relatively well.

"Don't worry, I won't let them hurt you," Peter said close to her ear.

"I'm not the one who should worry," she told him. "I think they're after you."

"Oh, okay, Jayce."

"Really, mister, put her down. You can't come to our town and hurt people, you know," the man said, swinging his rifle around in his agitation.

The second chimed in. "We'll shoot you if we have to."

Peter glared at them. "Move aside, I have to get her home."

Man number two stepped forward. "Looks like you've done enough damage. Let her go."

Crap. Enough is enough. She was ready to tear into these two, but the area flooded with light, piercing her already sensitized eyes. "Police, hands up," echoed through the woods. Jayce didn't know if man one or man two had been startled most, but one of them pulled the trigger on their rifle, and a burning pain shot across her thigh. "Holy shit," she screeched.

Then darkness swallowed Jayce.

Chapter Twenty-nine

TIARA HAD NO idea how long or far she'd ridden Majestic, however she felt immense relief when a Jeep came into view, pulling over as soon as she appeared in the headlight's beam. Majestic, intuitive as he'd been the entire time, slowed to a stop by the drivers' door. If her nerves weren't so shot, or Tiara hadn't been mad at Slim, she would have cheered at seeing her father behind the wheel. Instead, she slid from the saddle and peered into the jeep.

"We have to hurry." She pointed in the direction she'd come. "Jayce has been hurt, and needs a doctor."

Edna slammed a fist into his shoulder. "Damn it, Edward Michael, I told you." To Tiara's relief, Edna took charge. "Mo, take the horse to the ranch." Elmo hopped from the jeep and grabbed the reins from her. "Tiara get in the back. Slim, break the sound barrier," Edna ordered. Tiara had no sooner closed the door than the jeep leapt forward.

Now that Tiara had found help and was heading back, she worried about Jayce all over again. Edna asked questions, which Tiara answered absently. Her focus was on the road ahead, worry consuming her about Jayce's condition. "Please, sweetheart, be okay," she whispered in prayer.

"What was that, dear?" Edna asked, closing her cell phone, after letting Darla know the status of the situation.

Tiara shook her head in reply.

"Hey, look," Slim whooped, "a sheriff's vehicle." Tiara shifted to see out the windshield.

Happiness flooded Tiara, knowing she truly had brought the Calvary. Jayce would get all the assistance she needed. "Hurry, Dad," she encouraged. As she watched, Alison stepped out from the driver's side, pulled her pistol from the holster and rested her forearms on the car door, announcing, "Police, hands up."

The echo of a gunshot exploded through the forest.

SARAH SAT TENSELY, Darla's hand clasping hers in a death grip, waiting for Mark to disconnect the call and tell them all what news he'd received. Sure, the call only lasted about half a minute, but it felt like thirty to her. "Well?" she asked as he clicked the phone off.

"They found Tiara and Majestic and were going to get Jayce." He paused, glancing at Darla. At a nod from her, Mark said, "Peter punched Jayce, and she needs stitches and might have a concussion."

Sarah thought she might pass out. "I should get to the hospital, wait for them." She got up from the couch, but couldn't move further because Darla's grip tightened.

"We all need to go to the hospital," Darla hissed through clenched teeth. "My water just broke."

"Oh, shit," Craig muttered.

Sarah agreed. Mark and Craig hadn't moved, and she knew Darla wasn't getting to the hospital by wishful thinking. "Okay, then. Darla, sweetie, we need to get you to the car. Mark, go get her overnight bag. Craig, bring the car around front by the porch. Now, people," she bellowed hoping to kick everyone into action. "Okay, here we go," she said, pulling Darla up from the couch. After alternating a lot of heavy breathing and groaning, Sarah had Darla out the door, down the porch and to the car. Craig stood by the back, holding the door open.

Mark flew down the stairs with a small overnight bag, which he tossed on the floor in the rear. Gently, he took hold of Darla's hand and helped her crawl into the back seat, then following her in. "Let's go."

"All right," Sarah said, climbing into the passenger seat. "Craig, you drive."

"I have no idea where to go," he admitted.

"No worries, I've got your back," she told him. He got behind the wheel and headed down the drive, as Sarah gave directions. Sarah wondered how long it would take Edna to get Jayce to the hospital, even as she listened to Mark giving Darla directions on breathing. They made their way through the streets, and Craig reached across the console for her hand and squeezed. "She's gonna be okay, you know."

"I know," Sarah said, glancing toward the backseat. "She's probably happy to have it over with after so long."

Craig chuckled. "Jayce, honey. I meant Jayce will be fine." A warm rush of pleasure filled her that he understood her worry. He lowered his voice a little. "Darla will be in delivery for a bit, we'll wait by the doors so we see when Jayce arrives."

Squeezing his hand, Sarah realized Craig understood her better than anyone had, with the exception of Jayce. Someone had finally been able to see her as Sarah Marsh, not defined by her career. Hope for a normal future wasn't lost after all. "Here we are," Craig said, pulling up to the emergency room doors.

Darla eased into a wheelchair, with the help of the medical staff and they whisked her off to the maternity ward, Mark following behind. Craig left to park the car, as Sarah's cell rang. She recognized Edna's number. "Edna, did you get Jayce?"

Edna's strained voice said, "Sarah, Jayce has been shot."

Sarah didn't know what else Edna might have said, because the next thing she knew Craig grabbed her and wiped away the rush of tears.

TIARA JUMPED FROM the jeep, fresh tears falling down her face.

She ran down the road, hoping she'd find Jayce and Peter unharmed. Parallel to the sheriff's vehicle, Alison grabbed her arm, stopping her forward momentum. "Whoa, hang on," Alison ordered.

"I need to get to Jayce! She's already been hurt," Tiara cried.

Alison nodded. "I understand, just let me go first. We don't need these boys more freaked than they are. Give me a minute, okay?"

Tiara nodded, reluctantly.

Up ahead Peter cradled an unconscious Jayce protectively in his arms, slightly turned away from the men with rifles. He seemed torn between beating the two men up, if the dangerous glint in his eyes were any indication, and worry about Jayce, who had fresh blood darkening her jeans-clad leg.

Alison, pistol pointed at the two men, shouted orders. "Drop the rifles, boys, and put your hands behind your heads." They complied. "Drop to your knees and cross your legs at the ankle." Only when the men were in position did Alison move forward, stepping in front of Tiara. Alison looked over her shoulder, "Breathe, Tiara. Jayce is a fighter, but she'll do better if you're calm. You might want the first-aid kit under the driver seat."

Nodding, Tiara inhaled deeply. "You're right, Sheriff, thank you."

Flashing a beautiful smile, Alison said, "Let's go save Jayce from herself, or them from her wrath when she wakes up." Tiara waited as Alison slapped cuffs on the two men. Holstering her gun, Alison cocked her head in Jayce's direction. "Go on. I'll be right there."

Tiara rushed to Peter and Jayce. The moment Peter realized Tiara was back, he burst into tears. "They shot Jayce, and I couldn't stop them. Should'a been me got shot."

"No, Peter, it was an accident." Tiara told him. "Can you hold on to her for a little longer?" she asked him.

Peter nodded, and sniffed noisily. "She's not that heavy."

"Okay," she said moving close enough to see the rent in the fabric and fresh blood from the bullet. Luckily, though deeper than a graze, the wound didn't look life threatening. Tiara took a roll and a three-by-three square of gauze from the first aid kit and applied it to Jayce's wound. "Are you able to carry her to the jeep? It's behind the sheriff's car."

As they approached Alison's car, she was closing the back door on the two men sitting on the bench seat. "How bad is it?" Alison asked, peering under the material Tiara laid on the wound.

Tiara said, "It'll need more than a band-aid."

"Right. Here's the game plan." Alison pointed to the backseat. "They have some thinking to do, and aren't going anywhere. I'll turn the cruiser around, and you have Slim follow me, and don't worry about speed. I'll take it a bit slower on the rutted roads, but once we hit pavement I'll go like a bat outta hell. Ready?"

Tiara nodded, telling Peter to carry Jayce to the jeep.

"Tiara?" Alison put a hand on her shoulder, and Tiara saw the concern in her eyes. "Hang in there. She'll be fine. Let's go break some speed limits."

Beside the jeep, Peter stood stiffly. "Slide in and I'll pass her through."

Tiara jumped in, telling her father Alison's plan. Once she slid in, Peter leaned nearly completely inside, gently laying Jayce on the seat, carefully resting Jayce's head on her lap. Then, Peter bent her legs and closed the door. "Hurry, Peter, climb in." He shook his head. Tiara watched him rush toward the cruiser and climb into the passenger seat. "Every boy's dream, I guess, to ride in a cruiser. Hurry, Dad. Follow Alison. She's our escort."

With them finally on their way, Tiara rechecked the leg wound to make sure the bleeding was controlled, and the bandage on Jayce's forehead didn't show any fresh blood. Tiara's full attention was on the woman on her lap.

How could any of this have happened in only two weeks? Being around Jayce had been an emotional roller coaster ride. Jayce had been kind and funny the entire time, as she had always been when they were younger. A decade ago, Tiara had remembered that one kiss as mind-blowing. Later, she had downplayed her reaction to the fact that it was her first, so it had left an impression. Though Tiara hadn't really put any effort into dating, she had been kissed by other women, but remained unimpressed. Of course, she believed that was because she'd held her first kiss in such a high regard. And earlier today, Jayce's kiss in the barn had again been overwhelming, and Tiara realized no other woman could kiss her as Jayce did. Then Jayce professed her love. Tiara concluded that was the deciding factor for her response to be so eye-opening. Jayce loved her.

And Tiara loved Jayce. She'd loved Jayce since childhood, why else had she allowed Jayce to play her games? Were those pranks to get Tiara's attention? Had Jayce been giving signals the entire time?

Jayce moaned, and Tiara looked down into her pale face. Tiara ran her fingertips lightly across Jayce's cheek, and her forehead where it wasn't covered with the bandage. Life would be so different without Jayce in it. Empty was the first word to come to mind. No more laughter, no gentle caresses, and no love shining in those beautiful blue eyes.

But one major question still loomed overhead. Could Tiara give up everything for one woman, even Jayce?

Abruptly, the jeep door swung open, Edna and a nurse stood there. "We're here," Edna said. "Time to let go."

Tiara nodded, and let the medical personnel take over Jayce's care. They placed her on a gurney and rushed through the emergency room doors into the hospital. Tiara watched and noted Sarah, held by Craig, already standing by the ER doors and realized she should let Darla know everyone would be okay. Tiara became distracted. Edna's words rang in her head, and Tiara worried it was an omen.

Time to let go.

Tiara wondered, let go of what? Her old life?

Or let go of Jayce?

Chapter Thirty

JAYCE HATED HOSPITALS. Hospitals meant confinement to a bed while being poked and prodded by strangers. And she'd only been in the room for less than an hour. Of course, if the nurses had been cute enough to flirt with, not the grandmotherly type, it might have changed her opinion. She waited for someone other than hospital personnel to come see her. Her leg hurt like the dickens and she had a headache the size of Texas. "Where is everyone?"

On cue, a knock sounded on the door. "Please, whoever you are, come save me?" Jayce called out.

The door opened and Alison strode in. "Why, what trouble have you gotten yourself into now?"

"Hey, Ali." Jayce craned her neck to see if anyone else was behind her. "Where is everyone?" she asked.

Alison chuckled lightly. "Translation, where is Tiara?" Jayce shrugged, not willing to confirm her conclusion. "You haven't been forgotten, my friend. I've asked everyone to hold off visiting until you were settled and we had a chance to talk."

"So this is an official call?"

"Afraid so, even if you had plain-ole-Ali scared witless."

Jayce raised an eyebrow, but the sharp pain the action elicited made her stop. "Sweetie, a body can't use 'plain' and 'Ali' in the same sentence when referring to you and expect the observation to be believable. It's impossible."

"That's sweet, but not necessary. I'm not here to arrest you, or give the third degree."

Shifting to take some pressure off her thigh, Jayce tried to get comfortable. She'd had plenty of time alone in the last few hours to give a lot of thought to what could be expected. "Okay, shoot." Ali raised an eyebrow. "Not literally. If this is about pressing charges, I won't have Peter arrested for anything. Not only didn't he comprehend what was going on, Peter kept me safe. Now, for the other two morons, I hope you put the fear of Lady Justice into them. However, dumb as their actions were, ultimately they meant well."

Alison smiled at her, a bit of mischief of her own sparking in her eyes. "Yeah, I started the process and have them both locked up already. Those two will suffer some consequences from me for discharging their firearms." Ali ran her fingers through her blonde locks. "Mostly I wanted to check on you before everyone else monopolized your attention. You gave me a bit of a scare. I hope Jimmy stops whining about 'Bubba's gonna have his way with him.'"

Jayce knew Ali was worried more than as a local law enforcement official. As if noting Jayce's observation, Ali held up her hand. "The worry is as your buddy and friend, Jayce, nothing more. I just hope I can find someone who makes me giddy and has my face light up the way Tiara does for you. And, now that I've used my law enforcement position to jump the line, I'm going to get back to work and let the horde loose." She walked to the door and paused. "I've heard rumors, and even as I hope it won't be necessary, I'm a good listener, just in case things don't go too smoothly." At Jayce's nod, she left.

Jayce would probably have to take Alison up on that offer, knowing how hell-bent Tiara was on leaving Silver Waters.

Over the next hour, Sarah and Craig, then Slim and Edna had come to visit with her. She wanted to ask after Tiara, but feared she'd learn Tiara had already gone home, knowing Jayce would survive. Once again, Jayce had let herself hope that her love alone was enough to make Tiara stay. Finally, she couldn't stand it any longer. "Aunt Edna, where—"

"Gosh, sorry it took so long," Tiara said, pushing a wheelchair into the room. "I had to get permission to take Jayce for a ride from this little old lady nurse at the desk, who insisted on patting the top of my head for no reason I could fathom."

If Jayce could have jumped off the bed, she would've, to plant a lip-lock on Tiara for not leaving without at least saying good-bye. "Hey, Red. Are you breaking me outta this joint?"

"Not exactly, handsome," Tiara said, steering the chair along the side of the bed, leaning over and kissing Jayce's cheek. "Since Darla decided to have the baby while you were getting shot and probably so you wouldn't have to stay overnight by yourself, I figured you might want to go see the baby."

Jayce had never been happier to see anyone in her life. "I thought maybe—"

Before she could finish, Tiara kissed her on the lips, then drew back and whispered, "Hold that thought a minute." Tiara turned to Slim. "Would you mind waiting in the hall while I get Jayce ready for a trip to the Maternity Ward."

"Be still my heart," Jayce said, holding her chest. "I haven't proposed, yet." She knew Tiara didn't appreciate the comment, because her expression reflected distress. "All right, I'll shut up."

"We do need to talk, but I wanted to see the baby first."

It felt like the breath had been forcibly knocked from her. "Ah, back to the 'need to talk' line, which is never good." Jayce tried to appear composed. "Help me into my new wheels, Red."

Tiara did, wiping the sweat from Jayce's forehead with a tissue, before she bent eye level with her. "Don't go making yourself sick, honey. You've got to trust me."

Much as she wanted to trust Tiara, Jayce's gut told her the talk wasn't going to be an announcement of the outcome she wanted. Rather than trust her voice, Jayce nodded.

"Let's go take a peek at the baby," Tiara said, standing.

Jayce put on a happy face, but her heart felt like it was breaking all over again. "And the race is on," she said when Tiara set the wheelchair in motion.

They joined Slim and Aunt Edna in the hallway and made the trek to maternity. Sarah and Craig were standing in front of the nursery window making cooing noises. When they got closer, Jayce noted Mark was in a mask and scrubs cradling the newborn in his massive arms. At their approach, he brought baby Chester closer so Jayce wouldn't have to strain in her wheelchair.

"Oh my gosh," Jayce said, "look at all that hair."

Sarah put a hand on Jayce's shoulder. "Her name is Tina Claire Chester and she's six pounds, eight ounces and nineteen inches long."

"Little Tina is beautiful," Tiara said. For about fifteen minutes, all six stayed and stared in amazement until the nurse ushered Mark and the baby away. Tiara said, "I should get Jayce back to her room before they kick us out of here."

Jayce was grateful that the floor nurse followed them into the room to assist with getting her back into bed. Her head and leg throbbed in synchronicity, and it began to take a toll on her already sapped strength.

"She really needs some rest," the nurse told Tiara. "You need to say your good-byes."

Jayce's breath hitched at the choice of words the nurse used. Tiara must have noticed, as a hand clasped hers in a gentle squeeze as she nodded her agreement.

Tiara pulled a chair closer to the bed. "You know I've got to go, but I promise to be back as soon as can."

"For the wedding."

"And to see you," Tiara said. "So much has happened in such a short time and I'm having a hard time processing. But I'm trying, Jayce. One thing hasn't changed, honey. I have a responsibility elsewhere. I can't abandon my business."

So it really is good-bye, let's be pals, Jayce thought as her chest constricted tightly. "Will you still leave tomorrow?"

"I'll see you're safely home, first, however long it takes."

"You don't —"

"Of course I do," Tiara said. "I'm not going to abandon you, silly. I'll try to stay in touch as best I can." She laughed. "Hopefully no one will hide my correspondence this time."

Jayce smiled, though it was weak. "Or attack it with a red marker."

"Yeah, there's that, too." Tiara squeezed her hand. "Get some rest." She kissed Jayce's forehead and started for the door.

"Tiara," Jayce said before Tiara walked out of her life. "If you need me, please call. I promise to come to you. I love you, Red."

"I know. Sleep now," Tiara said, blowing a kiss before leaving the room.

Closing her eyes against the tears, Jayce let the despair consume her. Guess that's it. She's leaving, not giving a specific return time. It was over. Worse, Tiara didn't return her proclamation of love.

How long, Jayce wondered, did it take to heal a broken heart? Too bad she couldn't ask the grandmotherly nurse for a pill to fix it—or at least numb it from future use.

Chapter Thirty-one

NO MATTER HOW tight she clasped the pillow over her head, Jayce couldn't stop the incessant pounding echoing through her skull. Two months after getting clobbered by Peter, she still had residual headaches, and the banging wasn't helping. Well, she thought, at least her leg had healed. Unable to stand it any longer, Jayce glanced at the alarm clock: 5:15. What the hell? I've got Edna's wedding to deal with today. Throwing the covers off, she vaulted out of bed, threw on a bathrobe, and tromped out the bedroom to investigate. Going down the stairs toward the noise, Jayce realized it was coming from the front yard. Flinging open the front door, Jayce saw a pickup off to the side, the bed loaded with pallets of flowers. Off to the right side of the house, hammer swinging, was Tiara pounding on something just out of sight. Jayce couldn't control the rush of excitement, but wasn't about to let her emotions run wild. "Do you know what time it is?" she hollered to be heard over the racket.

Tiara stood and turned to face her. "Hey, sleepyhead. Good morning."

"Do you know what time it is?"

"Not exactly, I had a project to finish today, and wanted an early start. Got it done, too." Tiara dropped the hammer into the back of the truck, walked up the porch steps, and grabbed Jayce by the hand. "Come see what I was doing." Reluctantly, Jayce allowed herself to be tugged to the side of the house. What she saw had Jayce dumbfounded, her mouth gaping open. Tiara's arms snaked around her waist, her head rested against Jayce's back, as she asked, "What'd'ya think, Baby?"

Jayce didn't know what to say. Tiara had put up a four-by-four section of white picket fencing on the side of the house. She knew what this meant to her, but confusion still coursed through her. "Did I miss something, Red?"

Tiara squeezed her waist then grasped her by the hips, nudging her to turn around. "Jayce?" She took a deep breath. "I could use some coffee. Would you be opposed to making a pot, while I pull the flowers off the truck?" Jayce nodded, hoping she could pull herself together.

Fifteen minutes later, Tiara joined her in the kitchen. As she watched from the table, Tiara washed her hands in the sink, poured herself a mug of coffee, and sat in a chair facing her. Jayce waited, hoping Tiara would start the conversation.

She did, but with a question. "You've been getting my cards?"

Jayce nodded.

"So, you knew I was coming back. I wrote you I'd see you soon."

Jayce shrugged. "I guess I thought it might be a euphemism for 'when hell freezes over', that kind of see ya."

Surprise flashed across Tiara's features. Immediately, Tiara left her chair and kneeled before Jayce, clasping her hands around Jayce's. "Point taken. I didn't handle this very well."

"You left the same day I came home from the hospital."

"I told you I had some things to work out, and that I'd come back." Tiara frowned in confusion. "You understood 'come back' meant to you permanently, right? That I had stuff to settle, first?"

"Red, all I know is you couldn't wait to leave here. I know you have feelings for me, but not in the way I have for you."

"You're wrong. I love you, Jayce." Tiara stood up, only to shift onto Jayce's lap.

Jayce was astonished. "That's the first time I've heard the words."

"Please, honey, be patient. Some things are going to take time. Obviously, just because I think I've made myself clear, doesn't mean it isn't clear as mud." She grasped Jayce by the cheeks, and held her gaze. "Look at me, because I know you'll see the truth in my eyes. I've placed my current foreman in charge of Summers Construction as manager. I've signed the house over to Mark and Darla, so the baby will have a yard where she can play. Craig and I will run Summers and Walters Renovations here in Silver Waters. All this has already been arranged. However, I've already told Craig he'd have to open the shop without me this week. I'd come in after the honeymoon." Tiara finished this soliloquy by pressing her lips firmly against Jayce's.

When Tiara had released her lips, Jayce asked, "So you'll be coming back to Silver Waters, for good?"

"Yes." Another kiss, deeper than the last.

The honeymoon part baffled her, but at least Jayce had Tiara here for Slim and Edna's wedding. "And you won't start work until after they come back from their honeymoon?"

Tiara's lips moved to Jayce's neck, she nibbled gently at her earlobe, then whispered softly, "No, sweetheart, until we come back from ours." Tiara shifted so she could remove something from her pocket, which turned out to be a ring box. Smiling wickedly, Tiara asked, "Jayce Mansfield will you marry me?"

If Jayce hadn't already been sitting, she would probably have fallen. "Tiara, do you know what you're asking?" Then, Jayce understood the symbolism of the white picket fence on the side of the house. "You want to be my wife?"

Nodding, Tiara said, "If you'll have me." Taking Jayce's hand, she put the ring on Jayce's finger. "I thought we could have a double wedding with Edna and Dad. Actually, it was Edna's idea, but I'd hoped you wouldn't mind, so I've made arrangements if you're up for the idea."

Jayce realized Tiara expected her to refuse the offer, since Tiara had begun to ramble. She reached up and cupped Tiara's face with one hand, then dragged her thumb across Tiara's lower lip. "I can think of only one other thing I'd like to do right now." Jayce dropped her hands and grasped Tiara tightly to her as she stood. "We have a bit of time before the ceremony starts."

Tiara winked at her and Jayce's heart did a flip. Tiara's mouth claimed hers once again, as she groaned like a starving beast. Pulling back slowly, Tiara whispered, "This is an appetizer. We have a lifetime for me to prove I love you."

Chapter Thirty-two

Fourteen months later, Thanksgiving Day

TIARA PLACED THE last of the silverware on the table and stood back to view her masterpiece. She felt the flush of accomplishment at the near catalog-perfect table setting. Shaking her head, Tiara wondered how she could *not* have known this excitement would feel so phenomenal. Arms snaked around her waist from behind, just as the warmth of Jayce's breath caressed her ear. "The table looks gorgeous, sweetheart." Tiara leaned into the embrace. "Just like the woman who set it."

"Ah, well," Tiara giggled, "you're a little bit prejudiced, don't you think?" Tiara turned in Jayce's arms until they were chest to face, and glanced up.

"That would make me shallow," Jayce feigned hurt shock, even going so far as to let her bottom lip quiver. "How could you think so little of me?"

Pulling Jayce tighter, Tiara lightly kissed her pout. "I think the world of you." The gleam of Jayce's pleased smile filled Tiara with joy. Impulsively, Tiara placed a hand behind Jayce's neck, running her fingers through the thick hair at the nape, and drew her close gently kissing Jayce's lips, pressuring them open tenderly with the tip of her tongue, hoping to confirm how she felt. Tiara felt herself respond, the heat that pulsed through her body, and pebbled her nipples. The kiss left her gasping. "Oh, my," Tiara purred. "If we didn't have guests arriving any moment, I'd be dragging you to the floor to have my way with you."

Jayce tucked stray hair behind Tiara's ear, her gaze following her fingers with tender care. Tiara's heart fluttered and she groaned, wondering at her luck in being loved by this handsome woman. "Well, sweetheart, I could put up a note letting them know we're indisposed."

"You continue looking at me like you are, and I'm liable to let you, since you've made me so wet I ache."

Leaning back, Jayce gazed at her, whispering, "As you've done to me." The doorbell chimed from the front of the house. "Guess we'll have to continue this later, Red." She smiled mischievously. "Can we invite them in, put the food in plastic-ware and hurry them off? That way, I can give thanks in the way I love best."

Tiara laughed. "You're incorrigible. Go get the door." Caressing Jayce's cheek, she added, "Shoo, now. We have all night, and a lifetime, for us."

"I'm going to hold you to that—and to me," Jayce said, latching onto Tiara's hand, and then tugging her toward the front door. "Let's get this started so we can send them home."

Opening the front door, Tiara saw Craig and Peter standing on the porch. Mark held a diaper bag in one hand and Darla's elbow with the other, guiding her as she clutched Tina, their sleeping one-year-old, in her arms. All were ushered inside where coats were taken, and hugs exchanged, before congregating in the living room.

"Did you all come together?" Tiara asked.

"I drove with the Chester's, after forcing them to stop by so I could show off some of the changes at the house." Craig nudged Peter in the side with his elbow. "This big lug was sitting on the stairs, waiting. Didn't want to arrive alone, he said."

Tiara smiled at Peter. "You're family, now, Peter. You don't have to be worried that you aren't welcomed, alone or otherwise." Peter nodded, though hesitantly. Even after more than a year, Peter hadn't forgiven himself for harming Jayce.

"So, is Sarah not coming?" Jayce asked, sounding disappointed. Tiara knew Jayce had wanted all their friends together this Thanksgiving Day, so she could make a special announcement.

"No, no, she'll be here. She had to finish a few calls, so I wanted her to have some privacy," Craig said.

Mark chuckled. "Tell the truth, Craig." Mark shook his head, and smiled at Darla who giggled. "Sarah kicked him out because he wouldn't keep his hands to himself, while she was on the phone."

Blushing, Craig said, "I thought she'd just hang up. It's a holiday, after all."

"Not in Hollywood," Jayce and Tiara said simultaneously. This had everyone laughing.

"I'm glad the holiday has started jubilantly," Slim said from the hall, Edna behind him. "The back door was open, Princess," he said to Tiara, "so we let ourselves in and left some food on the counter. My wife," he beamed a broad smile in her direction. "Damn, woman, I can't say that enough, 'cause it feels too damn good. Am I right, Jayce?"

She winked at Tiara and nodded her response.

"Anyway, what say we put the game on and you women catch up while getting chow on."

"I'm not sure that's how it works, Dad."

Slim shrugged, plopping down in Jayce's recliner. "That's how it works on television."

Jayce shook her head. "The remote's where it's always been, Slim. We'll get started soon."

"We're not all here, yet," Peter murmured. Tiara knew he had a crush on Sheriff Stewart. The first time she recognized it, Tiara worried he couldn't understand it would never amount to anything but, luckily, it soon became clear he adored the idea of a pretty, lady cop being in charge of men. "Sheriff Ali and little Jennie haven't come yet."

"Plus, Sarah is AWOL," Craig said.

"None of us is in that big a hurry to get started, Edward Michael," Edna said. "If you're that impatient, get yourself 'ta home and make a jelly sandwich."

Slim slunk down in the recliner. "Sorry, Edna, honey."

Edna just *humphed*, and turned to Darla. "Your little one sure has grown into a beauty." As if the attention had been noted, Tina squirmed a bit in her mother's arms and grinned at Edna. "Oh," Edna cooed, "the little angel knows it."

Mark rolled his eyes. "And already she flirts with anyone who'd give her what she wants."

Darla handed their daughter over to Mark. "She can use it on her father, now. We ladies are adjourning to the kitchen while we wait for Ali and Jennie."

As the men arranged themselves in the living room, the women headed for the kitchen. Not long after, Alison arrived with her niece at the back door, Sarah close on their heels. "Hope you don't mind," Alison said, taking off her coat, "using the door that brings you to a kitchen seems so right." With the fluidity of people having worked together for years, the women put the final touches on the food preparations, placed the finished dishes on the dining room table, and called everyone in. The conversation flowed freely and comfortably, food was consumed in great proportions, until everyone sat back in their chairs totally satiated. Tina had lost interest early, and now investigated various items in the room, tittering at objects that caught her fancy.

Peter stood and pushed his chair back. "Miss Jayce and Miss Tiara, thank you for letting me have dinner with you. And thank you for letting me work here after — after —"

"Peter, we like having you around," Jayce said.

"Yeah, you're part of the family," Tiara told him. In fact, Peter had been learning about horses from Jayce, and working on an odd job here and there when Craig needed more muscle than she could provide.

He nodded. "Can I take Tina into the living room to watch some cartoons?" At their assent, he picked Tina up and left the room. That was the incentive the rest needed, each taking turns stating what they were thankful for this year. Darla for Tina; Mark for Tiara giving them her house; Craig and Sarah for each other; Edna for Slim, and Slim for Edna and the return of Tiara; Alison for the chance to spend time with Jennie; and, Jennie, with a devilish smirk, for the autographed picture of her heartthrob crush.

"Careful, young lady," Craig admonished. "That's my girl you're drooling over."

Jayce got to her feet then. Tiara knew she was going to make the announcement, so she stood also. Taking that as encouragement, Jayce moved behind her and embraced her in a comforting hug.

With a quick peck to her brow, Jayce said, "I'm thankful for Tiara, returning to my life and giving me her love."

Patting the arms around her, Tiara said, "I am thankful that Jayce had the patience to wait for me to realize how much I love her, and showing me my place has always been in Silver Waters." She gazed up at Jayce, the sparkle of excitement bright in her eyes. "Go ahead, honey."

A joyous grin spread across Jayce's face, as she glanced one at a time at everyone present. "And we are grateful to share with family and friends..." Jayce paused, rubbed her hands gently across Tiara's stomach, as everyone leaned toward them expectantly. "Tiara and I, we're having a baby."

"Hot, damn," Slim hollered, jumping up so fast, he knocked his chair over. He rushed to Tiara and Jayce, locking them in a tight embrace. "I'm gonna be a granddaddy. Yee-haw!"

AFTER THE WELL wishes, the football game, dessert, and one final cleaning everyone had gone to their respective homes, leaving an exhausted Tiara and Jayce behind. Tiara wrapped her arms around Jayce, kissing her quickly, and laying her head against Jayce's chest. "I had a great time, but I'm just as glad it's over."

"Me, too. Come on," Jayce said, taking her hand, they walked up to the master bedroom and prepared for bed. Once settled, with the light turned off, Jayce turned to her, snuggling close. "I love you."

Tiara loved the husky tones, the affection staring back from those remarkable eyes, when Jayce spoke the words. "And I love you, forever."

"I hope so, because I shall never release you, Red."

"You don't want to deal with child support?" Tiara teased.

Jayce smirked, before pinching her areola. "Not funny, please don't tease about that."

"Ouch." Tiara didn't know why she'd pushed, other than sometimes she needed reassurance that her new life wasn't a dream. "I'm sorry, honey. That was uncalled for."

"You're forgiven. Now, we have further things to be thankful for."

"Yeah?"

Jayce's tongue snaked out and slowly caressed her lips. Tiara's gaze latched on to Jayce's breast, a taut nipple straining against the material covering her. The heat in Tiara's body quickened, and finally she couldn't stand the delay any longer. She needed Jayce, and knew with all her heart, the feelings were returned. "I'll love you forever."

The End

More Titles by Sharon G. Clark:

Tears Don't Become Me

GW (Georgia Wilhelmina) DIAMOND, Private Investigator, dealt in missing children cases—only. It didn't alter her own traumatic childhood experience, but she could try to keep other children from the same horrors. She'd left her past and her name behind her. Or so she thought. This case was putting her in contact with people she had managed to keep a distant and barely civil relationship with for fifteen years. Now the buried past was returning to haunt her. When Sheriff Matthews of Elk Grove, Missouri, asked her to take a case involving a teenaged runaway girl, she believed it would be no different from any other. Until Matthews explained she had to take a cop as partner or no deal. A cop who just happened to be the missing girl's aunt...

ERIN DUNBAR, received the call concerning her niece from an old partner, Frank Matthews. It should have been from her sister, but their estrangement, compounded by her having moved to Detroit, kept that from happening. Now she would have to work with a PI. One had nearly killed her and Frank years ago; she expected this one would be no different. Matters were only made worse by discovering it was a "she" PI—a Looney-tune one who gave new and literal meaning to: "Hands Off." For the sake of her niece, Erin would put up with just about anything, until...

GW seemed to be strangely affected by this case and Erin, to her chagrin and amazement, was strangely affected by her. If Erin could solve GW's past, give her hope, could they have a hope of finding her niece?

ISBN 978-1-932300-83-3
eBook ISBN 978-1-61929-039-6

Into the Mist

Lieutenant Kasey Houston has snuck off the USS Console, to join the Marines in their fight against the Japanese soldiers, in May of 1945. She is a psychiatric nurse, and when the Marines of her unit are all killed, she attempts to take out the enemy. However, a strange gray mist is in the cave, and the enemy soldier releases a grenade that buries her in rubble.

Captain Andrea Knight is locating the occupants of an exploded building. She comes upon a woman without identification and in WWII era uniform. Andrea after learning Kasey is from the past procures documentation to establish Kasey as a Military Advisor to the Militia.

Andrea and Kasey are to meet with the officials and militia, who want them to be a bodyguard for the Ambassador of the United Church. His mission: to explain the severity of the threat of the terrorist gangs and Bad Billy. The United Presidents refuse to believe the threat bad. The Ambassador tries to explain he's capable of stopping Billy by using powers they both possess.

Bad Billy requests a rendezvous and stipulates that Andrea come alone. Kasey pleads with Andrea to ignore the message, and is shocked to learn later that Andrea has gone anyway. Meanwhile, Andrea realizes how much she loves Kasey although she is afraid to admit it. Can she avoid her worst fear that Kasey could be returned to her own time before an opportunity ever presents itself to act on her feelings?

ISBN 978-1-935053-34-7
eBooks ISBN 978-1-935053-34-7e

Other Yellow Rose books you may enjoy:

Amazonia: An Impossible Choice
by Sky Croft

A year after the events in *Amazonia*, Blake and Shale have joined as one. But only days after celebrating their union, a savage storm hits the Amazon village, unearthing a long lost secret—a clue to the location of a sacred relic, which was once stolen from the Amazon tribe.

Accompanied by Kale and Amber, Blake and Shale set out on a quest to reclaim the treasured artifact. Away from the safety of their village, the four women encounter thieves, deadly foes, and predatory animals.

Their search leads them underground to a vast cave system, where darkness is a constant enemy, and one mistake in the perilous terrain could mean death.

As echoes from the past come back to haunt them, Blake and Kale are both put into life-threatening situations. With only time to save one, Shale is faced with an impossible choice—her wife or her twin? Who will she choose?

ISBN 978-1-61929-180-5
eBook ISBN 978-1-61929-179-9

Moving Target
by Melissa Good

Dar and Kerry both feel the cruise ship project seems off somehow, but they can't quite grasp what is wrong with the whole scenario. Things continue to go wrong and their competitors still look to be the culprits behind the problems. Then new information leads them to discover a plot that everyone finds difficult to believe. Out of her comfort zone yet again, Dar refuses to lose and launches a new plan that will be a win-win, only to find another major twist thrown in her path. With everyone believing Dar can somehow win the day, can Dar and Kerry pull off another miracle finish? Do they want to?

ISBN: 978-1-61929-150-8
eBook ISBN 978-1-61929-151-5

Beyond Always
by Carrie Carr

Set a year after the events in *Trust Our Tomorrows*, everything is going well for the Walters family. The ranch is prospering, the kids are growing-and Lex & Amanda have never been happier. When an unimaginable tragedy strikes close to home, everyone handles it in different ways. Will the family be able to survive?

ISBN 978-1-61929-160-7
eBook ISBN 978-1-61929-161-4

White Dragon
by Regina Hanel

The story of Halie Walker and Samantha Takoda Tyler continues a year after they first met in *Love Another Day*. Halie's efforts to reestablish a career while still recovering from previous injuries consume her time and focus, leaving Sam far from the center of her attention and their relationship under emotional strain. Adding to their troubles, someone unknown begins a campaign of attacks. Sam's horse Coco winds up missing, their home is vandalized, and worse. As anxiety builds, Halie's childhood friend, Ronni Summers, provides welcome support, but no one can figure out who is involved in the attacks.

Ronni's brief encounter with Cali Brooks taunts her dreams, but finding her potential soul mate again proves most difficult. As Thanksgiving approaches, a series of events bring Cali into Sam and Halie's life, and almost into Ronni's. New and old friends join together on Thanksgiving Day, but snowfall cuts the gathering short. What follows brings not only the White Dragon, but also revelation, love, and death; the question is: which is brought to whom?

ISBN 978-1-61929-142-3
eBook ISBN 978-1-61929-143-0

The Gardener of Aria Manor
by A. L. Duncan

Janie O'Grady is a woman quite adapted to her life and circumstances as they are, living in New York City during the Great Depression. A hint of cynicism clouds the cold winter streets and keeps the rum runners strange bedfellows to the Irish mob's bounty in and out of speakeasys, daring to brush shoulders with the neighboring Italian mobs. At a moment where Janie fears for her life she is presented with circumstances which seem like a harsh nudge from the heavens to decide her own destiny.

Feeling there is no other choice, Janie makes the fateful decision to change her identity and move to the Devon countryside on the coastal shores of England, as a Head Gardener to a 17th century manor, where déjà vu and the intrigues of a past life and murder mystery over shadow her life in the big city.

This tale invites you to peek into the pages of one woman's life and follow her incredible story of self-discovery of a very different kind; where looking back at one's past includes connecting the threads of passions and desires of a life lived before. A life lived where one's odyssey must wait to complete the circle in the next life.

ISBN 978-1-61929-158-4
eBook ISBN 978-1-61929-159-1

Jess
by Pauline George

Jess is a modern day lesbian Lothario who was so hurt from an emotionally damaging relationship that now she doesn't let anyone get close. She protects herself by keeping her relationships short and sweet. When Jess's sister Josie challenges her to get to know a woman before she jumps into bed with her, Jess is intrigued. How hard can that be?

Although she's a serial monogamist, Jess has deep-seated morals that will be tested to the limit by her carefree acceptance of Josie's challenge. When she falls for her sister's best friend Katie, she suddenly finds her life upended, and she's left wondering if she actually has what it takes to have a lasting and fulfilling relationship. Is she destined to spend her life bed-hopping? Will her ever-growing attraction to Katie be the catalyst for romance, or will Katie's indecision about her life prove to be Jess's downfall?

ISBN 978-1-61929-138-6
eBook ISBN 978-1-61929-139-3

Second Chances
by Lynne Norris

Alex Margulies is a self-driven chief attending physician in the emergency department of a large community medical center. She is fierce and merciless with her staff, expecting the same tireless dedication from her peers as she does from herself.

Driven by her recent failures, Alex struggles to put her troubled past behind her. With the annual influx of new residents to the hospital, she meets one of her new charges, Regina Kingston, a bright, young, promising doctor. Before long, Regina finds herself irresistibly drawn to the enigmatic physician despite the woman's fiery personality and maligned reputation.

As professional differences come to light and personalities clash, Alex and Regina both struggle to overcome their own demons. It is within each other that they will find the strength to overcome their darkest moments, surviving to live and love again.

This is an Author's Cut Edition released in eBook formats only

eBook ISBN 978-1-61929-172-0

OTHER YELLOW ROSE PUBLICATIONS

Regina A. Hanel	Love Another Day	978-1-935053-44-6
Regina A. Hanel	WhiteDragon	978-1-61929-142-3
Jeanine Hoffman	Lights & Sirens	978-1-61929-114-0
Jeanine Hoffman	Strength in Numbers	978-1-61929-108-9
Maya Indigal	Until Soon	978-1-932300-31-4
Jennifer Jackson	It's Elementary	978-1-61929-084-6
K. E. Lane	And, Playing the Role of Herself	978-1-932300-72-7
Helen Macpherson	Love's Redemption	978-1-935053-04-0
J. Y Morgan	Learning To Trust	978-1-932300-59-8
J. Y. Morgan	Download	978-1-932300-88-8
A. K. Naten	Turning Tides	978-1-932300-47-5
Lynne Norris	One Promise	978-1-932300-92-5
Paula Offutt	Butch Girls Can Fix Anything	978-1-932300-74-1
Surtees and Dunne	True Colours	978-1-932300-52-9
Surtees and Dunne	Many Roads to Travel	978-1-932300-55-0
Vicki Stevenson	Family Affairs	978-1-932300-97-0
Vicki Stevenson	Family Values	978-1-932300-89-5
Vicki Stevenson	Family Ties	978-1-935053-03-3
Vicki Stevenson	Certain Personal Matters	978-1-935053-06-4
Vicki Stevenson	Callie's Dilemma	978-1-61929-003-7
Cate Swannell	A Long Time Coming	978-1-61929-062-4
Cate Swannell	Heart's Passage	978-1-932300-09-3
Cate Swannell	No Ocean Deep	978-1-932300-36-9

Be sure to check out our other imprints,
Quest Books, Mystic Books, Silver Dragon Books, Young Adult
Books, and Blue Beacon Books.

About the Author

Sharon G. Clark lives in beautiful Colorado with her partner, her adorable dogs Kiko and León, her talkative cat Sophie and devil-cat Rum. She enjoys the hiking in the mountains, reading and playing mahjong (not simultaneously), and especially family time.

VISIT US ONLINE AT
www.regalcrest.biz

At the Regal Crest Website You'll Find

- The latest news about forthcoming titles and new releases

- Our complete backlist of romance, mystery, thriller and adventure titles

- Information about your favorite authors

- Current bestsellers

- Media tearsheets to print and take with you when you shop

- Which books are also available as eBooks.

Regal Crest print titles are available from all progressive booksellers including numerous sources online. Our distributors are Bella Distribution and Ingram.

Lightning Source UK Ltd.
Milton Keynes UK
UKOW03f2210180814

237149UK00005B/437/P